...works wi... ...em full time
2 0 ... /Children's literary agent, and lives back in East
... with her boyfriend and pet fish. *Editing Emma* is
... book.

CHLOE SEAGER

EDITING EMMA

THE SECRET BLOG OF A NEARLY PROPER PERSON

ONE PLACE. MANY STORIES

HQ
An imprint of HarperCollinsPublishers Ltd.
1 London Bridge Street
London SE1 9GF

This paperback edition 2017

2
First published in Great Britain by
HQ, an imprint of HarperCollinsPublishers Ltd. 2017

Copyright © Chloe Seager 2017

Chloe Seager asserts the moral right to be
identified as the author of this work.
A catalogue record for this book is
available from the British Library.

ISBN: 978-0-00-822097-6

Printed and bound by
CPI Group, Croydon CR0 4YY

My Dingy Internet Cave
Tuesday, 2 September i.e. Day 45 of Despair

posted by MissH 15.03

Leon Naylor is in a relationship with Anna McDonnell.

3 mins

Huh… That's funny. Because I thought he was in a relationship with me.

posted by MissH 16.05

My phone rings. And rings. And rings. It's Steph. Then Faith. Then Gracie. I know they mean well (except Gracie, who will be not-so-secretly enjoying this) but I really don't want to speak to anyone. Maybe ever again. I will limit human contact to only when it's strictly necessary, i.e. my mum when I need food. Maybe she'd even consider getting a little hatch put in my bedroom door.

posted by MissH 17.14

Staring at the status as it gets more and more comments and likes, becoming more and more real as I become more and more discarnate.

I guess that explains why he hasn't spoken to me all

summer, then. How could he do this? Am I not even worth a proper break-up? Was I that unimportant, that he can just act like I never existed? I wasn't even made Facebook official. I didn't even have the dignity of him ending our relationship in person *or* online before starting a new one. I have been left in the shadows, invisible and unacknowledged.

Has he been meeting up with her all this time? All this time I've been sending out deranged, thinly veiled tweets that are OBVIOUSLY about him? Or posting photos that say, 'LOOK AT ME IN THIS REVEALING OUTFIT HAVING SO MUCH FUN. I'M COMPLETELY FINE WHO NEEDS YOU LALALA', when really Steph had put me to bed by 7 pm sobbing in my heels. Through all of that, he's been *starting another relationship*? For how long? I did see her on a group shot on that day out to Hyde Park, but I thought she knew one of his friends, or something.

posted by MissH 19.36

This is what the inside of my brain looks like:

Leon Naylor is in a relationship with Anna McDonnell.
Leon Naylor is in a relationship with Anna McDonnell.
Leon Naylor is in a relationship with Anna McDonnell.
Leon Naylor is in a relationship with Anna McDonnell.
Leon Naylor is in a relationship with Anna McDonnell.
Leon Naylor is in a relationship with Anna McDonnell.
Leon Naylor is in a relationship with Anna McDonnell.
Leon Naylor is in a relationship with Anna McDonnell.
Leon Naylor is in a relationship with Anna McDonnell.
Leon Naylor is in a relationship with Anna McDonnell.

Leon Naylor is in a relationship with Anna McDonnell.
Leon Naylor is in a relationship with Anna McDonnell.

posted by MissH 21.05

It almost feels better, now that I know for certain. (*Almost.*
But not quite.) He really has been ignoring me. As if all the
other evidence wasn't enough:

He started to 'miss' my calls, and didn't call me back.
Even when I got Steph to phone him from her mum's number,
and he answered, I convinced myself it was probably a coincidence. Maybe the twenty or so times I called him, he really
had been in the shower.

He stopped replying to my texts.
I was so sure they'd been accidentally swallowed into an
abyss by O2. (Who I did ring, frantically, several times.)

He detagged ALL pictures of us.
I still can't believe I was kidding myself about that one. I
thought maybe it was a weird error, or his friends did it as
a joke. But really, it seems like quite an extreme length to
go to, to break up with someone... Surely just telling them
is easier?

posted by MissH 23.37

The Forgotten Photos
Can't sleep so I made a list of my favourite pictures of us, that

he so coldly detagged. Because we did have a relationship, it did exist and I am not hallucinating. I am *not* hallucinating.

4) **Us doing our best smize. (November.)** We put it up for people to vote on and I won, 82 per cent. It was raining A LOT and my eye make-up was running down my face in a way which Leon said was 'haunting' and gave me an unfair advantage. He demanded a rematch.

3) **Us lying on the school field. (March.)** Our faces are red and puffy because a football had just hit me in the face (thanks Steph). After laughing for about a zillion years, Leon stood in front of the goal and let a football whack him in the face, too.

2) **Us in Gracie's garden the night he asked me to 'go out' with him. (June.)** Gracie did a barbecue (or her parents did after she caused a smog). The sun was going down and we were lazing in the back garden, choking from leftover fumes and laughing. I can't remember ever feeling so happy. (Apart from maybe when I won that magazine competition for designing my own red carpet outfit. They made the dress and sent it to me, and put a picture of me on the back page. It's pretty sad that these are the best moments I can pick out in my life – in one I was eleven, and one has been completely ruined.)

1) **Us at the end of term, before summer break. (July.)** We are TOGETHER in this one. (I am not hallucinating.) We have

been together for two weeks. We are lurking outside the Sixth Form Centre, peering in the windows and scoping it out for next year. I remember being excited by the new beanbag chairs, and Leon saying, 'Good luck getting out of those when I sit on you.' We laughed. I threatened to protect myself from suffocation by stabbing him with a snooker cue. We kissed.

And now I'm in this place, and I'm not sure how I got here.

Wednesday, 3 September i.e. Day 46 of Despair

posted by MissH 11.30

Sitting in the living room, steaming my stye with a bowl of boiling water. My hair has not been brushed for three days or washed for six, unless you count dry shampoo. There is a dark stain on my pyjamas from where I was too eager with a tub of chocolate mousse. According to all the TV shows that ever cast glamorous twenty-five-year-old women to represent me, this is NOT how my teenage life is supposed to look.

It also seems a little unfair that I get dumped, *and* grow a big, red, painful lump on my eye from the stress of it. Still, maybe it's an important life lesson to learn. Give someone your undying love, they give you a stye.

posted by MissH 11.32

Not even dumped. *Avoided*. I had to work out for myself that I was dumped.

posted by MissH 13.03

I can't seem to get off Anna's profile. There are lots of pictures of her doing sports (I think she is the Hockey Captain). Should I have paid more attention in Games instead of using the time to chase Gracie around with my stick? And she has… wait for it… a *baking blog*. It's called, I kid you not: *Scrumptiously, Anna*. There are lots of videos of her whisking cake mixture whilst looking, quite seriously, into the camera. Should I have paid more attention in FT?

I want to say she's not, but she's indisputably pretty. I have named her Apple in my head to make her less threatening.

posted by MissH 17.48

Still, she might be pretty, but there's something really bland about people who always have the same expression in photos. Boring face. Boring face. Boring face. Boring face. I mean, yes, we all have our standard poses (I am a fan of the tongue-poke), but seriously… PHOTO after PHOTO of that insipid smile. She may as well just have one photo. The only way you can tell it's even a different night is because she's changed her cardigan.

posted by MissH 18.56

APPLE AND EMMA: THE PRO/CON LIST
NB: evidence gathered only from photos (not totally solid) and self-reflection (notoriously difficult)

APPLE
CONS: She can't quite smile properly. This may or may not mean something very significant about her personality.

PROS: She's all nice and pretty and wins sports tournaments and things for the school. She has a baking blog and makes cakes for her friends.

EMMA
CONS: I have been told my smile is 'demonic'. I can't do ANY form of sports (though I have been told watching me fall over provided 'light comic relief' on Sports Day. Should this go in the Con or Pro list?).

PROS: I'm not *not* nice. I'm not *not* pretty, when I bother to brush my hair. I have an encyclopedic knowledge of rubbish TV shows. I have a blog, too, though it's mainly dedicated to self-pity, and it never results in cake.

Looking at it this way, I think I know who I'd choose, too.

posted by MissH 21.14

God, look at me. I have now, officially, wasted the entire day staring into the vacant eyes of my ex-boyfriend's new girlfriend. Still, as Jennifer Lawrence once said, 'You try being twenty-two, having a period and staying away from Google! I once Googled "Jennifer Lawrence Ugly".' If J-Law isn't strong enough to resist the self-destructive charms of the internet, then what hope do I have?

posted by MissH 23.58

Going to sleep, stroking the plaster under my pillow.

The plaster under my pillow

It is, obviously, Leon's. One night, Mum went out and in a very thoughtless act of selfishness she left ingredients in the fridge, but failed to put them together into a shepherd's pie. So, I was VERY hungry and wondering what I was supposed to do with this pile of meat and vegetables, and I Snapchatted Leon a picture of me holding a peeler, looking confused. He sent back a picture of himself holding up his hand, with a message that I remember very clearly because I screen-shot it and had it as my background for a month,

'PUT THE PEELER DOWN. I'll be there in 5. I quite like your fingers and I'd hate to lose one to a pie.'

(Message to Steph ten seconds later: 'He likes my fingers! He likes my FINGERS!')

I stood around dithering, hopping from one foot to the other and shaking my arms above my head. I kept trying to position myself in ways that felt natural, but I seemed to have forgotten how to stand. Then there was a knock that vibrated through the house. My heart pounded like it was Jack Nicholson at the door holding an axe, and I slowly edged towards it. When I let him in I was so nervous I couldn't even look at him. I turned round, and he collapsed in a fit of laughter.

'Thanks for the warning,' he spluttered, pointing at my shoulders.

I completely forgot I was wearing my pyjamas that say, 'I Fart. What's Your Superpower?' on the back.

'What? Oh... Steph bought them for me as a joke!!' I turned to face him, dying a little inside.

'So you *don't* fart?' he asked.

'I... No,' I said, carefully walking backwards into the kitchen.

'What? Never?'

'No. Never.'

'I'm going to have to call you out on that one, Emma, because that's a physical impossibility. The average person produces half a litre of farts every day.'

'...Well... *I* don't.'

'If you hold them in they come out in your sleep. Maybe that's why Steph got you the pyjamas. You think you never fart but actually by night you are Explosive Emma.'

'You seem to be worryingly full of gas knowledge.'

'You seem to be worryingly full of gas.'

'Are you going to help, or did you just come to insult me?'

'Pass me the knife.' He smiled.

As he began chopping, I remember feeling very solemn, like it was some kind of pivotal moment in our relationship that I should honour. *Leon was in my kitchen. Chopping a carrot.* He passed me the little pieces of vegetable and I took them very delicately, like he was handing me a baby.

'You'd better not start calling me Explosive Emma.'

'Already changing it in my Contacts,' he said, reaching for his phone.

I threw a potato at his head.

'It works in reference to your violent nature, too.'

'I hate you.'

'Do you?' he asked, looking straight at me. I suddenly felt like I was made of glass and all my insides were on show. My stomach started backflipping, as he moved imperceptibly towards me...

'Bollocks,' he said, breaking eye contact.

It took me a second to register he'd cut his finger.

'The irony,' he said sheepishly, as I ran to get a wet cloth and started dabbing at him.

'Haha, yes, irony, yes.'

Touching Leon, touching Leon, touching Leon.

'Thanks, Emma.'

'No problem.'

I would gladly clean up your blood by licking it off the counter.

'Can I have a plaster?'

'Sure.'

Take all the plasters. Take everything. That fruit bowl. That pile of Vogue *magazines. My shoes. My vital organs.*

So… yes. That is the story of the plaster. I can honestly say I don't think I've ever found anything so satisfying as putting on that plaster. Before he left he put it in the bin and took another one, and I took it *out* of the bin, wrapped it in cling film and put it under my pillow. Yes. Fine. I admit it. I'M NOT PROUD OF IT, OK. As long as I remember that this is freakish behaviour, it's definitely *sort of* OK. And luckily I have Steph to remind me. ('THROW IT AWAY NOW YOU COMPLETE WEIRDO' I believe were her exact words.)

I put the sacred pie in the fridge, ate some toast and went to bed. The pie didn't last very long because Mum ate it the next day. She didn't understand why I was so upset, though.

Thursday, 4 September i.e. Day 47 of Despair

posted by MissH 12.03

Only just got up and already wish I hadn't. Not a *single* Snapchat or WhatsApp. You'd think someone might have bothered. I mean, I'm not speaking to anyone, but you'd think they might have tried a bit harder.

posted by MissH 14.59

A picture of them has been uploaded. A PICTURE OF THEM HAS BEEN UPLOADED. They're at London Zoo, in front of the squirrel monkey exhibit. Anna is standing half smiling and Leon is crouching down pretending to be one of the animals. He looks like he's having so much fun.

Are they there now? Are they there now having fun whilst I'm here sitting looking at them having fun and feeling as if I'll never have fun again???

I can't believe they went to London Zoo. On a date. A date to London Zoo like a real couple. A real couple in a real, *Facebook official* relationship. UGH. It's like celebrities who have a verified tick on Twitter. It just makes them more valid as a human being, somehow.

posted by MissH 15.30

Mum came back from a meeting with a new client and started babbling at me from the hallway. It did actually feel nice to hear someone talking in the real world, even if it was about mood lighting and sinks without plugs.

'Anyway, I told her I don't care how *nice* they look, a sink without a plug is insane. I refuse to be *that* kind of designer…'

She came in, looked at me, and sighed.

'Lovely, is that how you greet me now?' I demanded.

'I'm sick of you, quite frankly, Emma. Look, I know you're upset,' she blathered on, 'but it doesn't mean you can lounge around here being moody, not cleaning up after yourself.'

One time I forgot to clear up my breakfast tray, and now I will never hear the end of it. And if she chooses to refer to my heartbreak in such diminishing terms i.e. 'being moody,' then I will obviously choose not to answer her.

She stood in the doorway, scanning me with judging eyes.

'You're not the only one who's ever been upset in a relationship, you know. What about me? The Poison Penns? The entire world?'

(Who are the *Poison Penns*?)

'I *know* you've been upset, Mum.'

I wanted to add, 'because you make poor decisions,' but I didn't.

'Get up and get on with it,' she said, walking off before I could get another word in.

I hate it when she does that!!

Of course, I could get up and get on with it, but I'm too comfortable. Why *can't* a girl have a few months where she lies in her own filth and literally doesn't move unless it's to urinate? I'm hardly going to start taking life advice from her.

<u>**Reasons I will not be taking life advice from my mother:**</u>

1) **She's seeing a man who takes off his clothes in front of other women for a living.** Bit of a red flag when you're already a possessive person. Which she pretends not to be, but she is.

2) **She *knew* that about him when she chose to go out with him.** It's not like she met him, liked him and then found out. It was listed on his online dating profile.

3) **He's about ten years younger than her.** Absolutely fine, in theory, if only she didn't keep going out with younger men and then moaning when they want different things. 'Mum,' I said once, 'you know there's a solution, and match.com have made it really easy for you. See that little bar? Where you put your age range in? You just need to shift it along a bit.' Then she threw something at me.

4) **I'm her own daughter, and I don't even know if she's still seeing him.** Who knows what's happening with her love life? Does she even know? They're on and off like Ross and Rachel, but weirder and in no way romantic.

posted by MissH 22.31

Still, I can be mean about her online dating antics all I like but she *may* have a point. I thought it was time to finally communicate with the outside world and get a valid, non-parental opinion. So Steph came over. When she arrived I heard Mum say, 'She's somewhere in the darkness. Just follow the smell.'

'How are you?' Steph asked cautiously, perching on the edge of the sofa. I looked even more pale and sickly next to her gorgeous dark skin, and she looked really good in her football kit. It sort of made me *maybe* want to get changed out of my giant, stained pyjamas, but only for a moment.

'Fine,' I replied.

'Clearly,' she said, glancing at the huge pile of tissues at my feet.

We sat in silence for a moment, and then I broke down in tears.

'He's got another girlfriend,' I sobbed.

'I know,' she said, putting her arms around me.

'And he didn't even tell me.'

'I know.'

'I'm nothing.'

'You're not nothing. You're definitely something.'

We stayed hugging for a while, until she said, 'Emma, this is all lovely and everything, but on second thoughts can we hug after you've had a shower?' She moved away.

'Oh God. Look at me. This happened two months ago and I still feel exactly the same about it. I mean, yes, that status only just came up. But we stopped speaking at the beginning of summer. In two months I have made zero progress. How is that possible?'

'Maybe because instead of actually trying to make progress you keep stewing over how you've made no progress.'

I sensed her annoyance, then. It was time to ask the important question.

'Steph, am I being truly unbearable?'

'No, I mean… well…'

'It's OK. You can tell me.'

She took a deep breath.

'Well, the rate at which you ask me how I am has definitely gone down in proportion with how much you sit around pretending to be Miss Havisham. But that's fine, there's definitely an allowance for this.'

'Ugh, for about two weeks, not two months. I'm so sorry.'

'Emma, it's OK, I don't mind. I'm just a bit worried. Don't you think it's time to move on? I mean… Leon has.'

'Owch.'

'I'm sorry, Emmy, I'm not trying to be mean. I just really want you to see it like it is. I know you liked him, that's probably an understatement, but…'

'But he's with Anna now. Who is categorically better than me. I know, I have the proof.'

'What are you talking about?'

'I made a pro/con list.'

'I… You did WHAT?!'

For some reason this made her truly, deeply angry with me. Angrier than she has been with me all summer, angrier than she was when Oberyn's head got squished on *Game of Thrones*. She launched into a full on rant,

'EMMA. A PRO/CON LIST?! Come on!! Where's your dignity and… sense of self worth?! Where's your feminism?! You're not like… objects to be compared!!! You're both PEOPLE. Leon treating you like this has nothing to do with Anna, or you, and by the way… you completely *don't deserve to be treated like this*!!!'

She took my phone and made me delete the pro/con list. Eventually, she calmed down, and started breathing normally again. Before she left I said, 'I'm not pretending to *be* Miss Havisham, by the way, I'm channelling her.'

'Whatever you say.'

posted by MissH 23.18

Ugh. Steph is so, so right!! *An Emma/Apple pro/con list???* Is this what I've been reduced to?! Measuring myself against another girl? I should never have been left to sit around wondering what I did wrong, and I definitely shouldn't be sitting around comparing myself with Leon's new girlfriend!!! Making myself feel bad, or feeling the need to insult her when this is completely not her fault! People are different, and you know what, if he didn't like me and he liked Bland Face then he should have had the guts to say it to my face. Or at least my direct message inbox.

An Ode To Steph

Oh Steph you make the skies seem blue, which they are in fact and that is true, but without you they might as well be poo, because without you oh what, oh what would I do?

Quite like that. Sent it to her. She said:

You are a freak. Sx 23.14

Friday, 5 September i.e. Day 48 of Despair

posted by MissH 12.46

Ghosting – Is This An Actual Thing?

Got an email from Gracie. It said, 'I know you don't want to talk but this might help xx' and then she linked me to some article about something called 'ghosting'.

The Urban Dictionary definition of 'Ghosting', just in case you were wondering:

The act of suddenly ceasing all communication with someone the subject is dating, but no longer wishes to date. This is done in hopes that the ghostee will just 'get the hint' and leave the subject alone, as opposed to the subject simply telling them he/she is no longer interested.

Was this supposed to make me feel *better?!?!*

posted by MissH 18.28

Spent the last five hours reading horror stories about ghosting. One woman was dating a man for eighteen months, had met his parents and agreed to move in, and one day he was just... gone. She went round to his flat and he'd moved out. She eventually got in touch with his old flatmate and apparently he was living in Scotland with another girl. Even more bizarre, one woman had been married (yes, MARRIED) to a man for twelve years (TWELVE YEARS) and one day they went to the local swimming pool. One moment he was there, doing his lengths nearby, and the next he was gone. Just like that. Did he get up and go in his trunks?? It's two years later and she's still technically married to him.

Aghh, I must stop this! YET ANOTHER DAY HAS BEEN WASTED FEELING SORRY FOR MYSELF. I need to focus on something else, anything else!! THE TIME HAS COME. Something good has to come out of this pathetic, miserable summer!! I *will* forget about Leon and his complete, utter rejection of me that makes me want to do nothing but lie in darkness watching serial killer documentaries on Netflix. I WILL NOT BE LEFT LOST AND CONFUSED IN A SWIMMING POOL.

I deserve so much more than a 'ghosting', and so does every other human being on the planet! I always knew it, in a sort of vague way like how you know you should floss, but now I'm really starting to *feel* it. Ugh. What a JERK. He had me feeling bad about not *baking*. I HATE BAKING. AND THAT IS FINE. It's not like he's so perfect, either... Let's take a moment to examine Leon's CONS, why don't we!!

posted by MissH 18.57

Reasons Why Leon Naylor Is NOT Worth Any Girl's Time or Virginity
1) He ends relationships by pretending girls no longer exist.

Do I need to go on? No, but I will anyway because there's more.

2) He eats far too many Chewits. There are other foods, you know.

3) He finds fart humour way too funny. Sometimes it is, but there's a time and a place.

4) Relating to my last point, he is completely juvenile.

5) He's actually kind of stupid. He's always getting me to help with his Maths, Physics & Chemistry (he really struggles with anything vaguely numerical). He pretends like he doesn't care but he tries SO HARD in everything and usually gets bad marks anyway. He once confided in me that he felt like his parents loved his brother more, because he was the smart one and applying to medical schools. I told him it wasn't true, but it probably is.

Oh, and his brother is better looking than him, too.

I hate him.

posted by MissH 23.48

I'm going to bed consumed with rage. I'm shaking a little bit and my teeth are chattering, I'm so angry. At least, I am for about five minutes and then I feel sad again. And then angry. And then sad. It feels good to finally be angry, I think, but it also feels like my body is too small for everything that's going on inside me. It's like a cage. How can everything that I'm feeling be contained in me, in this little room, in this little house? And everyone else's feelings inside them, in their little rooms, in their little houses? All trapped inside ourselves sitting alongside each other in this big mess? Why hasn't the world imploded?

I think anger must mean I'm feeling a bit better, anyway.

Saturday, 6 September i.e. Day 1 of Recovery

posted by MissH 10.50

Fuelled by a new outrage that has lasted for over twenty-four hours now, I have decided to take some action in my life. This has seemed a very remote and unreachable possibility all summer, and my reasons for feeling this way now are four-fold:

1. Anger and disbelief that I have been sitting around being *this* pitiable, for *this* long, over someone who has yet to even pay me the courtesy of a rude break-up text.

2. Panic that my own mother and best friend will stop talking to me if I don't stop being so annoying. It's not like I'm exactly swimming in friends as it is.

3. The realisation that not only have I succeeded in alienating all my friends, I seem to have estranged myself. (When did that happen? When did I become this pathetic person I really, intensely dislike?)

4. A belief (or hope) that there must surely be a better use for the internet than for self-involved moping and stalking my ex-boyfriend.

For these reasons I have started redesigning my blog, which is as pathetic as I am. Goodbye, My Dingy Internet Cave.

posted by MissH 11.01
Should I also throw away my Chewit wrapper collection of all the Chewits Leon ever gave me?

posted by MissH 11.04
Let's not go too far.

Editing Emma
(The Secret Blog of A Nearly Proper Person)

posted by EditingEmma 11.47

Today is the day. Today is the day that I, Emma Nash – in light of the above realisations – set upon a mission that I hope will change lives, beginning with that of my own, and then maybe my mother's. From this moment on I shall no longer be Emma, but Editing Emma, striving to make positive changes to my life (or 'edits', if you will).

I have made a discovery of what I consider to be one of the human race's biggest untapped resources... the internet. OK, so the internet has already technically been discovered and has in fact become the world's most important tool for communication. BUT, when it comes to DATING, I strongly believe we've been using it the wrong way. Here's why:

For the past two months I have used it to stalk the same, not-worth-anyone's-time-or-virginity waste of space over and over, thus never getting over it and perpetuating the myth that we are still somewhat involved.

I have used it only to make myself feel more alone and focus on the person who abandoned me, rather than for connecting with other human beings (i.e. THE WHOLE REASON IT WAS INVENTED).

Though my mother does use it to 'connect', as it were, I often observe her on whatever new dating site she is currently a member of meeting EXACTLY the same kind of creeps she meets down the pub.

For these reasons, I feel we have been missing out on all the internet has to offer. Over 50 per cent of people in THE WORLD have a presence on a social network, and we are each and every one of us connected to hundreds, maybe thousands of other human beings… Amongst these there is bound to be someone out there for all of us – someone maybe even *already in our life*, who we may well have met and overlooked.

From now on, instead of using the internet to obsess over the same person, I will try using it to get to know someone different. What's more, someone NOT AT ALL LIKE LEON. I am determined to prove to myself and my fellow comrades in the search for an at least 50 per cent functional relationship that, with the internet's help, it can and will be found. (I think. Maybe. Let's give it a try.)

RESOLUTIONS
1. **Stop isolating myself.**
I will do this by:
    A) Resuming regular washing, so that people want to go near me.

    B) Dedicating more time to real-life people than characters
       in TV shows.

2.   **STOP obsessing about Leon, and stalking him online.**
I will do this by…
    A) Trying instead to use my phone/laptop to meet someone
       else, someone who will actually be nice to me.
    B) Recording my findings here for the rest of the world to
       see!! (Steph and my mum.) No more will I lurk around
       moping in my dark, crusty little internet hovel, but I
       will use this space for something productive!
    Behold… my new blog.

posted by EditingEmma 12.07

Experiment 1
Facebook: Because the Person You've Been Looking For Could Be Right Under Your Virtual Nose
Right. Time to start on my resolutions… If I want to begin the new term afresh, I'm going to have to stop stalking Leon. And, er… start stalking other people.

posted by EditingEmma 12.43
Or I could always go to my room and masturbate all afternoon. It does seem infinitely more appealing.

posted by EditingEmma 13.18
Six orgasms in half an hour. That's one every five minutes. If

you look at my daily activity based on masturbation alone, I'm actually an incredibly productive person.

posted by EditingEmma 15.02

I've bathed. It happened.

Mum knocked on my door.

'What do you want?' I grunted.

'I've run you a bath, and you're getting in it. You're revolting,' she called from outside.

I saw myself in the mirror, red-faced, bedraggled and be-styeed, with one hand down my pyjama bottoms, and I knew she wasn't wrong.

I'm actually feeling way more positive now that I'm clean.

posted by EditingEmma 19.41

Called Steph to tell her about my resolutions.

She said, 'I'm totally on-board. But I think you might need a new strategy.'

'Why?'

'How will you meet anyone new, from people that you already know?'

'Aha! But see, I've been thinking about this. How many of your Facebook friends are you *actually* friends with?'

'Oh God. I don't know. Err... I'm going to say about 15 per cent.'

'Exactly!!'

'So what? I still know what they all look like.'

'It's not just about looks, Steph.'

'Disagree.'

'But I didn't even like Leon, in that way, for the first two months of knowing him. I think we could already KNOW our soulmates, just not know that they're our soulmates yet.'

'So you're saying… Willie Thomas might have hidden depths?'

(Willie Thomas is a boy in our art class who looms way too close to girls to try and look down their tops. He also has really bad breath.)

'Well, maybe not Willie.'

Sunday, 7 September

posted by EditingEmma 12.46

Staring into the cold, harsh, glaring light of the computer screen, which may be the guiding light leading me towards my new life... Beginning the stalk. Hmm... Going through my 'friends', looking for boys I don't normally speak to.

posted by EditingEmma 14.05

As it turns out, I've actually only added people I *do* normally speak to. Or Leon's friends. And I know that I definitely don't want to date any of them.

Well, plan over.

posted by EditingEmma 16.33

Mum has been ranting on about how 'tired' she is and how her 'glands are up'. As is the case most of the time. She thinks she has a 'mild case of ME'. I'm not going to tell her otherwise, though; her hypochondria makes her more lenient when it comes to letting me stay off school. I thought I'd better lay the groundwork now, in case my stye doesn't disappear by Thursday, so I shuffled into Mum's room with a blanket wrapped around my shoulders.

'Mum,' I coughed, 'I think I caught your ME. I think you should consider keeping me off college next week.'

'You can't catch ME,' she says with a dismissive wave of her hand, as if to say, *You don't understand what I'm going through*.

She is so annoying.

posted by EditingEmma 20.42

Steph called:

'Did you start on your resolutions yet?'

'Yes, but you were right. Everyone I'm "friends" with I already know sort-of well enough in real life to know I wouldn't want to date them.'

'Ah.'

'My plan was fatally flawed.'

She munched away on something down the end of the phone.

'What about the people you haven't added? No offence but you've only got about three hundred friends.'

'...I'll try again tomorrow.'

Monday, 8 September

posted by EditingEmma 12.22

Back to the drawing screen. I'm discovering people I never even knew existed... who are apparently in our year at school... (Who is Umar Khan? Or Brian Fielding?) And there are lots of people I've seen around but never had ANY interaction with.

. . . Am I hugely anti-social?

Let's not dwell too much on that.

posted by EditingEmma 15.59

I have found a couple of possibilities... Laurence Myer and David Hudson. An elusive pair of technology nerds. You don't see them often, but when you do it's usually together and it's ALWAYS on a computer. I overheard a conversation between them once and it was about the relative differences between android and iOS operating systems. No idea what that actually means, but I sense that they're the kind of guys who will grow up to make millions inventing something to do with algorithms that no one else understands.

Adding them both. I'm actually kind of nervous. What if they don't accept?

posted by EditingEmma 16.04

I needn't have worried. Four minutes ago, Laurence Myer accepted my request, and three minutes ago, David Hudson accepted.

Evidence: Technology nerds get back to you quickly. Probably because they are always attached to their phones and/or their laptops.

I couldn't choose between them, so I'm going with Laurence Myer because he accepted first. As solid a reason as any. After going through his pictures for a while, I am astounded by the fact that I've never really noticed Laurence. He is, actually, quite attractive. My love for Leon has made me blind to everyone else around me. I save the most normal-looking picture of Laurence I can find for my case study, cropping out everyone else around him and enlarging his head.

posted by EditingEmma 21.00

I was feeling really pleased with myself until I spoke to Steph:

'Steph, I've done it. I've set off on an important journey.'

'Where are you going?'

'To a new beginning.'

'You're beginning a journey towards a new beginning?'

'Yes.'

'So you spoke to Laurence Myer?'

'Oh, no. I added him though. We've achieved virtual friendship.'

'Woah! Slow down, Emma!!'

'Oh. Really?'

'NO. Talk to him!!!'

'. . . I feel like that might be a step too far, for tonight.'

'Yes, you're right, you might end up achieving virtual pregnancy.'

'. . . Fine.'

Maybe he won't be online.

Of course he's online. OK, here goes... I'm going in for the kill.

posted by EditingEmma 21.46

Our conversation, which I have recorded (with commentary):

> **Emma:** hey
>
> **Laurence:** hi
>
> **Emma:** how are you?
>
> **Laurence:** im good
>
> There is a long pause.
>
> **Laurence:** you?
>
> **Emma:** im good thank you, what are you up to?
>
> **Laurence:** just listening to some music
>
> **Emma:** what you listening to?
>
> **Laurence:** nickelback
>
> **Emma:** ah cool, I haven't listened to them in ages...

Because the only reason I've *ever* listened to them is that my dad used to play them, and my ears would bleed liquid mediocrity. How old is this boy, sixteen or fifty-six?

> **Laurence:** do you have any of their stuff? I would

> download it but I have no money and I'm morally
> opposed to piracy and I hate the adverts on Spotify

That was way too much information. I suppose some of Dad's beige songs might still be cluttering up this ancient laptop.

> **Emma:** probably somewhere
> **Laurence:** could you send me anything?
> **Emma:** ermmm, hang on...

I'm in the middle of feeling a bit judgemental and superior, when something awful happens... Just as I'm about to send him a song Mum screams something about a missing eye-shadow, which I know is at the bottom of my handbag. I turn from the screen and call back that I have no idea where it is. I turn back and click 'paste' but instead of pasting 'How You Remind Me' into the conversation, I end up pasting the last thing I copied.

The enlarged picture of his head.

I sit for a second in utter disbelief.

'No. No. No. No. No. No. NO NO NO!!! Cancel! CANCEL!!!'

> **Laurence:** whats that?
> **Emma:** that... that is a picture of you
> **Laurence:** ok

Think of an excuse!! Think of an excuse!! Oh God... there IS no excuse! What excuse could I POSSIBLY have?!

Emma: I was just zooming in to see your teeth, I
noticed before you have very nice teeth
There is a long pause.
In fact, that's sort of why I added you, I was
wondering if I could have the name of your dentist
Laurence: er, I don't know her name
Emma: oh well. Ok
Laurence: ok
Oh my God, just STOP TALKING.
Emma: got to dash
Got to dash?
Laurence: ok. Bye
Emma: byeeeee ☺

Yes, the smiley face at the end makes everything better. Much
less scary.

Well, after that I may have ruled out Laurence Myer as
a potential case study. URGH. Now I feel worse than I did
before. Just when I thought my self-confidence couldn't sink
any lower, I fail to get a date with a Nickelback fan.

posted by EditingEmma 22.04
Oh God. If I can't even speak normally online, what hope
do I have in real life?! All physical awkwardness (like how
long you're supposed to make eye contact without coming
off as a psychopath) has been removed AND you get as
much time as you need to think of a witty response. Even if
you wait like ten minutes or something you can just pretend
you were 'getting a cup of tea' and not frantically trying to

sound clever. And it's not even like I was that anxious. That idiotic interaction is me at my most relaxed and most likely to come off as a real person.

No wonder Leon isn't speaking to me. I wouldn't speak to me either.

Going to bed. At ten. What is my life?

posted by EditingEmma 22.38

I can't even sleep. Mum is snoring in the next room. Usually, I would make a loud noise to wake her up then pretend it was her 'night terrors' but I can't be bothered. I don't even have the energy to cry any more. I'm exhausted, all the time. I never stop thinking about Leon. He never stops being there. One time I *made* myself stop thinking about him for a week or so. That was exhausting in itself. And then I fell asleep from the exertion and just dreamed about him all night anyway.

Tuesday, 9 September

posted by EditingEmma 18.52

Today I got to work on resolution 1B (stop isolating myself) and walked round to Faith's. I was quite afraid of leaving the house and lingered in the corridor for twelve minutes until Mum pushed me outside and locked the door. I'd forgotten what our street looked like. My irises felt quite assaulted by the amount of natural brightness, and I was feeling exceptionally beaten down by the time I rang the doorbell.

Faith's mum answered, dressed in an apron that said, 'My Husband Wears The Pants. I Just Tell Him Which Ones To Wear'. I couldn't help but think that my mum would have doused it in petrol and thrown it, with its frills and questionable presentation of gender roles, on a bonfire.

'Hi, Emma,' she said, tentatively, as if I might start crying at any moment. (Did she see the status, too?)

'Hi, Lillian.'

'Faith's upstairs, painting.' She smiled.

When I came into her room, Faith's blonde curls were covered in flecks of purple and red. She was wearing a long, blue shirt, also caked in paint, and she was, very earnestly, decorating her wall with a giant flower.

'Hello, Georgia O'Keeffe,' I said.

For a moment she said nothing, and then, 'Thank you, Emma.'

'Thank you for what?'

'Georgia O'Keeffe painted flowers – though only about 10 per cent of her work was actually flowers, you know – and was plagued by accusations that they were vaginas. She insisted time and time again that they weren't. I *try* to paint an expression of my sexuality; a giant, purple and red flower-vagina, in the middle of my wall, and my mother comes in and says, "What a pretty flower, Faith."'

It looks like I'm not the only one who's been too isolated this summer.

'I'm not sure "pretty" is the word I'd use. It's a bit of a monster,' I remarked.

She put down her brush, then, and looked at me. I looked at her. We both looked at the flower and burst out laughing.

Reasons That Faith is One of the Best Humans I Know

1) **She hardly ever moans, and keeps her bad moods to herself,** usually channelling them into something creative. I have no idea how. Imagine having a feeling and not examining it over and over until you've turned it completely inside out and bored your friends stiff with it.

2) **Despite her parents not accepting her being gay** (granted, she hasn't definitively told them yet), **she is one of the most accepting people I've ever met.**

3) **She has a strong moral compass.** (Something I'm still

developing. But as my teacher in Year 1 told me when I was trying and failing to tie my shoelaces, we all develop at different rates and that's OK.)

4) **She's a peacekeeper.** There have been many times when I've wanted to throttle Gracie, or Gracie's wanted to throttle me, and the only reason we're both still alive is Faith's soothing, balmy presence.

5) **She gives really good advice, which is probably a result of reasons 1–4.** I hardly ever listen to it, but it's reassuring to know it's there.

I spent the entire afternoon lying on Faith's bed looking at *Elle* and *Marie Claire* galleries on her computer whilst she painted. I told her about my plan and she said, 'Are you sure you're ready to date? You've cried three times since you got here.'

See. Solid advice, reliably ignored.

posted by EditingEmma 20.01

A Further Reminder of My Sadness
Mum came in and threw my mail at me.

'It's time to open it. I've had enough of you cluttering up my house.'

'You shouldn't have had a child, then,' I muttered as she walked away.

It was my new A level timetable, which I've been avoiding since it arrived three weeks ago. I'm taking Art & Design, English, French, Maths, Biology. Yes, that is five instead of four, and no, I'm not one of those super-intelligent and slightly unbalanced students who really enjoy learning and go to after-school clubs.

CONFESSION: I only really took Biology because Leon was taking it.

WHO AM I?????

Even writing it down makes me feel dirty. I rationalised that otherwise we wouldn't have had *any* of the same subjects (he's taking History, Politics, German and Biology). I didn't want to give up anything *I* wanted to do, so I just... took an extra one.

Mum was all,

'Are you sure that's not too many, Emma?'

'Are you sure you *actually* want to take Biology, Emma?'

'Since when did you like touching dead animals, Emma?'

And I was all,

'It's not too many, Mum.'

'I can handle it, Mum.'

'Of course I want to take Biology. Why else would I be doing it, Mum?'

EVIDENCE: Heed my warning. DO NOT make life decisions that will actually affect your future based around someone you like. Even if you think you may 'love' them. It is not worth it. You will end up like me. *I am doing a whole extra AS level because I am an idiot.*

posted by EditingEmma 22.25

I was just contemplating which series to start from the beginning yet again, when...

Laurence: hi

....What's this?!

Emma: hey

Has he hit his head? Does he not remember that I am a strange stalker?

Emma: you ok?

Laurence: yeah you?

Emma: I'm good thanks

Laurence: I got the name of my dentist off my mum... ;)

Is he being nice about yesterday?

Emma: haha... thanks

Laurence: now you can have teeth as nice as mine

Emma: I'm not sure they'll ever measure up

Laurence: haha. Do you want it?

Or does he really think I want his dentist's number?

Emma: er sure ta

Laurence: you'll have to get it off me in person

Oh. I see.

Emma: I see

Laurence: do you want to go to the cinema tomorrow?

Emma: sure

Laurence: ok, meet me there at 7, I'll get the tickets

Emma: cool see you then

Laurence: see you tomorrow

And the investigations are back on track!! Interesting. Very interesting. I'm quite taken aback.

Evidence: Technology nerds don't scare easily.

So, I have a date tomorrow… I hope he doesn't mind that I'm in love with someone else. Or that he's a case study. Going to sleep now. I feel marginally better about life. (Marginally.)

Wednesday, 10 September

posted by EditingEmma 10.10

Up bright and early. I'm not really nervous. Is that a good thing or a bad thing? Before seeing Leon, I used to shake like a leaf and feel sick. Even though I saw him a lot.

I miss him.

I wonder how often he sees Anna? I mean Apple?

posted by EditingEmma 11.37

I was looking through pictures of Leon on my phone when I realised something that I've never noticed before... he has quite a small head. And I have quite a large one. What was I thinking?? Trying to make a relationship work with someone who has such a smaller head than me??? I pointed this out to Mum.

She replied, 'Yes, that's probably why it didn't work out. He was afraid of your big, beefy skull.'

Must snap out of this. Focus on tonight. *I'm Louis Theroux, I'm Louis Theroux.*

posted by EditingEmma 18.07

I can't seem to motivate myself to put on make-up. Sometimes

I feel like there's nothing fun about it any more, it's just some cruel necessity… and I'm only sixteen. What am I going to feel like when I'm twenty-six? Thirty-six?

Mum came in and stared at me staring at the mirror.

'What are you doing?'

'Feeling resentful that half the population don't feel pressured to waste time and energy painting their faces every day.'

'You could stop doing it.'

'Then I'd feel bad about myself because I'd look worse than everyone else. It will only work if every single woman on the planet puts down their eyeliner and says, "no, this is what I look like, and this is how I am."'

'Someone's got to start the revolution.'

'Will you join me?'

'No.'

posted by EditingEmma 18.41

I suppose, if there is one small consolation to the injustice of dreary, habitual make-up, it's that I can cover up my stye. OK… I'm off on my 'date' now. Maybe it will actually be magical and we'll have lots of sex and terrifying babies that look like Chad Kroeger.

posted by EditingEmma 22:14

My 'Date': A Play By Play

Magical is definitely not the word I would use to describe tonight.

7 PM: I arrive at the cinema and Laurence is already waiting there, swaying awkwardly from side to side with his hands in his pockets. He's wearing baggy jeans and a baggy t-shirt with some sort of cartoon dog on it. It's a look, I guess. I walk over to him.

'Hi!' I say.

'Hi.'

Silence.

'So, you got the tickets OK?'

He nods.

'How much do I owe you?'

He shakes his head.

'Oh, well, I'll buy you some popcorn or something.'

He shrugs.

7.20 PM: We are probably in the seats by now. Conversation has been minimal so far. Minimal to the point of… well, non-existent. I tried a few topics and got mainly head twitches and grunts in response.

7.30 PM: Just before the movie starts.

'Do you want a Minstrel?' Laurence asks.

Yes!! We have conversation lift off! I think.

8.30 PM: No, we didn't. I'm ashamed to think of my enthusiastic hour-ago self.

I always thought cinema dates were just a bit of an excuse to sit in the dark and giggle at things. It seems Laurence actually really wants to see the movie.

9.20 PM: The film is over. We stand awkwardly at the doors of the cinema. So far the sum total of Laurence's conversation is still, 'Do you want a Minstrel?'

'So, you enjoyed the film then?' I ask.

He nods.

'OK, well, bye, then…'

'Oh, bye.'

I give him an awkward hug. And then he walks away. Seriously?! Is that… *it*?! Can that count as a date? Or even as an interaction? I say more to the cashier at Tesco when I'm buying some gum.

Evidence: Technology nerds are more charming over the internet.

posted by EditingEmma 22.28

I just got a message from Laurence: 'Lol that film wasn't as good as I thought it was gonna be. Disappointed. Did you enjoy it?x'

Evidence: And over their phones.

What? Just… what?! I can't even be bothered to reply. That whole evening was such a flop. Why does anyone bother stepping outside the front door? The odds that you'll have a better time doing anything on the outside than you will sitting watching TV seem pretty slim to me.

posted by EditingEmma 23.09

Until now I'd somehow successfully blocked that it was the night-before-the-first-day-of-sixth-form from my mind. It must have been all that scintillating conversation. Just think, before all this I was actually *looking forward* to starting sixth form. PAH.

Emma Nash @Em_Nasher
Whyyyyyyyyyyyyy

posted by EditingEmma 23.50

Imagining What Will Happen When Leon Sees Me Tomorrow
I'm listening to very intense music to set the scene. I walk into school, in my new black skater skirt and fitted shirt (that I bought from & Other Stories), finally liberated from the lumpy school jumper I've been stuck wearing for five years. My stye is barely noticeable. Our eyes catch... We keep making eye contact and he can't pretend to focus on the conversation he's having any longer. He strides over to me and puts his hand behind my neck and his other hand on my face and just kisses me...

And everyone is watching.

Thursday, 11 September

posted by EditingEmma 08.22

What Actually Happened When Leon Saw Me
Our eyes catch… He looks slightly awkward for a moment, but then keeps going with the conversation he's having. Neither of us go over to say hello. Or really acknowledge each other at all.

posted by EditingEmma 08.33
Sitting next to Steph in registration, comparing timetables. Gracie is going on and on about 'split ends' and keeps shoving strands of red hair in my face. It feels strange to be interacting with so many people at once. I feel like a rabbit caught in headlights, and everything feels very loud and terrifying. But it's nice… I think. I can't believe I'm saying this but it *almost* makes me feel relieved to be back at school.

Discussed the Leon meeting with Steph:

'I was so sure that the first time he saw me, *in person*, he wouldn't be able to ignore me. But nope. He did. Are we absolutely, positively, one hundred per cent certain that I didn't make the whole thing up?'

'No. He definitely exists. I've seen him many times.'

'I mean… the asking out thing. Maybe he never asked me out at all. Maybe he said, "Emma, will you HANG out with me?" And then my longing desire caused me to hear whatever I wanted to hear, and I took it to mean GO out with me, and then he was too awkward to say anything.'

'I don't think so.'

'Sometimes my granddad does it. Sometimes because he loves trifle, he'll say that my mum *said* we were having trifle, which she would never say in a million years, because she *hates* trifle. But he genuinely thinks it. He genuinely thinks she said we were having trifle, then gets all upset when she brings out yoghurt and fruit. What if that's me?? What if I've inherited it??'

'I think your granddad is eighty-nine, so you're probably not there yet. And I don't think he asked you to hang out because you were already hanging out. That makes no sense.'

'What if he said… "Emma, will you eat sprouts with me?" Or "Will you joust with me?"'

'Not impossible, but highly improbable.'

Emma Nash @Em_Nasher
Glad to be back at school for 5 seconds. Now chanting our stupid school motto in Latin. I take it all back. Hoc sugit.

posted by EditingEmma 11.22

The End of a Very Eventful Break
Coming to you nearly live from the Maths & Sciences Block girls' toilets.

11.00 AM: I am standing around with Steph, Faith and Gracie in the tuck shop, sweating profusely because Leon is in the room. Gracie is WAY too excited about her brother's party on Saturday.

'Andy says he's got loads of good drinking games for us to play,' she says smugly.

'You know it won't be *Drinking Articulate*, don't you?' I point out.

'Yes, of course,' she snaps, then adds, 'Though I don't see why that would be such a bad idea.'

'You could teach everyone all about how to raise their WPM,' I say. (Words per minute.)

She beams and my sarcasm goes straight over her head.

11.05 AM: Laurence Myer ENTERS THE TUCK SHOP. Moving away from the safe, secluded environment of the Tech Lab, he wanders in looking a bit dazed, head spinning, blinking at the crowds… My heart sinks. I know I'm going to have to admit what I did last night.

Steph sees and stares at him for a second. Then she says, 'I know what you did last night.'

Faith and Gracie look up from their hot dogs.

'… What *did* you do last night?' asks Faith.

'I… I…'

'She went on a date with Laurence Myer.'

'Thanks, Steph.'

'That's… interesting,' says Faith. 'I didn't know you spoke to Laurence Myer.'

'I didn't. I mean… I still haven't.'

11.10 AM: He keeps looking over at us. And he's all on his own, looking lost. And just as I think I'd better shuffle over for a bit of painfully awkward silence… Leon beats me to it.

Leon. With his dark, wavy hair and eyes like chocolate buttons.

The four of us stare in amazement.

'This is brilliant,' says Steph, opening up her crisps and settling in for the show.

'Stop staring!' I order, but then give up and stare.

Laurence looks inordinately grateful to have someone to talk to. Leon is just chatting away, lighting up the room with his casual charm and beautiful laugh, when Laurence says something and they both look over here.

Gracie practically chokes on her hot dog.

Steph throws her crisps up in the air.

I duck.

Faith is the only person who remains even slightly within the realm of a normal person, and looks indifferently out of the window.

'Emma… Emma…you know, they can still see you,' whispers Faith.

So I stand up pretending I've dropped some sort of invisible object on the floor… Then Laurence leaves, presumably to return to his inner sanctum, and Leon goes back to sit with his mates. From then on, he keeps looking over in our direction with a very *serious* face.

11.15 AM: The crowds are all cramming through the door to leave and, out of nowhere, Laurence pops up. (He must have been hiding…) He smiles at me and brandishes a bag of Minstrels.

'Hi, Laurence.'

More silent smiling and Minstrel offering.

'Err… thanks.'

ANALYSIS OF EVENTFUL BREAK

1. Is Laurence Myer going to keep bringing me Minstrels at break but say nothing, and think this qualifies as a relationship?
2. What did Laurence say to Leon?! Does Leon know about my 'date'??
3. Does he care?
4. Even if he does care, should I care that he cares?

posted by EditingEmma 11.45

In Maths nomming on delicious Minstrels. OK, so conversation might not be stimulating, but I sure would be well fed…

As I was writing this, Mr Crispin walked past and complimented me on my concentration (on my phone, under my desk). Well, actually what he said was, 'Emma's hungry for the hidden values!'

posted by EditingEmma 12.01

<u>Why I Stopped Reading *Frankenstein*</u>

'Did everyone read *Frankenstein* over summer?' Ms Parker asks, at the beginning of English. There is a dreary murmur in confirmation.

'Did you really, Emma?' Ms Parker smiles at me.

'I did,' I say.

Not exactly a lie… I started it, but I never finished. For about a week afterwards, I had dreams that I was the monster and parts of me kept falling off. In one of them I was on a beach, and Leon was picking up the bits of me, like my foot or my nose, and lobbing them into the sea. And I was crying and crying for him to stop and he wouldn't. Then I went to Gracie's house, and she asked me to leave because I was just 'too ugly to look at'.

posted by EditingEmma 12.33

A screenshot of mine and Steph's WhatsApping in English:

Did you know that Laurence talked to Leon? 12.19

No 12.19

Who knew?? 12.19

You know, just because you'd never talked to Laurence before, it doesn't mean that no one else ever did 12.20

I sense that I'm annoying you… 12.20

. . . But I'm carrying on. Do you think Leon will be in our Biology class? 12.24

I'm not psychic 12.25

I'm glad we're together, anyway 12.25

Me too 12.26

Are you actually? 12.26

Not if you keep talking about Leon 12.26

Point taken. Sorry, I'm really nervous 12.26

If he's there it will be awkward. But at least Crazy Holly
will be there, too 12.27

How does that help? 12.27

It's impossible to feel awkward around Crazy Holly 12.28

True 12.28

posted by EditingEmma 13:55

Sitting in the loos crying

Really, given the amount of time I've spent processing
Anna and Leon's relationship status, you'd think I'd have
been more prepared for their actual relationship. But I
wasn't.

Here's what happened:

I went and collected my stingy portion of food.
Considering how much money I (my mum) pays for these
lunches, you'd think they'd give us more than one sausage
and three bits of broccoli. Yes, they actually *count* the
broccoli. And if you get an abnormally large bit then you
only get two. I once said, 'That's broccoli discrimination.
You've made him feel fat,' and the dinner lady just stared
at me. But I digress.

So I sat down at the table with my tiny lunch and Gracie
kept looking at me very uncomfortably, like the sight of

me was giving her stomach cramps. Steph gave me half her sausage. I should have known something was up then because Steph would usually fight you to the death for half a sausage. I was about to bite into it, when I saw Leon across the room. Talking to Anna. Then he put his arm around her. The sausage sort of hung in the air, then whacked me in the face. I stared open-mouthed. Suddenly, it was all too much for me and I got up to leave.

And now I'm in the loos.

Steph came to find me.

'Not many people can make me feel sad with gravy on their face but you pull it off,' she said.

I laughed but it quickly turned back to crying.

'I knew they were together but, seeing them…'

'I know,' Steph said.

'And now we've got Biology. And he might be there.'

'I know.'

'Is it really obvious I've been crying?'

'Errr…'

Steph got out her compact mirror.

I look like I've been boiled.

posted by EditingEmma 20.37

The Rest of My First Day of Sixth Form

Biology

I tried to hide that I'd been crying but I still arrived looking like a puffy red frog. I felt so nervous about the possibility of

Leon being there that I was physically quivering. Within two seconds, I'd scanned the room with my ultra-fast Leon radar, sadly the most effective part of my brain, and assessed that he wasn't in the room. I actually felt *disappointed*. (What's wrong with me?) My nervous energy plummeted back into regular old glumness.

I had a feeling Biology would not make me feel better. Long and pointy Dr Penzik had a creepy smile on his long and pointy face. Which meant that we were probably massacring some sort of small animal for an experiment. And then, ah yes… I spotted them. The pile of organs. Lovely. (This is my punishment for taking a subject because someone I fancied was in the class. And he's not even in it.)

Dr Penzik handed round the sheep hearts looking a little too pleased. I started typing a post, when he said,

'Oh, no you don't. Emma, move up here.' He pointed to the front of the class.

'Erm. Why, may I ask, Dr Penzik? I only got here five minutes ago so I haven't been talking yet.'

'I can see you texting,' he barked.

'I'm not *texting*, I'm—'

'Look, let's just avoid any trouble and move you away from Steph. Put your phone away and find a new partner.'

I refrained from pointing out the obvious flaws in his logic. Suppose I was 'texting' Steph, why would separating us stop that? The whole point of 'texting' is that you can 'text' from across the room. Anyway, I looked around, scanning for a new partner. Crazy Holly was beckoning. Crazy Holly is fun and everything, but did I really want to see what she would do to a sheep heart?

No, was the answer to that. Five minutes later, I already had sheep blood on my nose.

'Holly, what are we even meant to be doing?' I asked, glancing at the abandoned sheet lying next to us.

She shrugged and kept hacking. I stared fixedly at the mangled mess we had created. It was like looking down at my own heart.

When I Arrived Home

The door was double-locked, which was just what I needed. (Mum calls it the Emma Lock, there just in case I plan on having any 'wild parties' when she goes away. She clearly thinks I have more friends than I do.)

I banged on the door. It opened a fraction and Mum's nose poked out.

'Oh… I wasn't expecting you home yet… awkward.' Then she turned her head and called out, 'Gerald, you'll have to leave!'

She let me in and ran into the kitchen. I heard, 'Gerald, put some clothes on!!'

When I walked in there was no one else in there. Except Mum, pissing herself laughing in a corner.

And now I'm in my room, contemplating the day's events.

What did Laurence say to Leon?!?!

posted by EditingEmma 22.09

I tried so hard not to but I'm stalking Apple again. Leon linked her to a scene from *The Rocky Horror Picture Show*. He really loves that film. He's probably going to make her watch it five million times whilst force-feeding her jam tarts.

I really wish I was her.

One day of sixth form felt like a lifetime. I'm going to bed now. Hopefully I won't wake up.

Friday, 12 September

posted by EditingEmma 07.30
Woke up. Darn.

posted by EditingEmma 13.38

Strange Things That Have Happened Today
(And it's only lunchtime. And only Day 2 of Sixth Form.)
    When I came downstairs to breakfast, Mum appeared to be pretending to surf.
    She said, 'It's my t'ai chi.'
    I said, 'Of course.'
    Steph wants to go to Mum's salsa class.
    This is pretty much how the conversation went:
    'How's your mum?' Steph asked.
    'Keeping herself busy with a range of different hobbies.'
    'Ooh, like what?'
    'Surfing in the living room.'
    'Is she still seeing the stripper?'
    'You never get tired of asking that, do you?'
    'No.'

'I'm not sure. But I do know that she's been going to salsa, because she keeps stealing Bear to dance with.'

'Salsa?'

'Yes, I have since discovered where my dancing incapability comes from.'

'Is she having lessons? Can we go with her?'

'You want to go to salsa? With my mum?'

After an hour of thinking that she was joking, it turns out she does actually want to go to salsa. With my mum. Curiouser and curiouser...

The Awkward Toilet Encounter

I was washing my hands when Apple came out of the cubicle next door. And she *smiled* at me. Because she's a really *nice* person. I think I managed to smile back relatively normally (like I haven't spent days scrutinising every single part of her face and wondering things like whether she masturbates a lot or how often she washes her bras). But I ruined it by staring at her lips for a little too long. I couldn't help thinking those lips have been on Leon's lips. How recently? If I grabbed her and kissed her, would it be sort of like kissing Leon?

When I came out of the loos, Leon was waiting outside. My whole body flooded with adrenaline which, for some unknown reason, prompted me to speak to him.

'Lurking in the shadows outside girls' loos is generally considered a bit creepy,' I said jokily.

'I'm waiting for Anna,' he said, without an expression. Maybe it's contagious. She has some weird disease where all her facial muscles become like hanging bits of flab and she's given it to him.

'OK…' I said, and started to walk away.

'I didn't know you were friends with Laurence,' he called after me, stonily.

'I didn't know *you* were friends with Laurence.'

'I used to sit with him in Maths.'

'Oh. Did he help you?'

'Oh, piss off, Emma.'

He said it with such force, and I was so taken aback that I felt like I'd been shoved backwards into the wall. The only person who has ever told me to 'piss off' in such an ugly way is my mother.

He stared at me all defiant and scowly, and I stood there looking back at him like a jellyfish with my mouth open. Then Apple came out of the loo and we all continued to stand there for a bit. She looked at us both and, I swear, *almost* managed an expression (one of confused awkwardness).

Then I quickly moved away.

posted by EditingEmma 15.32

Moping in Maths

I was hiding my phone under the desk but then I remembered it's Mr Crispin… Ah Maths. My free blogging pass.

So I told Steph all about what happened and she gave me a Chewit. After I ate it, I threw the wrapper away and she said,

'What? You're not going to save it and roll it up in a

ball with my hair and spit and keep it under your bed? I'm offended.'

'I never kept his hair. Or spit.'

'No, just his bloody plaster. Anyway, at least you've got Gracie's brother's party to look forward to tomorrow…'

I grunted. Then Mr Crispin asked me a question about 'cumulative frequency' and I just whimpered.

'Is that all you do now? Whimper and grunt?' asked Steph.

I grunted in response. She grunted back.

'It was like… he hated me.'

Steph bobbed her head in sympathy. 'I've run out of Chewits.'

'It's OK. I'm too miserable to eat.'

'Or maybe you're too full because you ate the whole pack.'

'Maybe.'

'Do you think we'd still be friends if we were guys?' asked Steph.

'No, you'd punch me.'

There was silence as we both visualised it.

'Yeah, I probably would.'

posted by EditingEmma 15.50

Crazy Holly asked to plait my hair (she just loves to plait hair). I must be feeling pretty low because a) I let her and b) I enjoyed it.

posted by EditingEmma 17.16

At Home

'Mum… ?' I say carefully.

'What? What is it *now*?' she spits.

How nice.

'Are you still dating the stripper? I mean, again?'

'Yes, I am dating *Olly* again and please call him Olly.'

'How's it going?'

'Yesterday it was great. Today not so much. Ask me again tomorrow.'

'OK.'

Silence.

'It can't be any worse than that guy who asked you what older birds had to offer over younger ones.'

'No, it can't. Thanks for reminding me.'

'Any time.'

Silence.

'So, Mum, what *do* older birds have to offer over younger ones?'

'Stop it.'

Evidence: When using the internet to meet people, one must learn to ignore half the stupid crap people feel more free to say than they would to your face.

'Oh, also, can we come to salsa with you tonight?'

She laughs.

'No, I actually mean it.'

posted by EditingEmma 19.57

At salsa. It's the break and Steph and Mum are queuing for the loos. I'm trying to at least pretend like I'm having fun, because I've been so crap over the past couple of months and Steph and Mum seem to be having a freakishly good time. But I will never be doing this again. Ever.

Why You Should Never, Ever Go to Salsa with Your Mum:

1) **You stand in lines, with men on one side and women on the other, and go round in a rotation.** There aren't enough men and so half the time you have to put your arms up and pretend to dance with an invisible person.

2) **The rotation also means you have no control over who you dance with.** You have to dance with *everyone*. There's one *really* smelly man and I had to hold my breath for the whole minute that we were partnered. There's this other man who trod on me A LOT (definitely his fault) and then when the music stopped said pityingly, 'Don't worry, it's your first time.' And another man who put his face way too close and got really into wiggling his hips against mine but didn't move in any way that resembled the actual steps.

3) **You are prey to watchful women who have come with the aforementioned men.** There's this one extremely hostile lady who keeps looking over with narrowed eyes at who-ever is dancing with her fiancé. I wish she knew how truly, deeply I'd rather *not* be dancing with him.

4) **You realise that you are so terrible at dancing, even your mum is better than you.**

Oh joy. The break is almost over and it's my turn to dance with the smelly man again.

Add another reason to the list:

5) **You might come face to face with your mum's strange taste in men.**

Back home now, thank God, but after class me, Mum and Steph sat down.

'Are you looking forward to Gracie's brother's party?' Mum asked.

'I'm looking forward to having her stop talking about it,' I replied.

'OK, so don't look now,' Mum muttered, 'but my ex-boyfriend was in the class.'

I thought back through the less than desirable bunch of men we had just danced with.

'Which one?'

'The dark-haired, dark-skinned one.'

'The wiggly one?'

'Yes, him.'

'Oh, God, Mum… Why?'

'What?! He's a good-looking man.'

'If you can see past the creepiness.'

'Well, for me it was more seeing past the good looks.'

'Did you meet him here?' Steph asked.

'Yes,' Mum sighs, 'this was a long time ago. Before I'd even tried internet dating or anything like that.'

Evidence: Most people use the internet merely to repeat the mistakes they make in the real world.

Saturday, 13 September

posted by EditingEmma 11.01

The Day of 'The Big Party'
Gracie has already rung twice asking me about what to do
with her hair. My answer both times was, 'I don't know' i.e.
'I don't care, you have a mind of your own.'

posted by EditingEmma 12.04
'What about my flower clip?'
   (What flower clip?)
   'Yes, definitely.'
   It's going to be a long day...

posted by EditingEmma 17.29

At Gracie's House
Getting ready. It's just me, Steph and Gracie. Faith said she
couldn't come because she 'didn't want to blow off her family
friends'. (I definitely think there is a line between being nice,
and too nice.) We are all crammed into one mirror. Gracie
keeps elbowing me in the face. She's so eager for tonight.

'And Andy's friend Jonno is so good-look

'Is he the one with the really small head?'

Gracie's lips tighten and she goes all pink. 'No, I don't think so.'

'I think he is.'

'I don't know who you mean, but it's not him.'

'Yeah, yeah! It is!' says Steph, laughing.

Gracie is incredibly pink by now.

'None of my brother's friends have a small head.'

'None of them? Does he have some sort of head-size screening process?'

'They're all really attractive.'

'So now you can't be attractive unless you have a large head?' says Steph.

'Just don't make fun of my brother's friends, OK?' she snaps.

'Why? They're not *your* friends.'

That did it. She slammed out of the room. Then came back in for her lipstick and left again.

posted by EditingEmma 17.44

It's so nice being able to do my make-up without being elbowed.

posted by EditingEmma 18.26

Eventually, Gracie came back into the room, but she left again when she realised Steph and I were talking about periods.

'Guys!! Ew!' she exclaimed, like she doesn't have them or something.

Anyway, apparently Steph's sister Jess was kissing a boy at uni, and he tried to go further but she told him she was on. His response was something along the lines of 'gross' and 'too much information'. This makes me angry for several reasons.

The Period Taboo

First of all, it's not like we can help it. It happens. That fact is unfortunately unchangeable (and I think I speak for all women when I say, we really wish there was a better way to be fertile). In that situation, was Jess not supposed to mention it? Would this boy have liked to get his hand covered in blood instead? No, I think not. Then why is she being punished for telling him? Either way, she loses. Which means she's effectively being punished simply for having an uncontrollable bodily function.

And, more than that, why *shouldn't* she be able to speak about it? I actually think women are generally very discreet about the whole thing (e.g. Gracie, who obviously bleeds rainbows). If guys bled out of their penises for a week of every month, you can bet we'd hear more about it.

posted by EditingEmma 20.30
I think I might actually feel a whisper of excitement. I'd almost forgotten there were other emotions aside from desolation and apathy. And I haven't thought about Leon or Apple in at least ten minutes.

We come downstairs and Andy is sitting at the kitchen

table on his phone. Surrounded by cans of beer. He looks a bit like Gracie around the eyes, but more... er... like a boy.

'So what time are people getting here?' Gracie asks, trying to act casual and failing.

'Some of the guys are coming here for pres at nine.'

'Cool.'

'I think Babs is driving them here.'

'Babs?' asks Steph.

'His last name's Babcock.' Andy looks up and smiles at Steph.

posted by EditingEmma 21.35

Gracie keeps jumping out of her skin every time the doorbell goes. (I'm actually feeling a little nervous too.) It's been thirty-five minutes since people arrived and we still haven't spoken to anyone except each other. We're all pretending it's fine, like we're some sort of incredibly exclusive club, not like a cluster of scared penguins huddled protectively together. I should probably stop running to the toilet and blogging.

posted by EditingEmma 21.42

OK, OK, just *one* more post because this was really satisfying. 'Babs' the designated driver for the evening is a real meathead. I said this and Gracie replied, 'What, just because he's got big arms?'

Then Meathead Babs called out, 'Shove it down your bra! Shove it down your bra!' across the room, and I just smiled at her.

posted by EditingEmma 22.09

PS The Answer to Nerves Is…
VODKA. Lots and lots of vodka. We're just passing it round, taking turns to burn our insides. It really is foul without a mixer but a) it's getting us drunk faster and b) everyone else is doing it and we don't want to seem lame.

posted by EditingEmma 22.27
I'm *only* in the toilet again because I had to leave the room. (I am having fun. Sort of. Maybe? I imagine this is what 'having fun' looks like, at the very least.) We're talking to people now, in a manner of speaking, playing some drinking game where you sit in a circle and someone asks another person the most embarrassing/awkward/disgusting question they can think of. If that person hesitates and doesn't instantly ask another socially inappropriate/repellent/horrific question to someone else, *straight* away, then they have to answer it. I'll give an example:

'Have you ever had a sex dream about Jonno's mum?'

'Do you fear that deep down you are secretly a paedophile?'

'Have you ever wanked with a parent in the room?'

I got up when that wanking with a parent in the room question came up, just in case it got directed at me. When you're eleven years old, having just discovered the glory of masturbation and stuck on holiday sharing a room with your mum, you really aren't left with much choice.

At some point Meathead Babs turned to Jonno and asked, 'Would you bang Andy's sister?'

Jonno hesitated and they all went 'ooooohhhhhhhh oh oh oh oh' in that really aggressive, loud way that makes 'laddish' boys sound like packs of gorillas.

'You 'ave to answer now, mate,' declared a satisfied Babs.

'No, he really doesn't,' said Andy.

'Yeah, not answering that,' Jonno said, shaking his head.

'But would you? Would you?' persisted Babs.

The circle descended into shouts of 'Answer, Jonno!' and 'Come on, Jonno!' until Jonno grinned and said, 'Yeah all right, all right, yes.'

More gorilla noises. Andy looked horrified and Gracie looked like she'd just accepted an Oscar.

posted by EditingEmma 22.34

Gracie is still smiling. She's going to be UNBEARABLE for the rest of the night. All because some slobbering idiot with a very small head said he wouldn't mind 'banging' her.

posted by EditingEmma 22.48

'Gracie's brother has a nice smile, don't you think?' Steph pondered.

'Steph, you realise if you went out with Gracie's brother, you'd see her face every time he kissed you.'

'Nooo.'

'Actually, she'd probably kill you before it got that far.'

'It's probably not worth it,' she sighed wistfully.

posted by EditingEmma 23.17

Steph seems to have gotten over it, as she's sitting on Jonno's lap with his hands around her middle. I guess she's gotten over Jonno's abnormally small head, too.

I was standing with Gracie and she started sighing.

'I can't *believe* Steph would do that.'

'Do what?'

She gestured to Steph, who was kissing Jonno so aggressively I wondered if she was trying to dislocate her jaw and eat him whole.

'Why?' I asked.

'Because, you know, of what he *said*.'

'That he would "bang" you?'

'Yes!'

'In all honesty, Gracie, I'm not sure if there's a single female in the room he wouldn't "bang". I think his getting with Steph, not to put a downer on their whole romance, was probably less about choice and more about chance. Sort of like breaking in pool. Doesn't matter which ball goes in the hole, as long as it's a ball. Steph was standing near him seven minutes ago, and you weren't.'

'I should have known you wouldn't support me,' she said, running off to her bedroom.

I honestly thought that was incredibly supportive!!

posted by EditingEmma 23.48

Back in the toilet, with a bottle of gin. Somebody left it unattended and I swiped it, thus teaching them an important life lesson about being careless.

I knocked on Gracie's room a few times but she won't come out. As a result of being ABANDONED I was targeted by a very lanky boy who was slurring his words and had beer down his shirt.

'What's so interesting?' he asked, gesturing to my phone.

'Nothing,' I defended, quickly hiding it.

Then he started showing me some game on his own phone where you have to get a pigeon or something safely across the road. I watched him stab drunkenly at the screen.

'Look, and then you…Oh,' he'd say, looking genuinely crestfallen every time the thing died.

After a few more minutes of wishing he would go away, I leaned on his arm slightly, the one holding his beer, so that it tipped up. Twelve seconds later he clocked and stared down bemusedly at his wet leg. I took the opportunity to slip away.

I wish Leon was here. Leon back when he was still talking to me, that is. Obviously his being here *now* probably wouldn't help my situation very much. But I used to have loads of fun with the old Leon. He would have laughed at everyone drinking their gross, straight vodka and we would have gone and sat in Gracie's empty bathtub, throwing Hula Hoops in each other's mouths and talking all night about everything and nothing.

posted by EditingEmma 00.36

Not that it matters. I am *not* with Leon. These random fifty people are all I've got right now. If I keep drinking maybe the alcohol will give me some semblance of emotion towards at least one of them.

posted by EditingEmma 01.07

Oh God, starting to feel a bit… peaky…But the alcohol may actually be working. Remaining on the edge of the crowd and talking to no one, I've yet to develop any individual bonds, but I've fostered a substantial, almost protective affection for this particular group. These aren't just *any* fifty people I don't care about, these are *my* fifty people I don't care about.

There's an empty bottle of gin in my hand. Did I drink that? Was that me? I thought I was drinking vodka…

posted by EditingEmma 01.35

Tried to find the bathroom but it seemed so, so far away. I've done really well, though, to make it to this doorway. I've sat down as a reward.

> EmmaNash @Em_Nasher
>
> People should put their heads in between their own knees it's lovely and cool and dark
>
> EmmaNash @Em_Nasher
>
> Tea floor is a really nice and peaceful place very good for thinking
>
> EmmaNash @Em_Nasher
>
> Thoughts

posted by EditingEmma 02.02

I don't feel like crying any more, in this safe little spot. None can touch me here.

Minus then rude people who keep stepping over. Me and kicking me.

posted by EditingEmma 03.28

How did I get on the bathroom floor? Someone's been sick jan here, it smells terrible.

Crying so much I am choking. Potentially choking on vomit. Don't have any tears left, I'm so dehydrated. I'm caught in a river of tears, like Alice. Except that the tears are the water at the bottom of Gracie's parents' toilet.

posted by EditingEmma 04.44

Staring into a bucket of sick. Is that mine? Surely that can't *all* be mine?

posted by EditingEmma 05.39

Sobbing into a pillow. Feeling so disgusting and alone. I want Leon so much. He's the only one who can stop me feeling this way, feeling so horribly, horribly lonely. Why doesn't he want me?

I feel as if a huge, gaping hole has opened up inside me that will never ever be filled. Except by Leon, and Leon wanting me. It's like if he doesn't see me, there's nothing to see. I can't ever imagine this ending. I can't ever imagine feeling differently. I am a void which I have no idea how to fill.

Sunday, 14 September

posted by EditingEmma 13.53
Oh God. I'm at home now and just... oh God.

This Morning

I woke up and my first thought was: *Where am I?* There were sounds of people laughing and a TV was on somewhere. Everything seemed too loud. I tried moving but quickly found this was not a good idea. My head was in AGONY. I wanted to ring Steph but I couldn't find my phone.

Then she popped her head round the door with a cup of tea. I was so happy to see her I wanted to start crying again.

'OH,' she said.

'What?' I croaked.

'Have you looked in a mirror?'

'No...'

'Don't.'

She began cleansing me with a face wipe. The pillow was covered in black eye make-up.

'We'll just turn that over,' Steph said.

'What HAPPENED?' I asked.

'You got completely wasted.'

'Yes, I've guessed that much. Where were you?'

'Err… Well I didn't realise you'd got so bad until…'

'Until?'

'Until you stumbled into the room threatening to throw away your Chewit wrapper collection – which, by the way, I don't think would be such a bad idea – then fell over into some girl's lap.'

'Oh. Did she laugh?'

'No. She wasn't very amused.'

'Oh.'

'Especially when you tried to stand up, then it happened again.'

'Oh…'

'And then your top came down.'

Silence.

'At least I was wearing a nice bra.'

'It really is a *very* nice bra.' Steph nodded.

'What happened after that?'

'Well, you declared that you'd "made enough trouble" and that you were going to "sit quietly". Then you sat in the doorway, obstructing everyone's path to the kitchen and the toilet.'

'Why didn't you MOVE me???'

'Various attempts were made. Greg actually got you to stand up but then you looked at him, quite intently, said, "You're not Leon" and sat back down.'

'Oh my God…'

'One good thing came out of it though. Apparently Meathead Babs came in here with a girl to have sex, and after she saw you sobbing next to a bucket of sick it really put her off.'

'I suppose that's something. I can't find my phone.'

'Oh, yeah, about that... I have it. It sort of, er...'

'What?'

'You sort of dropped it in the bucket of sick.'

'No.'

'Yes.'

'*No.*'

'Yes.' She nodded sympathetically.

'Did you... did you fish it out for me?'

She just laughed. 'No. Greg did.'

'I'm sorry but, who *is* Greg?'

'Er, the boy you got with.'

'I... what?!'

Ah, yes. The boy with beer down his shirt. It all came flooding back, then.

Fragmented Memories of the Night Before

1) Kissing The Lanky, Beer-Stained Boy

Who I'm guessing is 'Greg'. I really, *really* had to pee, but Greg was lurking outside the bathroom. I waited for a bit, pretending I was really interested in the coats on the banister. Then I realised it probably looked like I was trying to steal something. So I carried on to the bathroom...

I smiled politely and slid past him to get to the toilet door... when he stopped me.

'How old are you again?'

'Sixteen.'

Then he leant in to kiss me so clumsily that my head got bashed against the wall. I don't think he noticed. I was too drunk and slow to stop it. I think the inner monologue was something like this:

Why didn't I say something??? It just seemed too rude… Why am I so bloody polite?? If I don't WANT to kiss someone, I don't HAVE to kiss someone. I'd probably apologise to a murderer if their knife got stuck in me.

How long do I have to keep this going for? It's got to have been about forty seconds. If a knife DID get stuck in me… where would I want it to be stuck? My arse? Fifty seconds. Why would someone stab you in the bum, though? Do murderers take requests for stabbing preferences? They might think I was a bit odd if I asked for my arse. Over a minute now… definitely… How can I stop this?

My eyes were fully open. I could see people looking at us over Greg's shoulder. Eventually, I took a stand and pulled away.

'I'm hungry,' I announced and walked off forcefully.

And I didn't even get to use the bathroom. My bladder felt like it was going to explode.

2) Avoiding Lanky Greg

He came lolloping over to where I was standing in a group (in, on the edge of, whatever) crashing into one girl as he headed over, holding onto another for support.

'You! Did I kiss you?'

The group looked at me.

'Er, no. No… that was… her.'

And I pointed at Gracie. Thankfully he believed me and

went beetling after her. I smiled and shrugged at the others. They went back to their conversations, and I went back to watching their conversations fondly. I still really needed a wee.

3) Gracie Ignoring Me

Steph was still occupied with Jonno, but I finally found Gracie standing with Andy and a couple of his friends. When I walked over she cast her eyes over me, gave me a cursory smile and then carried on with her conversation.

4) Crying In Public

Greg came back to me. I must have looked a bit sad because he said, 'Are you all right?'

Then suddenly, it was all too much and I burst into tears. I could feel everyone staring at me and, in spite of the silent and uninvited devotion I'd come to feel for them in the past hour, not one of them rushed forwards to comfort me.

'What's the matter?!' Greg exclaimed.

'No, OK!! I'M NOT!!!' I blubbered incoherently and ran off.

5) Gracie Speaking to Me Again

This may only have been because I was obstructing her way to the toilet. I was on the floor and her familiar voice penetrated my tranquil bubble of queasy solitude.

'Oh my God, Emma!!'

'Graaaacieeeee!'

'Get up!! What are you doing??!'

She was all the way up by the ceiling.

'Why are you mad at me?'

'I'm not mad.'

'What did I do?'

'Nothing. Come on.'

'You're annoyed at me. You hate me. Just like Leon.'

'I don't hate you. Come on, get *up*.'

Then we were in the bathroom, and she was telling me everything was going to be OK and gingerly patting my back. She told me that she loved me. She thinks I don't remember that but I do. *Ha*.

Gracie popped her head round the door.

'Does this belong to you?' she asked, wrinkling her nose.

She had my phone, or what was left of it, in a tissue. There were little pieces of *stuff* I didn't wish to acknowledge... all over it. I imagine that's how parents feel about a newborn baby, full of love and affection but not really wanting to look at it until it's been washed.

'Is it working?' I asked, hopefully.

'Hmm, to know that I'd have to have touched it.'

I pressed the 'on' button and it made a terrifying sound, like a mouse being caught in a trap, and then it flashed green and blue.

'Maybe if I put it in a bowl of rice?'

'Well, I've never tried it with acidic bodily fluids, but it works a treat with water,' Steph interjected.

'Did you kiss Greg?' Gracie demanded.

'I didn't want to!'

She looked at me sarcastically.

'He cornered me!'

'So why did you go over to him?'

'I really needed to pee!'

'You didn't use the bathroom,' she laughed, and left the room.

'Urgh… I really want to PELT her with something.'

'Grapes?' Steph helpfully suggested.

'Yes! Giant grapes! Giant grapes that will engulf and suffocate her.'

Eventually I went downstairs to get some breakfast. I crept past the living room door, where Andy's friends had slept… You could hear calls of, 'Wake him up!! Wake him up!!' and, 'Stuff a jelly worm up his nose!' When I crept back, the door opened and Greg stepped out, looking flustered. He seemed different in the sober light of day, more boyish and innocent…His hair was ruffled and swept across his face, and his cheeks flushed with embarrassment. I was definitely the last person he wanted to see. He said 'Hi' and started hurriedly putting his shoes on and then he was out the door.

Gracie looked really relieved when I left her house. (I can't say I blame her, actually. Apparently I also threw up in the pile of coats on her parents' bed.) Then I walked home clutching my bowl of vomit-stained rice. All in all, pretty low.

posted by EditingEmma 15.24

For some suspicious reason, I am still thinking about Lanky Greg. I mean, Greg. Did he really fish my phone out of a bucket of communal vomit? Regardless, I must stop thinking about this. I already shouted, 'You're not Leon,' in his face and ran away crying. I think I've pretty much burned my bridges there.

posted by EditingEmma 16.09

Faith called. Thank God, someone who wasn't at the party last night.

'I heard about the party last night,' she said.

'Oh, goodie. Please please *please* can we not talk about it?'

'Only if you agree the next time I say that to you.'

'Done! How was your family thing?'

She took a deep breath. 'Hope's getting married.'

'Oh my God! To Simon?'

'Yes, to Simon.'

'Sorry. Stupid question.'

There was silence.

'Are you OK?'

'Of course. I'm happy for her.'

'What are you *not* saying?'

'I'm not *not* saying anything, Emma. It's great.'

'OK... great.'

There was another pause.

'After the announcement lots of aunties and uncles kept coming up to me saying "It will be your turn next," and asking me whether I'd got a *boyfriend* yet.'

'Ugh Faith, I'm so sorry. But I suppose they don't *know* that you're not straight.'

'They shouldn't assume. Why is straight the default?'

'They're old?'

'There's only so much you can let people off the hook for, just because of their age.'

'No, you're right.'

'Anyway, there was cake, so it was fine. Cake makes

everything better. You can shove it in your mouth when someone asks you an awkward question, and it's tasty.'

'Or maybe instead of arming yourself with cake for the rest of your life, you could… tell them?'

'Emma. Please please *please* can we not talk about it?'

'Oh damn you.'

posted by EditingEmma 17.15

The Thing That Girls Do When They Pretend Not to Be Mad with Each Other But They're Really, Really Mad

Gracie's passive aggression last night has inspired me to write a post about this. Here's how I figure it works:

It has to be noticeable ONLY to the victim. If anyone else notices, you have failed. This is because part of the process is making the victim look as if they're going mad. If I had said to Steph, 'Gracie's really mad at me,' then Steph would have said, 'Why?' and I would have said, 'Er… err… Like she smiled at my joke but it didn't reach her eyes, you know?'

In fact, it has to be so intangible as to be barely perceptible to the victim. This may involve moments of actual normality, where you think 'Maybe it *was* all in my head,' and then ten minutes later you think 'No, maybe it wasn't.'

It has to make it impossible to resolve the issue. So when I, the victim, say, 'I'm sorry for whatever I did,' she can say, with solid evidence to back her up, 'We're fine, Emma.' This is because IT IS A FORM OF PUNISHMENT, NOT A WAY OF FIXING PROBLEMS.

When you think about it, it's actually incredibly skilful.

I for one lack the required subtlety (I once ended up yelling 'BUTT FACE' in the middle of pretending I didn't notice Steph), but Gracie masters it with expertise.

posted by EditingEmma 18.39

Came downstairs and Mum was eating a bowl of egg fried rice. She offered me some, and I had a horrible, plunging feeling in my stomach.

'Mum, where did you get that rice? Did you order it? You bought it, right?'

'No, I made it. Why was your phone in it, by the way?'

Oh God. She must never know.

Emma Nash @Em_Nasher

Surely watching my mother eat vomit rice can't be the only thing to come of this day

Emma Nash @Em_Nasher

Found an old, hair-covered Oreo behind the sofa so there's always light at the end of the tunnel

Monday, 15 September

posted by EditingEmma 07.30

I think I'm still hungover.

posted by EditingEmma 07.38

Walked into the kitchen and Olly was in there... casually buttering some toast. He turned around when I came in and smiled. Then proceeded to eat it.

Well, look at that. A stripper. Just standing. Munching some toast, as you do. Huh.

I'm skulking in my bedroom until he's finished. I wasn't prepared for small talk this early in the morning. Especially not with someone who gets naked for a living... My conversational go-tos such as 'So what are you up to today?' or 'How's work?' are somewhat limited.

posted by EditingEmma 07.43

Still waiting. Come ON. How long does it take to eat a piece of bread!! Also, why is he even up?? What sort of strip clubs open at eight in the morning?

posted by EditingEmma 07.50

Finally got into the kitchen, now waiting for the bathroom. This is ridiculous. Mum emerged from her room, all preened and fresh like she 'just woke up that way'.

'Mum, I think we need to re-open the subject of an en suite bathroom.'

'What's wrong now?' she grunted.

She certainly wouldn't grunt like that if Olly was within earshot.

'Your *boyfriend* is making me late for school.'

Her eyes widen with concern. She grabs me by the shoulders.

'Did he really say he was my boyfriend??'

posted by EditingEmma 08.37

In registration. When I panted into the classroom Mr Morris raised one eyebrow, all his features (including his startlingly white beard) getting sort of dragged up his face with it.

'The resolution to be on time lasted well then,' he warbled.

Did I have a resolution to be on time?

Actual Resolutions for the Day

Get back on track with my internet investigations. Surely, one awkward cinema date with Laurence Myer can't be the culmination of my findings.

posted by EditingEmma 10.02

In Art Class
Lovely, soothing art class. I can paint the morning away and
forget about how much I hate myself. At least it would be
soothing if Steph would shut up about Jonno. They're messaging about ten times a minute. How on Earth does anyone
have that much to say to another person?! What could keep
happening every five seconds that is so riveting they have to
tell each other about it *immediately*?! Nothing, I tell you. I
know this because I'm sitting with Steph and she is doing
absolutely nothing of interest.

posted by EditingEmma 10.31
NOW she is uber excited about some lottery thing Jonno told
her about, where you get twenty-four friends and some sort
of statistics system that I can't even be bothered to listen to
her explain and then you have like a 0.00002 per cent higher
chance of winning or something.

posted by EditingEmma 10.49
Still listening to Steph list how many different kinds of *Game
of Thrones* collectables she's going to buy with her millions.
I'm so bored of this.

'And I'm going to get that real Valyrian steel replica of
Robb Stark's sword and hang it in the hallway...'

'Steph, do we have twenty-four friends?'

That shut her up.

Our List of Friends
(who would actually split the money and not run away to Barbados)

   Emma
   Steph
   Faith
   Gracie
   'So… just twenty more then.'

posted by EditingEmma 11.16

Told Steph about getting back on track with my resolutions.

'So, I've decided to embark on Experiment Two of my plan.'

'Which is? More friends?'

'No. Wait for it… FRIENDS of friends!!!'

She looked less than enthralled, but invited me over tonight anyway to get started. Given that there will definitely be chocolatey snacks, I'll let it slide.

posted by EditingEmma 13.32

Walking over to meet the others at lunch and spotted Laurence Myer shuffling around with a bag of Minstrels in hand. This is getting ridiculous. I'm going to have to 'break up' with him.

Oh. He's not giving me the Minstrels. He's *eating* them. *Well. Fine* then!

posted by EditingEmma 13.44

At lunch. Now he's across from me on another table... just nomming away. Awkwardly glancing over at me every now and again, staring me straight in the eye as he puts them in his mouth.

Is *he* breaking up with *me*?

Through a packet of *Minstrels*?

Faith said, 'I think he's doing some kind of weird voodoo. Every piece of chocolate is a bit of you... being crushed,' and now I keep feeling stabbing pains in my legs.

posted by EditingEmma 16.37

In the safety of Steph's bed, staring up at her Kurt Cobain covered ceiling, thank God.

The News at the End of Biology

I was just about to leave for the day with some sense of hope, when Dr Penzik ruined everything.

'Oh, before you shoot off, Ms Fray went into early labour last night.'

There was lots of gushing and cooing. (Is it the law to have to pretend babies are cute if you have a vagina? Or do they actually like them? And if so, WHY?)

'The substitute won't be here for another week so on Wednesday we'll be in the other lab, with Ms Fray's class.'

Leon's in that class.

'You'll be put into pairs by last name.'

Of course. Nash and Naylor.

Still processing this news with Steph.

'Please say there's someone in between us???? There's a whole five letters... someone must be called... Naweltzer? Nautter? Natella? Navskov?'

'Maybe the numbers won't work out? Maybe you'll be partnered with the person the other side of you?'

'Yes, yes!! Maybe I'll be with Abby Matthews? Lovely, lovely Abby Matthews who thinks she's above everyone else and can never remember my name?? God, I'd kill to be locked in a room with Abby Matthews for a *week* if it meant avoiding Leon!'

That's not strictly true. I *am* dreading it, but I also know, now, that if I'm not next to him there will be a small part of me that's crushingly disappointed. How does that work?

posted by EditingEmma 17.51

After about an hour of obsessing Steph shook me and said, 'EMMA. Remember what you came here to do.'

Now we're scanning all my friends' friends, searching for hidden possibilities. We haven't come up with anything very exciting, yet. For a while we discussed whether Steph's Weird Cousin Bart might have potential, but then we remembered that time he peed out of her bedroom window and realised we must be scraping the barrel.

posted by EditingEmma 18.07

Steph got bored incredibly quickly. I wonder at her lack of dedication to my love life.

'Ooh, I know, Jess is back from uni. Let's go on her TINDER!' she cried through a mouthful of chocolate.

'Why would I want to talk to strange older men who think I'm Jess?'

'We won't use it, obviously, just for… research purposes.'

'Will Jess be OK with that?'

'Having a phone without a passcode is practically an open invitation.'

I can't argue with that kind of logic.

Operation Get Jess's Phone

The plan is to wait until Steph's parents call for dinner, and when she goes downstairs slip into her room and get the phone. (This has been left down to me, as Steph said, 'If I am caught in Jess's room I will be murdered. If you're caught there will only be a mild beating.' So that's reassuring.) We'll ask to have dinner in Steph's room, because I can't bear to miss *Coronation Street* (again, I had to take the hit on that one because Steph's parents know that she, quite rightly, couldn't care less about *Coronation Street*). And then… voila!

posted by EditingEmma 19.12

SUCCESS. With only one minor hiccup. I bumped into Jess on the way out of her room, as she was coming out of the toilet.

'All right, Emma?' she said. Her hair is cut short like Steph's, except it's dyed dark blue. I wish I could pull off blue hair but there's absolutely no way in hell.

'Yes, er… yes, I'm all right. Why? Are you all right?' I stuttered, hiding her phone behind my back.

'I'm hunky-dory, ta,' she said, and walked past.

'Did she seem suspicious?' asked Steph.

'Er... she looked at me like I was a bit strange.'

'Oh, then we're fine. She always thinks you're strange.'

posted by EditingEmma 20.41

So. I have now officially used A DATING APP (sort of, I suppose technically I have committed fraud via a dating app). It's been an... *interesting* experience. Here's what I have learned:

1) **It's more like stalking than 'dating'**

Their whereabouts are listed before you even get to read anything about them! (In fact, most people haven't put anything about themselves at all, so it's purely a photo and their whereabouts.) Why is location so important? What if my soulmate lived a few stops along the Northern Line and I never bothered, and ended up with mediocre-but-highly-convenient Mr Down-the-Road??

Having said that, I did always hate getting the tube.

2) **Leon does not have Tinder**

I already knew that. Logically. But try telling that to the illogical part of my brain that looks out for him *everywhere*. The supermarket with my mum. The dentist's. The doctor's. The garden shed. The airing cupboard.

3) **There are a lot of people who look a bit *like* Leon**

Alas, they are not the original.

4) **There are a lot of people, full stop**

I am completely overwhelmed by the sea of choice, and a little bit terrified of how many people are on the planet. It's not that I don't *know* there are over seven billion other people living on Earth, but looking through Tinder really smacks you in the face with it.

5) There are a lot of WEIRDOS

Weirder than me. And I sleep with a blood-encrusted plaster under my pillow. There was one boy in particular doing a great Charles Manson impression.

'Does he want to date me, or induct me into a cult and convince me to stab unwitting strangers?' I asked.

And, finally, perhaps the most important lesson of all...

6) My mum has Tinder

Yes. You did hear me correctly. My mum has *Tinder*. It's so awful I can barely type it. Here's what happened:

Steph and I were just casually playing with the settings.

'Make the age range older,' I said.

'Why?'

'No reason. Just... for fun.'

'You want to see if Mr Allen is on here?'

'Naturally.'

So we did. Then Steph said, 'Shall we set it to women? See if there's anyone on here Faith might like??'

And we forgot to shift the age range back. A few seconds later we both saw the image which will forever be burned into my eyelids.

'Emma, is that... is that your *mum?!?!*'

I gaped, speechless.

It was, undeniably, my mother. My mother, ladies and gentlemen, in a very busty outfit. Her profile reads 'Allie Nash' 'I am not ready for a Zimmer frame. I'm chilled, but love a bit of heat ;) (I mean the weather, of course!!)'

Dear Lord.

Steph laughed, and laughed, whilst I tried to figure out a

way to take back the last five minutes. I'm hoping the vision of my mum's Tinder profile will fit into that little coffin in the darkest, murkiest corner of my mind, filled with memories never to be relived. Like the questionable objects I found in her drawer one time, when I was stealing her tights.

Tuesday, 16 September

posted by EditingEmma 08.31

Is There Such a Thing as TOO Good-Looking?

So last night, I was feeling a bit defeated and about to go home (after smuggling Jess's phone back into her room) when Steph had an idea.

'Ooh, go on Jess's friends!! She's older so her friends are twice as likely to be attractive than ours. Or at least taller.'

And then we found this BEAUTIFUL BOY. He is, without a doubt, probably one of the best-looking people I have ever seen, except on the big screen. Well, I guess he is sort of still on a screen, but you know. His name is PAOLO. Even after stalking him loads last night I can't seem to say his name in lower case letters. Probably because the name PAOLO sounds like it's made up.

'How do you think Jess knows him?!' I asked.

'Hmm. Definitely not uni. He's not friends with any of her uni friends.'

'You're a little too good at this.'

'AHA!' She stopped on a picture of him sitting in an armchair.

'What?'

She pointed to the corner of the photo.

'A table?'

'What's *on* the table?'

'A… mug?'

'Not just *any* mug, Emma. A mug from the coffee place down the road, where Jess worked over summer.'

She leant back and crossed and uncrossed her legs.

'Say it,' she said.

'Say what?'

'Say "STEPH HAS MAD SKILLS".'

'Steph… you have mad skills.'

'Not quite the enthusiasm I was looking for, but I'll accept.'

She carried on clicking. I glanced at a picture of PAOLO chucking a ball at his friend in the sea.

'Do you think he's *too* good-looking, though?'

'No such thing,' asserted Steph.

'There is.'

'There isn't.'

'There is.'

'There isn't.'

'There is.'

'LOOK AT HIM.'

'Yes. I am… I suppose, I mean, it doesn't look like he's really arrogant, does it? He's not like, posing with his shirt off or obnoxiously wearing sunglasses indoors.'

'He *should* pose with his shirt off.'

'You're not helping.'

'LOOK AT HIM.'

'This is supposed to be about finding someone who won't make me feel like crap.'

'How could kissing this guy make anyone feel like crap?'

'You know what I mean.'

'I do, but I think you're being a bit look-ist. Just because a guy is attractive, doesn't mean he's going to do a Leon.'

The mention of what he did stung me unexpectedly.

'Sorry,' she said, noticing me wince.

Anyway, now I'm in the girls' loos deciding whether or not to talk to PAOLO. Hmm.

posted by EditingEmma 11.17

Terrible Things That Have Already Happened Today

English Class

I was half thinking about Leon, half watching Crazy Holly's impression of Victor Frankenstein and feeling glad I wasn't sitting at the front… She'd backcombed her hair and was leaning in really close to people's faces, asking in a stern voice, 'What have I done? What have I done?' Boring Susan looked particularly uncomfortable. Then Ms Parker's voice interrupted, just as Leon was kissing down my neck… It was quite odd. For a moment I had a vision of her kissing down my neck.

'Emma? Emma? Earth calling Emma?' she called.

'I don't know, sorry.'

'Don't know what?'

'Er… the answer?'

The whole class laughed.

'It's your turn,' Ms Parker said.

'Ohh… right. I know I said this last time but could I possibly *maybe* go next week?'

'There is no next week. This is the last week.'

Bollocks.

'Ohh, right. Fine. Could I possibly maybe go after the next person?'

'There is no next person. You are the last person.'

Double bollocks.

Five minutes later, I was standing in front of the class like a lemon.

'Right, Emma, and which character are you going to be presenting?'

Crap. The monster can't speak much, right?

'Er… I… the monster.'

There was a snigger.

'Interesting—' Ms Parker leant back in her chair '—ready when you are.'

I searched my mind frantically for what was happening in the book the last time I looked at it… Think. *Think*. I remember the monster was wandering around in some woods?

'I feel… cold.'

Oh God… think more.

'Water come from my eyes but I do not know why. People are scared of my face but I do not know why. My face cannot hurt them. I see old lady in street who scream at me. More water come from my eyes. I say, "HEY, LADY! YOU UGLY TOO!" Then she hit me with her bag. It hurt me. I like the pain. It mean I feel something else that is not sadness.'

It was like being the captain on a sinking ship, with nothing to do but go down nobly.

'I like pain so I kick tree. I kick it again. And again.'

At this point I thought I might as well roll with it. I grabbed a chair and kicked it. Boring Susan had a glint of terror in her eyes.

'And AGAIN!! AND AGAIN!!'

The back of the chair broke so I stopped.

'Then the tree break. Even tree hate me. If tree could run, it would run. Then I think of tree with legs and funny sound come from me. It sound like… Hahahahah. What is this? What is this noise that I make? I like it so I keep thinking of trees with legs.'

I sat down on the floor.

'I do not need people. I have my ha-has.'

I thought I was done then, but the class was still looking expectant so I just kept saying 'hahahahah' and lay down and pretended to go to sleep.

Steph Not Letting English Class Go

'You er, *might* not have failed… I mean, you never know.'

'It's OK. You don't have to…'

'It was different, at least.'

'Can we not talk about it?'

'Oh, yes, sure.'

Silence.

'Can I just ask one question?'

'What?'

'Why the German accent?'

posted by EditingEmma 13.51

Summary of Lunchtime

Steph stole my phone and followed Paolo on Instagram, because she's so mature. Faith's sister is having an engagement party and Faith's pretending that she's excited, but I can tell she's dreading it and won't admit it for fear of seeming selfish. Gracie was moaning because there was a suspicious lump on her fishcake.

posted by EditingEmma 17.41

I came home to the sound of high-pitched giggling, and knew instantly that Mum's friend Heather was here. When I walked into the living room she exclaimed, 'Oh, Emma, you look lovely!'

'In my uniform?'

'Such pretty colours.' She nodded.

With anyone else I'd assume they were lying, but Heather has very strange taste in clothing. She once unironically wore a cork hat.

Mum's Friend Heather

Heather is a bizarre but lovely woman, who mostly travels a lot, floating from job to job. She did a lot to help my mum when I was growing up and my mum was trying to juggle raising me alone with starting her own business, though to this day I'll never understand how because Heather is possibly the least organised person I've ever met. Apparently, she was supposed to arrive on Friday but missed her flight, because she saw a cat that she thought looked 'distressed' and wanted to stay with it.

posted by EditingEmma 18.09

We Have Achieved Insteraction

I'm actually quite proud of that pun. Anyway, I was just sitting around muttering to myself, 'Don't think about Leon, don't think about Leon…' whilst flicking through his photos, when I got a notification. This is unusual as I am more of the 'silent observer' on Instagram.

Then I saw it was from PAOLO. He liked one of my photos, of the beach in Tenerife where me, Mum and Steph went over Easter. THEN he commented: 'You like waterskiing too? :)'

I flicked onto his profile and saw that Steph had liked about a million photos of him waterskiing earlier. Thanks for that, Steph.

Still, why not?

'I love it!' I reply.

Then we had a really long comment-conversation, and he messaged me.

Hi Emma. Would love to chat with you. How are you?

Paolo x

OH MY GOD. He would LOVE TO CHAT WITH ME. What do I say back?!

How Am I?

How *am* I? Terrible, actually. I've only ever really liked one person and he's pretending I don't exist. I spend most of my time obsessing over him and hating myself for it. But wouldn't it be great if I wasn't terrible? If I was having way too much fun to care? If I had tons of really glamorous friends and went to parties all the time, where I didn't get so drunk that I lost my phone in a bucket of communal sick? (My heart wrenches briefly as I imagine Greg fishing around in there…)

> Hi Paolo! I'm great thanks, just going into London with some friends :D we're going to this new bar which is meant to have an amazing view & do really good cocktails. How are you? Emma x

I am SO adventurous that I try new and sophisticated places every night. Note also that I said 'some' friends, not 'my' friends, because this Emma has more than one set of friends. She has friends ALL OVER THE PLACE. She is LOUSY with friends.

posted by EditingEmma 19.24

HE'S MESSAGED BACK.

> That sounds fun! Maybe we can chat when you're back…?
> Enjoy cocktails x

YES, WE CAN CHAT WHEN I'M BACK FROM COCKTAILS.

posted by EditingEmma 19.38

Watching *EastEnders* with my mum and Heather. I am such a fraud.

'Mum, do we have any cocktail stuff in the house?'

'Why?'

'Can we have one?'

'Er . .. well there's my whisky, and a bit of old Crème De Menthe...'

'Any mixers?'

'Ribena?'

Now I am drinking Ribena and whisky. Mum is laughing her head off. At least I feel a bit less like a liar now.

> **Emma Nash @Em_Nasher**
> Whisky is truly disgusting. Especially with Ribena
>
> **Emma Nash @Em_Nasher**
> Controversy. Mum's friend Heather declares it is 'delicious'

posted by EditingEmma 21.59

Have I been out drinking long enough? What time do sociable, older people get back from central?

Best give it another hour.

posted by EditingEmma 23.15

Experiment 2 : Maybe I Can Be Someone Else Entirely
The moment has come.

> Hi! How's your evening?
>
> Oh hi! You're back :)
>
> Yeah, getting an early one tonight *yawns*
>
> I hope you don't mind if I ask... how old are you?
>
> Hmm.
>
> How old are you... ?

Haha. 18. And you?

Hmm.

Me too.

I *could* be eighteen. If I was born one and a bit years earlier.

posted by EditingEmma 00.55

We're still up talking. It's AMAZING. We're getting on SO WELL. I mean, it's easy to get on well when you just agree with everything the other person says and pretend like you like everything they do, but still!!! Screen shot of my favourite bit of the conversation:

I am really glad we started chatting. I need cheering.

Cheering like cheering up or someone standing beside you screaming 'YAY PAOLO' at everything you do?

Haha.

I guess I could be your personal cheerleader. Depends how well you pay

You are very funny

Why thank you

But I am really missing Italy and it is nice to talk to some-one who loves it, too

I probably *would* love it, if I'd ever been.

One day I will take you waterskiing on the beach in Bardolino. It sounds like you will give me a run for my money

Yes, I did say that, didn't I? Thankfully there's no waterski-ing on the Thames so he'll never know.

Wednesday, 17 September

posted by EditingEmma 07.46

Came downstairs and Heather was asleep/passed out on the sofa. At first all I saw was a limp hand hanging off the side. It was quite a shock. Then when I sat down she squealed, 'Oooooh!' and startled me again.

Now listening to her talk about a dog that got shot three times and survived and how incredible it was and then about how she couldn't watch *The Way We Were* because it upset her too much and then about funny German words like '*kummerspeck*' which literally means 'grief bacon' and refers to the extra weight you gain from emotional overeating.

How does anyone have this much energy at seven in the morning?

posted by EditingEmma 10.43

In Maths

Talking to Paolo last night was like discovering a new, magical world, except instead of a lion and a witch I had waterskis and a beguiling sense of humour. I genuinely felt like I had been sucked into my phone and given a brand-new cyber-life, matched by my awesome new cyber-personality. Now, sitting in Maths watching Crazy Holly hide and replace Mr Crispin's glasses every time he turns around, I find myself somewhat deflated. How can I be expected to develop a beguiling sense of humour when my peers are amused by such juvenile pranks?

posted by EditingEmma 10.50

Watching a blinded Mr Crispin point at Boring Susan instead of Crazy Holly to tell her off was pretty funny (both have curly, brown hair and the similarity ends there). But I refuse to crack a smile. I am above such infantile behaviour.

'Why are you being so quiet today?' Steph asked.

'I'm actually working on being sophisticated.'

'You mean boring?'

posted by EditingEmma 11.05

In the Girls' Toilets

I've wasted *five minutes* of break waiting for the loo. Whoever is in there is taking a really, *really* long time.

Oh *come on*.

posted by EditingEmma 11.09

Finally, Crazy Holly came out (of course) and said, 'Sorry, I was dismantling a bomb.'

I smiled and went into the loo. Then I heard her say, 'No need to thank me for saving your life.'

posted by EditingEmma 11.21

The Strangest Places to Masturbate

Crazy Holly's toilet activity somehow segued into a very interesting discussion. I sat down with Faith, Gracie and Steph.

'What were you doing?' Steph asked.

'Crazy Holly was in the stall for AGES. Do you think she was masturbating?'

'Ew, Emma!' Gracie exclaimed.

'Do people do that in school?' Steph asked.

'I don't know. Maybe Holly.'

'My sister has a friend who goes to the beach at night, takes off his socks and puts his feet in the water, and masturbates,' continued Steph. 'He says it's a very sensual experience.'

'My brother knows a boy who does it when he's driving the car, and he makes eye contact with other drivers and everything,' Faith added.

This somehow led to various confessions.

Faith – has done it in a plane bathroom. ('It was a long flight,' she added. I commented that this sort of qualifies her for the mile-high club.)

Me – I have done it in a Topshop changing room. (It was actually M&S Clothing, and there were lots of old people around doing their shopping, but Topshop sounds distinctly less creepy.)

Steph – has done it in my bed. ('I hope I wasn't in it at the time,' I said. She assured me that I was not.)

Gracie – 'doesn't masturbate'. (Which I refuse to believe.)

'How can you *not* masturbate?' I goaded her again.

'Because… it's *weird*.'

'But sex isn't?'

'No. Sex is with another person. On your own it's just… awkward.'

'I'd say it's probably much more awkward with another person.'

posted by EditingEmma 13.07

Thoughts I Had in French

I wonder where other people have masturbated?

Has someone masturbated on the chair I'm sitting on?

Did Madame Fournier say '*les orgasms*'?

Oh, no, she said '*les* organes'.

And *now* I can't stop picturing Madame Fournier masturbating. Get out!! Get out!!!

Think of something else!!

Leon masturbating.

NO.

Paolo masturbating.

NO NO.

At one point, they were all in a room doing it together. It's been an exhausting few hours.

posted by EditingEmma 14.20

Sitting Outside English Class

I was walking over to English, trying to distract myself from thinking about Biology with Leon tomorrow. I was imagining myself as a well-travelled eighteen-year-old who does sports and wears fancy clothes, and ignoring that I am actually a sixteen-year-old who has been on a couple of holidays to Tenerife, can barely walk without falling over and whose mum still buys her oversized knickers 'in case I grow out of them'.

I was just in the middle of forgetting Leon, when Leon sprang on me from round a corner. I was so startled I threw my folder up in the air, then when I realised it was him my heart started pounding so hard I was a little scared it was actually an alien life form readying itself to explode out of my chest.

He just stood, watching over me as I scrabbled for my papers on the floor.

'What are you doing? I mean, what do you want?' I asked.

'Nothing. I have a message.'

I stood up and looked him in the eye. (The big, brown, incredibly beautiful eye.) He was staring really hard at the bit of wall behind me.

'Laurence wants to know what's going on with you two.'

I was speechless.

'Come on, Emma, I think he has a right to know.'

'I...'

'You're being a bit cruel, don't you think?'

The *hypocrisy*.

'Oh yeah, because, it's not like you ever dumped anyone without saying anything, or anything. Is it?'

He started to walk away.

'In fact, I was never even going out with Laurence! You're *worse*! Or maybe you didn't dump me… maybe we're still going out!! How would I even know??' I shouted at his back, running a little bit to keep up with him.

So now I've literally been reduced to chasing him around school. How did that happen?

Ten minutes later I got to English.

'Emma, you're really, really late,' said Ms Parker.

'I know, I…'

'No, don't bother. Wait outside. I'm sick of you to be honest.'

Ouch… And now I'm sitting outside crying. I never thought the day would come… Crying because I'm banned from English class.

Could this day get any worse?

posted by EditingEmma 16.02

End of School

Oh yes, it could. Mum just rang, saying she got a call from the school and 'what was I playing at'. And we haven't even been back a week. I'm going round to Steph's tonight, to hide.

posted by EditingEmma 17.28

At Steph's

Having tea with Steph, Faith and Gracie. It won't be long now until Gracie suggests getting a board game out, then gets so competitive she throws something at my head.

posted by EditingEmma 19.11

Gracie: 'Shall we play a game?'

We're now playing something called *The Definitions Game* where Gracie reads out a really complicated word and we all have to guess what it means. For every word I put 'Gracie's Mum' and every time she reads it out she goes all pink and tight-lipped and you'd think it would get old but it just doesn't.

posted by EditingEmma 20.03

When I sloped in the door I thought there was going to be an unwelcome, lung-sapping fight. But Mum's out with Heather, which means I can safely avoid her until this time tomorrow.

I can't believe that tomorrow I may actually have to sit next to Leon for a full hour and twenty minutes. How can I bear it? And why does he care what I'm doing with Laurence Myer? I refuse to believe he's actually that concerned on his behalf. They're not *that* good friends, and Leon has never been so self-righteous before. I know for a *fact* that regularly he steals from self-checkouts and sticks his gum underneath desks. Those are not the actions of a moral person.

I've got to do something else to distract myself. I'm venturing back to Narnia.

posted by EditingEmma 20.15

Ciao Paolo

Ciao Emma

How are you?

Better give it a minute or two before saying something else, you know... Build up the suspense. He can see that I've 'seen' his message so it looks like I'm just super casual. I LOVE THAT. It's a little hard to be casual with Leon when I lose the ability to speak English and fail to restrain myself from staring fixedly at the little moles on his neck.

posted by EditingEmma 23.58

In My Room (Still Talking to Paolo)

Paolo and 'Emma' are having yet another great conversation, whilst real-life Emma intermittently stalks Leon and Apple's profiles. I see that Leon has made a guest appearance on *Scrumptiously, Anna*. I hope they drown in a giant vat of their raspberry buttercream.

posted by EditingEmma 00.16

Mum got back ten minutes ago and I quickly turned out my light. She came in and peered at me, feigning sleep, then went away again. As I lay there hiding from her beneath the duvet, phone in one hand and laptop in the other, I suddenly felt inexplicably desolate. I'm getting to that phase when you've been online for so long you start feeling a little bit empty. The real world tugs at you with its wholesome charm but you can't seem to leave behind the bizarre YouTube videos and scrolling through people's mindless updates. You stumble across some very strange things you wish you could unsee. The longer you stay on it the less likely it seems that you will ever get off again.

Hmm, trying to log off, but it's like my fingers aren't listening to my brain…

posted by EditingEmma 00.44

> Once again, I have kept you up too late, Emma. Would you maybe like to come and see this band with me on Saturday?
>
> That would be nice, let me just check my diary

Hmm. My check of my 'mental diary' tells me I have no plans this weekend other than sitting around watching *Goodnight Sweetheart* with Steph and her nan.

> Out Friday with the girls but could do Saturday, yes :)
>
> Bellissimo. Hang on, I will send you a link. I know you will love it, if you like techno
>
> Amazing!!!

(So I like techno now. Why not? All music, when you really examine it, is just noise anyway right?)

I feel like I am two different Emmas. When I talk to Paolo I'm this other person, I'm confident and fun and things don't bother me or hold me down, they just roll off me like water. Internet Emma has a much better life and is happy in herself.

But then I close the laptop and it doesn't stick.

posted by EditingEmma 01.02

Can't sleep. When I think about seeing Leon tomorrow and actually sitting next to him for a full hour and twenty minutes I feel like I'm sinking into the bed and through the floor and falling really fast into a vast, cavernous hole. But let's pretend it's because I have a date with a sexy Italian man.

And he is a man. He's *eighteen*. He can legally buy alcohol and go out to bars and probably has chest hair.

Thursday, 18 September

posted by EditingEmma 08.20

Registration
I'm actually early because I woke up at 6 am. I'd probably be tired if adrenaline wasn't surging through my body. Gracie reached behind me to get something from her bag and I jumped out of my skin.

'What's the matter with you??' she squealed.

'I thought your arm was a snake.'

I think I might be on edge.

posted by EditingEmma 08.31
Mr Morris looked very startled to see me when he came in.

'I'm glad you're making an effort, Emma, but I'm afraid Ms Parker's suggested I put you on work report.'

'What does that mean?'

'It means you have to take this to your teachers at the end of every lesson, and get it signed for good behaviour. If you miss three signatures then you get a detention.'

Another day I might have cared, but not today. I know

his words are aimed at me, but they miss and fly out the open window.

posted by EditingEmma 13.24

The Slowest and Fastest Day of My Life

Time is moving so SLOWLY and yet racing past at the same time. It's like I am a ghost watching my own life play out, in a zone where time is meaningless.

Break

I bought two coffees and I'm not sure why. Coffee is disgusting. I keep shaking. Actually, physically *shaking*. I don't think the coffee helped.

English

Mr Allen brought in finger puppets and pretended they were Marlowe and Shakespeare having a fist-fight about Marlovian conspiracy theory AND I COULDN'T EVEN ENJOY IT PROPERLY.

French

Leon. Leon. Leon. Near me. Leon. I tried to focus on the lesson, but I had absolutely no idea what Madame Fournier was saying. Then I tried thinking about Paolo and our date. I put up my hand.

'Madame Fournier, do you know any Italian?'

She looked almost aggressively puzzled, shook her head and carried on with French. I guess not.

Lunch

I tried to consume food but it tasted like cardboard because my mouth was so dry from nerves. I heard Faith say, 'We're just background noise to her today.'

Were they trying to talk to me?

posted by EditingEmma 13.36

Twenty-four minutes to go.

posted by EditingEmma 13.37

Twenty-three minutes.

posted by EditingEmma 13.41

I can't keep going like this. I desperately, desperately want to be in Biology, sitting next to him, forcing him to interact with me. But I'm also dreading it in every single part of my body. How is that possible?

posted by EditingEmma 13.55

Walking to Biology

At least, I'm trying to walk to Biology. My brain can't work out what it wants. One minute I'm half running, the next I've stopped, quivering by a bush. I was standing, frozen, pretending to be really interested in a leaf and Holly walked past me. She paused and frowned.

'Are you all right, Emma?'

Crazy Holly is concerned by my behaviour.

posted by EditingEmma 13.59

Outside the Classroom

It's taken me ten minutes to walk about thirty metres, but I am finally approaching the classroom. I'm taking a moment outside, peering through the window in the door.

OH there he is. I knew that he was going to be here, but somehow didn't quite believe it. But yep, he's here. He's here. I'm here. He's here. With his hair and his toes and elbows and cheekbones. Every single part of him is here. It's funny, isn't it, how we're all just bones and skin strung together by cartilage and muscle? What makes Leon's bones different to another set of bones? Why can't I just attach myself to another bag of organs?

There's a spare seat next to him. Looks like we are together then. I'm heading in.

posted by EditingEmma 15.00

I've Left College in the Middle of the Day

Yep. I've left school. In the middle of the day. I'm currently moving like a zombie towards home. It was surprisingly easy, actually. I half expected alarms to go off or for Mr Morris to leap out from behind a corner and rugby tackle me to the floor, but nothing happened.

Why I Left College in the Middle of the Day

I entered the classroom and he, the bag of organs that I so desire, didn't even notice me come in. He was too busy looking intensely at something on his phone. I find it incredible that I can be consumed by knowing that he's present on the same *planet*, and he doesn't notice me standing three metres away, but whatever. When I came and sat down, he jumped.

'Hi.'

He quickly fumbled to put his phone away and looked down at his sheet. Suddenly this made me irrationally angry... Is this what I'd been building up to? Just to be ignored for an hour and twenty minutes, leave the room and carry on?

'I said HI?'

'Emma?' called Dr Penzik from the front. 'Am I disturbing your conversation?'

'No,' I muttered.

I already knew by this point it was going to be a *long* lesson, then I picked up the dried yeast and Leon grabbed it from me, spilling it over the desk. We both stared at it.

Yeast is kind of gross.

He wouldn't let me touch *anything*. It was completely ridiculous. Fifteen minutes into the lesson everyone else was already miles ahead of us.

'Leon. Let me hold it while you do that, you're going to spill it everywhere. Just let me help.' I leant forward to take the test tube.

'Get *off*,' he hissed in the most vicious, horrible tone, which really should be reserved exclusively for blood relatives. A big lump rose in my throat and tears welled up. From that moment on I sat back and refused to do or say anything else, for fear of breaking down in a fit of sobs. This would have been fine, if Dr Penzik wasn't circling like a vulture.

He came over to our table and loomed over us. He really is incredibly tall.

'Emma. You haven't done a single thing all lesson. You might as well be lounging at home.'

He looked at me expectantly, and I looked at Leon who was pretending not to listen and looking oh so diligently at his little tubes. Dr Penzik sighed and ambled over to a different group. Once he was gone I said, 'I think I will. Go home, that is.'

'Finally,' Leon said.

And then I walked out. Just like that.

posted by EditingEmma 15.55

Examining Every Single Moment of Our Short-Lived Relationship With a Microscope

I usually love staying home and watching daytime TV but I feel all lonely and weird. I turned it on and burst into tears. Potentially, Jeremy Kyle's face was the last straw.

How could he be so horrible to me?! What did I *do*?! I'm completely stunned. He seemed genuinely hurt and angry. I keep coming back to this question: *is* there something I've done to justify it? All summer I racked my brains, and I keep reaching the same conclusion: No. There is 100 per cent nothing I've done. The only thing I can think of was going out with Laurence, which was *after* he ignored me for two months, and which I was completely entitled to do.

It's so unfair. *I'm* the rejected one, so *I'm* supposed to be the one who gets to be hurt and angry. Everyone knows that!!

He should be acting guilty whilst I tell *him* to go away!! He's acting like *I'm* the one who broke up with him... Or worse!! Like I killed his family pet or something. I don't know what he's acting like...

As if it wasn't enough to get broken up with, now I'm getting bullied by him too. Sitting there as he yanked those test tubes out of my hands, I felt like I was about five years old. It was as if he couldn't *bear* to look at me. This must be how Frankenstein's monster felt, out there in the woods.

I'm actually looking forward to Mum coming home.

posted by EditingEmma 17.03

Steph rang.

'Dude!! What the hell?!'

'What?'

'You just... *left*.'

'I know.'

'What happened?'

'I don't want to talk about it.' My voice wobbled.

'Oh, Emma.'

I cleared my throat. 'Am I in huge trouble?'

'Well... er... no one really noticed. I did, obviously, but I thought you were just doing a huge poo.'

'At least I won't get in trouble, I guess.'

'Uh... yeah, well, you probably could have got away with it. But then Leon put up his hand and... sort of... told Dr Penzik.'

What. The. Hell.

'Emma? Are you still there?'

'I'm here.'

'Are you OK?'

'I think I just need to go to bed. I'll see you tomorrow.'

'OK. Night night. I love you.'

'I love you, too.'

posted by EditingEmma 18.20

En-sausaged

All sausaged up in bed where no one can hurt me. The door slammed and Mum came raging up the stairs shouting, 'EMMA! EMMA!' But I am unperturbed in my roll. Sausages do not have thoughts. She stormed in, her face all red, then she saw me and softened. She leant down.

'What happened?'

I tried to talk but a sort of strangled wail came out.

'Emma, I've had another call from Mr Morris. I don't care how bad things seem, you must never, EVER just walk out of school. OK?'

I nodded. She tried to coax me out with a shepherd's pie, and sat on the floor next to my bed spoon-feeding it to me. I couldn't help but laugh at how ridiculous we must look. She laughed too until I accidentally spat a bit of pie on the floor.

posted by EditingEmma 21.06

Had to get out of bed to wee. Stupid body. Feeling so miserable I could barely be bothered to put in a tampon. I just sort of stared at it for about fifteen minutes, gathering momentum to use it. I went on my phone briefly. It felt like everyone's photos were saying 'We are SO MUCH HAPPIER THAN YOU' and it just made me feel even more lonely. Saw Paolo was online and put my phone under my pillow. I don't feel like I have the energy to be anything but my miserable, pathetic self right now.

Friday, 19 September

posted by EditingEmma 08.39

Losing My Mind

I was so distracted this morning I've forgotten to wear deodorant and brush my teeth. I am actually repugnant.

posted by EditingEmma 10.34

In Maths

'Holly, do you have any deodorant I can borrow?'

'No, sorry. I just get Botox in my armpits.'

'I... What?'

'My aunt's an anaesthetist,' she says, like that explains
it all.

I pause for a second.

'So you just... don't sweat?'

'Oh, no, I do. But it comes out other places. Like my
boobs.'

posted by EditingEmma 13.07

Ms Parker handed out our grade sheets for the presentations. She didn't look at me as she gave me mine. I think she's annoyed at me for putting in zero effort. Agh, as if I don't have enough to worry about without mothers and teachers constantly showing that they're people with emotions, too.

'You read it,' I said to Steph.

She scanned her eyes over the sheet, her mouth agape like a fish.

'I don't believe it,' she said, handing it back to me.

'What? How bad is it??'

'You got an A.'

'What?? You're lying!'

She wasn't lying. Curiouser and curiouser... My comments read:

Well, Emma, you could have been better prepared but after watching twenty-five Victor Frankensteins I decided to give you an A for originality. Don't make me regret it.

P.S. German???

I was feeling pretty smug until Steph pointed out that no matter what happened today, it would always be the day I forgot to brush my teeth.

posted by EditingEmma 13.24

Mum drove up to the school with a toothbrush. She quickly handed it over, glancing around her all shady-like.

'Mum, you know you're not selling me marijuana.'

'Just take it and get back inside.'

I looked back at school and it seemed very bleak... The car looked so warm and cosy.

'Mum, can I come home with you?'

She rolled up the window and sped off.

posted by EditingEmma 13.51

The Burden That is Food Technology

'What are you making in FT, Emma?' asked Gracie.

Oh bollocks. I forgot. Every week we have 'activities' and Mum thought it would be a good idea to choose FT, so that I learn how to survive without her.

Now I'm frantically going around collecting pieces of fruit. So far I have Steph's apple, Faith's orange, a banana I bought from the tuck shop and a lemon from Crazy Holly. She was reluctant to let go of the lemon at first but I let her plait my hair for a while and she gave it to me.

> Emma Nash @Em_Nasher
>
> What can one make with an orange, banana, apple and a lemon?
>
> Emma Nash @Em_Nasher
>
> Dammit! The orange rolled under a bush. Make that a banana, apple and a lemon. HELP.

posted by EditingEmma 15.14

Got to dreaded FT and, of course, *Apple* is in our class. UGH. I know that Gracie's talking to me, but all I can do is watch Apple, sitting there smiling and... SHE JUST LOOKED AT HER PHONE. Is it Leon??! Is he messaging her?! Oh God.

This is going to be so bad for my 'stop obsessing over Leon' resolution.

At the beginning of class everyone sits with their ingredients in front of them explaining to Ms McElroy what they're going to make, and the method. Apple is making *rainbow rose meringue cookies*. My apple, banana and lemon look a little sad.

'So, Emma,' Ms McElroy glanced at the fruit, 'what are you making today?'

'Uh, fruit salad.'

'I see. And how are you going to do it?'

'Well, Ms McElroy, I thought I'd chop up the apple first, then the banana, and then squeeze the lemon juice over it.'

I cut the fruit reaaally slowly. But now I'm done. Hmm. What to do now? Stare intensely at the back of Apple's head? Yes, that will pass the time.

posted by EditingEmma 15.57

Ms McElroy went around tasting everyone's food. She said Apple's cookies tasted like 'fresh, spring buds opening up to the sun', and I had a really vivid daydream that she started choking on one.

When she tried my salad she closed her eyes and said, 'Mmm, yes, the lemon really harmonises with the banana and the apple.'

She is mad. But at least I sort of got away with it.

posted by EditingEmma 19.32

Why Do Parents Have to Be People?

I could hear Mum on the phone to someone.

'I just don't know what to do… I think it's that boy again.'

'MUM! CAN YOU PLEASE NOT DISCUSS MY PRIVATE PROBLEMS WITH YOUR FRIENDS.'

'Hang on,' she said, and slammed the door to her room so I couldn't hear her any more. As if *I s*houldn't be hearing a conversation about *my life*. Ten minutes later, she came into my room.

'Finished discussing me, have we? I'm sorry, I do hope I didn't interrupt.'

'That was your father.'

'*What?*'

'I feel I really needed some backup, Emma.'

'Backup?? I'm not an armed criminal.'

'I'm *worried*.'

'What is my *dad* going to do? *Talk* to me? Have a little heart-to-heart? We're awkward enough when we're speaking about my homework, without admitting that we're both human beings with feelings. Ugh, I can't believe he knows I'm upset, ugh.'

'It was more for me. But yes, it was a stupid idea.'

She did look genuinely sorry. Which wasn't good enough, but it was a start.

'He's not going to come over here, is he?'

'No.'

'Good.'

There was a silence. She must be really worried if she's calling my dad...

My Dad
He travels around a lot doing work for various charities. (So he says, anyway, really I'd have absolutely no idea. He could be concealing himself in a house down the road for all I know.) He sends a postcard from time to time and shows up for a couple of hours at Christmas with some sort of generic present, wearing a novelty jumper. We do a vague catch-up as if it were a job interview and then he pats me awkwardly on the shoulder and leaves again until the next year.

'Mum, it's OK,' I said gently, 'I'm fine, really. I even have a date tomorrow night.'

'A *date*?'

'Yes.'

'With who?'

'His name is Paolo.'

'PAOLO? And where did you meet *Paolo*?'

'He's friends with Steph's sister.'

'All right. Well don't go upsetting yourself even more.'

'Why?! Because my date's going to be a disaster?! Is that what you're saying?!'

'I'm just not sure you're in the right frame of mind to be going out on *dates*, my love.'

I can't believe this. I was just trying to stop her worrying, and she starts criticising me.

'Well, I didn't ask for your opinion.'

She slammed out of the room then. How mature. Five minutes later, she came back.

'You know, I have my own problems too, Emma.'

I stayed silent.

'But of course, you don't care,' she went on.

'What? Have you and Olly broken up again? It's hard to stay sympathetic when it happens every other week.'

She folded her arms.

'Yes, we have. We're over for good this time, and you can stop being so patronising. But aside from that, I'm trying as best I can to look after your granddad, I'm struggling to raise you alone with no support, I'm trying to keep my business afloat and I'm *constantly* tired and I'd *love* to actually relax now and again, but I can't.'

'Fine,' I snapped.

Suddenly I felt so overwhelmingly guilty I wanted to break down into tears and throw myself at her feet. But I just sat there. She left the room, and didn't come back.

My Mum
She is really the best, despite having questionable taste in men and an embarrassing Tinder profile, and she's right about everything. I feel like a worm. I'm going to bury my head under a pillow and never, ever come out.

Saturday, 20 September

posted by EditingEmma 11.04

When I got up Mum was already downstairs making pancakes. I think this means we're OK now. She dropped most of them on the floor attempting to flip them and they were covered in little bits of dust, but I ate them with good grace.

posted by EditingEmma 12.35

Trying to focus on tonight, and not the fact that I seem to have engendered hatred in a place where I only ever tried to inspire love. There must be something terribly wrong with me. Yesterday, Leon was standing at the gate with his friend, and when I walked past he actually *scowled* at me. His friend looked a little bit shocked, so at least I know I'm not imagining it. It might almost be comical, if it didn't make me want to repeatedly bash my head against the wall.

But there is nothing wrong with Internet Emma. Internet Emma ONLY inspires love, admiration, and sometimes a bit of casual envy. She's the kind of girl who doesn't stare at other people's social media profiles as a form of morbid self-persecution, or focus too much on the angle of her selfie or pitching her tweet exactly right. She *just tweets*. She doesn't care about what other people think and *never* compares herself to others.

Internet Emma is who Paolo will be meeting in a mere matter of hours. At a *gig*. Which is what cool people like Internet Emma and Paolo do... And then it dawns on me. Internet Emma might be eighteen, but real-life Emma certainly isn't. Do they check ID at gigs?!

posted by EditingEmma 12.44
Looked at the link Paolo sent me: 'If you are lucky enough to look under 25 years of age we will ask you for ID when you enter the event.'

Nooooooo.

Guys... I don't have any ID 12.29

Stephanie Brent
I'd love to help but don't think you'll get away with using Jess's 12.32

For obvious reasons 12.32

Faith?! 12.33

Faith Connelly
You don't really look like Hope either 12.36

Yes, but otherwise I'm trying to pass as black with blue hair 12.37

So I'm not looking for perfection here 12.37

FAITH?! 12.38

Faith Connelly
All right all right 12.42

posted by EditingEmma 13.57

The Stress of Being Under 18 When You Are Internally a Sophisticated Adult

At Faith's to get her sister's passport. You'd think I was asking her to steal the crown jewels. She opened the door and let me in, without making eye contact.

'Do you have it?' I asked.

'Yes.' She sulked, putting it in my hand.

'Hope won't notice.'

'I'm not a *natural thief*,' she said, implying that I am.

Oh God. I really look nothing like Faith's sister. I suppose I could have dyed my hair. (Though anyone dyeing their hair my murky colour seems unlikely.) Probably couldn't have changed my eye colour, though…

posted by EditingEmma 14.35

Faith Finally TALKS

It was an incredibly brief window but IT HAPPENED. I stayed at hers for a while and she kept snipping at me (she said *Pretty Little Liars* was 'crap'). At first I thought she was just moody about the ID, but then she opened up a bit.

'Are you OK?' I asked. 'You seem a bit…'

She sighed. 'I've been at a flower market with my mum and Hope.'

'Ah.'

'Mum's so excited. I mean, I'm excited too. But she's *so*

excited. The woman can really talk about flowers. And colour schemes. And salmon blinis.'

'I do love a salmon blini.'

'She's practically delirious. And I just… I just keep thinking.'

'Go on?'

'Would she be this excited for *me*? If I was getting married? And instead of a groom there was another bride?'

I sat awkwardly for a moment, thinking about the right thing to say. Because I really don't know. Thankfully, Faith didn't let me answer,

'It's like it's about so much more than two people finding each other and falling in love. It's like getting married is some sort of *achievement*, and for the love to be celebrated it has to fit into this traditional mould. And mine will never be worth as much, because it doesn't. Hope said she might carry a bouquet of herbs instead of flowers, and my mum laughed like it was the most outrageous thing ever. She said, "Well, dear, as long as you're happy," like she's so… *accepting*… when all it is, is about friggin' *flowers*. I bet if I said, "Hey, Mum, I'm marrying a woman instead of a man," she wouldn't say, "Well, dear, as long as you're happy."'

'Maybe not. BUT… I do have to point out that you haven't tried.'

She ignored that one.

'Oh, they were just so… *smug*, Emma. And I really wanted to stop and scream "I'M GAY. I LIKE GIRLS." But all I did was stare at my shoes. Like always.'

Faith took a breath.

'Agh, this is stupid. This isn't *about* me. God, all I keep thinking about is myself, feeling jealous like a five-year-old.'

'Faith, you're *not* being stupid! It's not like you want to take away what Hope has. You just want the same excitement for your own life.'

She nodded.

'You should go get ready for your date.'

'Are you sure? I can stay, talk some more?'

'No. I've talked too much already.'

On my way out I held up Hope's passport. 'Faith, I need your honest opinion. Do you think I'll get away with this?'

She shrugged and said, 'You're the same race, I guess.'

posted by EditingEmma 17.26

Getting Ready for Date No. 2
Steph turned up at the door, wearing a leather jacket, crop top and purple lipstick.

'What are you doing here?!'

'You didn't think I was letting you go alone?'

I felt like I was going to cry.

'Emma, please don't cry.'

'Sorry. You look AWESOME.'

'Thanks,' she said. 'I know.'

'Do you think I could pull off purple lipstick?'

'No.'

When Steph came into my room she screeched, 'Agh, what IS that?!'

'That… that is the band we're going to see.'

'How is that *music*?!'

'I happen to like it.'

Not strictly true, but if I keep saying it enough maybe I'll believe it.

posted by EditingEmma 18.58

Still in my room, desperately going over 'my' birthday and 'my' star sign and 'my' address. Why can't I just be older? Why can't I just be BETTER? Why can't I feel like Internet Emma all the time? Why can't I turn the clock forward and be twenty-five?! And then stop the clock and never turn twenty-six?!!

I'm suddenly starting to feel all nervous about having lied about my age. And about almost everything else. I'd feel so much better if I had my blanky dress.

My Blanky Dress

Steph calls it this, because it's essentially my teenage equivalent of the 'blanky' to a five-year-old. It's black, the skirt is sort of skater-esque, and the sleeves are three-quarter-ish length. It sounds like a fairly standard dress, but IT'S SO MUCH MORE. The black is not just any black; a really subtle, softer grey-black, which sets off smoky eyes. The length of the skirt is perfect. I don't know... I've just never found anything that I like as much, or that I feel as comfortable in. I've worn it so much it's essentially just a rag now.

Faith messaged:

Good luck! 18.47

Thanks 18.47

I'm with Gracie. She says avoid dancing, if you do get
in 18.48
Tell her THANKS 18.49

Please, please, please say I don't get turned away at the
door. Oh God. It would be the worst thing to get turned
away at the door.

posted by EditingEmma 19.24

In the Queue With Steph

'Now, we have to split up,' said Steph.

'Why?'

'We're less likely to get in if we go together.'

'But I'll miss you.'

'Be cool, Emma.'

Now I'm standing way ahead in the queue alone. I turned
around and winked at Steph a couple of times but she pretended not to notice.

posted by EditingEmma 19.33

I'm In. Sort of

UGH!!! The man on the door was so EVIL!! When I arrived
I tried to look as natural as possible.

'ID, please,' he ordered.

He scrutinised the passport and for a blissful second I
thought I'd got away with it, because he flashed me a big grin.

'I have a daughter about your age,' he said, stamping my
hand with a giant, red circle.

Then he waved me past. I started doing a jig until I got to the bathroom and saw that, in the middle of the red circle, it says 'UNDER 18.' I've been scrubbing for at least five minutes!!! AND IT WON'T COME OFF.

Steph strolled in and saw it. She said, 'I told you to be cool!!'

'I WAS COOL.'

'Evidently not.'

'Did yours work?!'

'YES.'

'HOW?!'

'Probably because I wasn't stuttering and moving my eyes from side to side.'

AGHHHHH.

posted by EditingEmma 23.25

How to End a Date By Ten-Thirty

At Steph's. I ended up dragging her out before the main band even played. Thankfully her nan has gone to bed so there's no more *Goodnight Sweetheart* on. It really is a very morally dubious premise. Anyway, here are my top tips on being a terrible dater:

Do the Dorky Wave

Paolo walked in and faithful Steph scampered off to lurk in a corner. He spotted me and nodded his head slightly. Unfortunately, I'd already broken into the 'dorky wave' and for some reason, once I'd started, found it very hard to stop. He actually looked away uncomfortably.

Talk About Your Stye

He sat down and kissed me on either cheek like my aunt does, when you're not really kissing but just sort of bumping faces.

'*Ciao*, Emma!'

'*Ciao*, Paolo!'

'*Come stai?*'

'What?'

'*Come stai?*'

After three attempts to understand him and a second of sheer panic where I thought my stye was back and he was pointing it out to me, I realised that this means 'How are you?' in Italian. The moment was somewhat lost, and to fill the conversation gap I started explaining about my gross eye-lump.

Cough in Your Date's Face

'What would you like?' he asked.

'Errr... what are you having?'

'A beer.'

'Yep. Sounds good.'

I was sure it would taste fine. People drink beer all the time, right? It's UNIVERSALLY LOVED so it must be all right. Wrong. It's disgusting. I had a WHOLE PINT to get through and every gulp made me splutter.

Keep Your Left Hand Under the Table at All Times

This doesn't sound like it would really affect the date but it made any natural movement very difficult. Still, at least he didn't see my glowing mark of underage humiliation.

Reveal Too Much About Your Family

'So, Emma.' Paolo folded his arms. 'Tell me another story about your mother. She sounds so amusing when you speak of her.'

'Err… Gosh. A story? I don't know. Today she broke an egg cup that she was really attached to and yelled and swore at me for about half an hour for not "helping" her.'

He grimaced a little. Not such a good story I guess.

Act Like a 90-Year-Old

The music was SO LOUD and, with his accent, it was near impossible to hear what he was saying. I kept yelling 'WHAT?' like my granddad.

Dance

Gracie was right.

posted by EditingEmma 23.42

Discussing with Steph.

'Oh God. It was so, so awful.'

'Did you not think he was attractive?'

'No no, he was REALLY attractive.'

She looked at me as if to say, *Then what's the problem?*

'I don't know. We just didn't bond.'

'How did it end?'

'He offered me another beer but I said no, thanks. He shrugged and went off to get another one… Then when he came back there was a really long gap in our forced conversation and he downed it with a really pained expression on his face. Then I said I wasn't feeling very well.'

'Oh, Emmy, I'm sorry.'

'He looked genuinely *relieved*, when I said I was leaving. I feel like a popped balloon.'

'I'm just so confused.' She frowns. 'I thought you got on really well before?'

'We did.'

'I don't understand that.'

'Me neither.'

But I do understand. I'm too ashamed to say that I lied about certain things, and that I felt more confident and witty behind my phone. In real life my bravado fell completely flat.

Evidence: Online connections do not necessarily entail real-life connections. Especially when you've e-tweaked yourself a little bit.

posted by EditingEmma 00.12

Oh my God… I'M LAURENCE MYER. Maybe I should just go out with him and live in a Minstrel-made house of silence.

posted by EditingEmma 00.21

Got a message from Paolo.

'Emma, thank you for meeting with me tonight. But I do not feel that I want to see you again.. You were different, I cannot explain. Maybe you weren't drinking enough. Forgive me and it was lovely to meet you, you are a wonderful girl. *Tua*, Paolo. x'

Maybe you weren't drinking enough???????????

MAYBE YOU WEREN'T DRINKING ENOUGH?????????

As if in order for me to POSSIBLY be any fun I'd have to be DRUNK?

posted by EditingEmma 00.28

Sent a message back: 'You were different too. You said your music was good.x'

A minute ago that felt really cutting and edgy and now, looking at it sitting there on our message thread, it looks like something a petulant five-year-old might say.

Aghhhhhhh.

This is one of the worst things about technology. You can say something stupid in real life and it will essentially just disappear into thin air. You say something stupid on a phone, and the message will hang there in cyberspace, haunting you with proof of your stupidity. It's permanent. It's out there forever. Even if *you* delete it someone else will still have it. They can hold it up and say, 'Look at this message Emma sent me. Look how stupid she is.'

I wish I could go back to the gig and pour the gross beer all over his head.

posted by EditingEmma 00.56

Spooning Steph as she sleeps, very lightly so that she doesn't wake up and push me off. I feel so low. For a brief time, I really felt like talking to Paolo over the internet was helping me discover myself, or something, but now I feel like all it did was remove me from myself. And introduce me to a complete buttface.

Sunday, 21 September

posted by EditingEmma 11.18

'Maybe you weren't drinking enough???????' The phrase keeps resounding in my head. For a brief moment I (sort of) stopped thinking about Leon. I started feeling good about who I was. Now I'm back to thinking about Leon constantly, and self-loathing.

posted by EditingEmma 17.08

Sitting on the toilet just letting my period drip out because I am sick of always having to change my sanitary towels. It's quite satisfying. Animalistic. Natural. Almost regal. I bet, if I sat in the middle of a gallery, people would say I was an amazing feminist performance-art piece.

How comes, when you do really mundane things on your own, it's not art, but as soon as you invite people to look at you doing it, it can be art? I feel like that's a rule that should change. I can be art right here, right now. I can be still, unthinking, unfeeling *art*. Some might say I was just a person sitting and staring into space on a toilet, but they would be wrong.

posted by EditingEmma 17.49

Mum and her stupid bladder interrupted my art.

posted by EditingEmma 19.05

You know what else I'm sick of? SHAVING MY LEGS. Why must I shave my legs in order to feel attractive? Boys don't have to. Stupid, horrible boys like Paolo can be as hairy as they like and people actively LIKE it. You know what I want to do... Reclaim leg hair for women!!! I'm going to grow it out, and really make myself see it as fine. You know why, because it *should* be fine. There is absolutely no reason for it *not* to be fine. It's just a stupid decision that society has made, and I can just as well *un*-make it.

posted by EditingEmma 20.36

Sitting in my room, willing my leg hair to grow faster so that I can start liking it.

    Emma Nash @Em_Nasher

    Sum total of my day: sat on a toilet for an hour for no reason. Watched my leg hair grow. I suppose it could be worse.

    Steph Brent @Brentsy

    @Em_Nasher You're not supposed to admit these things on social media

Monday, 22 September

posted by EditingEmma 08.35

All Dates Should Come With A Reference

Steph sat down next to me.

'I told my sister about you and Paolo,' she said.

'What did she say?'

'She laughed and said, and I quote – "Next time you rifle through my acquaintances looking for someone to rub up against, just *ask* me and I'll tell you which ones are dicks."'

'Noted.'

posted by EditingEmma 10.20

In Art

I dropped a pencil on the floor and Ms McElroy came and stood beside me. She put her hand on my shoulder and said, 'Every time you drop a pencil, it dies.'

Then she floated off to stare out the window. Probably having a moment of silence for the dead pencil.

posted by EditingEmma 14.46

I forgot to ask my mum to sign my work report, and Crazy Holly offered to do it because she 'forges signatures all the time'. I'm just about to hand it in when I look down at the signature she did...

> Oh God.
>
> Emma Nash @Em_Nasher
>
> Would anyone buy that my mum's signature was 'Emma's Mum'?
>
> Emma Nash @Em_Nasher
>
> If I slide it over to Ms Parker, keep talking & maintain freakish eye contact maybe she won't notice...?
>
> Emma Nash @Em_Nasher
>
> SUCCESS!!! Can't believe that worked @HoHoHo
>
> Holly Barnet @HoHoHo
>
> @Em_Nasher Told you I'm a pro

posted by EditingEmma 18.33

At Home

I turned down my music a little and heard this sort of wailing noise coming from downstairs. I thought, what *is* that? Is Mum singing? Has she stubbed her toe? I went downstairs to investigate and Mum had her arms around this thing in a blanket. I thought for a moment she had uncharacteristically taken in a stray animal, but the thing turned out to be Steph.

'I found her on the doorstep,' Mum explained.

'You are making impossibly inhuman sounds. What happened??'

'I, I… he…'

'I'll make tea.' Mum nodded sternly.

It turns out that on Saturday night Jonno went to a party and got with some girl. Andy saw and told Gracie.

'Oh no, you had to hear it from Gracie.'

'She was actually sort of nice about it. But she took AGES to build up to it, like she was announcing the winner of *The X Factor*. And I was the loser to be pitied.'

Steph has stopped crying now. She actually seems OK, except Jonno won't stop phoning her.

'I'm not answering,' declared Steph. 'I sent him a message saying this wasn't how I wanted to be treated, and he's made his choice.'

'What did he say?'

'That he didn't think we were "official" yet, so he thought it would be fine. Which I suppose is true. But I think if you like someone enough, you just don't get with someone else.'

She looked down at her phone in horror.

'Oh my God, he's outside.'

posted by EditingEmma 18.57

Steph came back in.

'He's gone now.'

'What happened?!'

'He was all upset and asking me to be "official" now, and I said no.'

'Good!'

'Eventually he got me to agree to think about it. But all the time he kept running his hands through his hair, and I re-noticed what a small head he has and knew that it was over.'

posted by EditingEmma 22.53
Still thinking about what happened with Jonno and Steph. Why does she always go for the Jonnos of the world?? (The boys who are nice-looking but not very nice?)

It sort of made me want to start up my internet mission again, but then I remembered my date with Paolo and the 'maybe you weren't drunk enough' message.

Tuesday, 23 September

posted by EditingEmma 11.17

I'm Sad To Say, Steph Has Joined My Ranks
I looked over at Steph just as she was stalking the girl that
Jonno got with, and I felt a stab of anger. She should not be
thinking about this girl. She should not be comparing herself
to her, wondering whether she's funnier or smarter...

'Steph, stop this,' I said.

'You were on Anna's profile about five minutes ago.'

'Yes, well... You're better than that.'

'No I'm not.'

'You are. You're strong.'

'Tell you what. I'll stop, when you hide Anna AND Leon
from your feed.'

We both know that's definitely never going to happen as
I don't have the strength, willpower or self-respect and on
some level seem to actually enjoy torturing myself. But I don't
want *Steph* to become like me.

posted by EditingEmma 13.53

Lunchtime Motivation
'How's your double life going, Emma?' asked Faith.

'Huh?'

'How did it go with the Italian boy?'

'Oh. Er. It… went.'

'That means it went badly,' said Gracie.

'Thanks for translating. Yes, it went badly.'

'Why?'

'Well, I got a message from him saying that maybe I needed to drink more.'

'Nooooo!!!'

Told Faith and Gracie all about the evening and how flat it was (and loyal Steph, who had to hear the story for the millionth time but politely feigned an unwavering interest). I actually feel a lot better.

Faith said, 'It sounds like *he's* the boring one.'

'I think some boys never admit to themselves that it might be their fault in any way. Or just… that a girl doesn't like them. I mean, if a girl isn't attracted to them, instantly there's something wrong with her. One time this boy tried to kiss me and I didn't want to, and he made me feel like I was really uptight,' said Gracie.

'Or they call you a lesbian,' added Steph, 'because, of course, if you don't like them, you must not like any boy.'

'And they say "lesbian" in a derogatory way, like it's something inferior. Like women turn to other women because they can't get a guy. Paolo sounds like one of those. I don't think you want to be wasting your time with him,' said Faith.

'No... I don't,' I said.

And I really meant it.

posted by EditingEmma 15.07

In Maths

My friends are completely right. In all this, I was so focused on how he perceived *me* that it's overtaken how I perceived *him*. And he didn't exactly come off well. I know I fibbed about a few things here and there (ability to do sports... age) but nothing that actually had any bearing on my real, core personality. And who doesn't fib a bit online, anyway?? Mum once told me every single man on this dating website had clicked 'average/tall' for their height. Not ONE short guy on the whole site?? I think not.

And OK, so I did feel more confident online... but who doesn't?! Hidden away behind a screen in the comfort of your own room in your pants is very different to having someone stare right at you across a table.

Reasons The Gig With Paolo Was Just As Much His Fault As Mine

He Was Firing Questions Like He Was Alan Sugar

I felt like I was in an interview or something. That is no way to date... It's not like you have to learn everything about the person straight away, surely you just want to see whether you get on?!

Being Judgemental
When I said something he didn't like he just made me feel really bad and inferior. Even when I thought my date with Laurence Myer was going terribly, I was still… *friendly*. You just have to be polite and get on with it.

Suggesting A Gig In the First Place
It isn't just me because I'm deaf. No one can have conversations at a gig.

Reasons the Date Was No One's Fault
Some people just don't click. If you hadn't heard, dating is notoriously difficult.

Conclusion: I DO NOT NEED TO DRINK ALCOHOL TO MAKE MYSELF INTERESTING.

posted by EditingEmma 18.39

Just When You Think You're OK With Your Mum…
I came in the door, put my bag down, and took off my shoes. Then I went to the toilet. As I was coming out, Mum ran out of her room screaming,

'You're so RUDE, Emma!!! What did I ever do to raise such a rude girl!'

'I… What?!'

She came up really close to my face.

'I exist, Emma. I EXIST just as much as you do!!'

Then she ran back into her room and slammed the door. I could hear loud sobbing coming from her room. Eventually, I thought I'd better go and see what I'd done, so I crept over to her door and knocked…

'Mum… Mum, it's me…Can I come in?'

I went in anyway. Mum was sitting on the floor in a little ball.

'Mum, if I've done something to upset you, I'm sorry. But could you tell me what it is?'

She sniffled.

'You never say hello to me when you come in. You treat me like I'm not even here.'

Is she serious?

'Are you serious? I'd literally taken my shoes off and gone for a pee.'

'Get out!!! Just GET OUT!!!!'

Emma Nash @Em_Nasher

Almost 7 and Mum hasn't emerged from her room. Hmm. Getting a bit hungry. I wonder if… I should make something for dinner?

Emma Nash @Em_Nasher

I'm DOING it. It will be excellent practice for when I'm a real person and 'have friends over for dinner' at my own house

Emma Nash @Em_Nasher
Which, given what I'm always hearing about 'current
house prices in London' will probably be never

posted by EditingEmma 19.38

Bolognese By Disgustingly, Emma
Chop the vegetables.
    Put the pasta on.
    The pasta will be done and the Bolognese will lag behind
somewhat.
    The pasta will form a GIANT PASTA LUMP.
    Add the Bolognese to the lump.
    You think maybe it will taste better than it looks, but no.
    I definitely shouldn't start a food blog.
    When I called Mum down for dinner, she came into the
kitchen, took one look at the pasta lump and just burst
into tears. Is she crying because I did a nice thing? Or at
the thought of eating it? Maybe it's because she's raised an
almost-adult-human who can't even make pasta; a sad reality
for which I do blame her entirely.

posted by EditingEmma 22.37
Mum is sitting in the darkness listening to Joy Division. I
want to ask her to turn it down as it's really bumming me
out, but I don't want to get attacked again.
    I went into her room.
    'Mum, do you want to talk about it?' I said cautiously.

'It's just… you're all grown up and it would be nice to have someone solid in my life,' she murmured.

'I know.'

'My best friends can't even catch their bloody flights to see me.'

'I'm not sure it's fair to generalise using Heather as an example.'

posted by EditingEmma 23.05

I'm feeling motivated to continue with my resolutions tomorrow. This is partly because Steph and Mum are both upset again about relationship stuff. Partly because I'm not going to let someone like Paolo stop me. And a little bit because – confession – I actually thought, or hoped, or something… in some small, irrational part of my brain, that tweeting about cooking alone might make Leon come over again. Like he did last time. But he didn't. Obviously. What did I think, he was going to say, 'Hey, sorry about the last three months, let me help you chop some leeks'?? We're not there any more and it's time to move on.

Tomorrow, I will venture once more into the dark recesses of the interweb to do just that.

Wednesday, 24 September

posted by EditingEmma 07.34

Experiment 3: Back To It – Because I Am Beyoncé
Right. It's a new dawn, it's a new day. Today, I am going to be ENTIRELY MYSELF online.

Or at least a version of myself that is vaguely sustainable in reality.

I am taking a step forwards… hmm… What step exactly? What is my next step going to be?

posted by EditingEmma 11.05

Leg Hair Watch
'Emma, why do you keep itching your legs?' Steph asked.

'I'm feeling the prickles.'

'Ew,' said Gracie.

'It's actually a very important thought experiment, Gracie.'

'Go on,' said Steph.

'So, as you know, at the weekend I decided to grow it.'

'Mm,' she said, like she didn't really remember at all.

'Because I want to change my attitude towards it. But if

I'm going to change my attitude towards said hair, I need to interact with it.'

'You mean, stroke yourself like a weirdo.'

'Every time I brush the hair I naturally shudder, but then really try to put that to one side, and *enjoy* the feel of it on my hand. Essentially, I'm rejecting my own rejection of leg hair.'

Gracie looked like she might vomit.

'If I were a guy,' I went on, 'you'd react like that if I *had* shaved my legs.'

'Yes,' she said.

'Is that not weird to you?'

'You're weird to me.'

'So what... you're just... never going to shave again?' interjected Steph.

'Never.'

'What about when we go on holiday?'

'I will walk proud.'

'What about when you want to lose your virginity?'

'If he minds then he doesn't deserve my virginity. I'm very passionate about this, Steph.'

'I give it a week.'

posted by EditingEmma 13.06

Faith Withholds Important Information
Me, Faith and Gracie were just on our way to lunch when this boy in Upper Sixth, Alex Griffin, walked past us and *waved* at Faith. Gracie and I turned to her in shock.

'You know Alex Griffin?!' I demanded.

'Er… yes.'

'Alex Griffin in the year above us? Attractive Alex Griffin? Alex Griffin who played Hamlet last term?'

'Yes. The very same Alex Griffin.'

'WHAT?! Since when?!'

'Jeez, sorry I have other friends, Emma.'

'No, I mean *actually* since when.'

'Er, since we were born?'

I digested this news.

'Are you telling me Alex Griffin is one of your "family friends".'

'Yes.'

'And whenever you go to one of your "family friends" gatherings, they involve Alex Griffin? Alex Griffin is present?'

'Yes.'

'I don't believe this.'

'I guess I don't find him as exciting as you do. What with liking women, and having seen him poo himself.'

'Ew,' said Gracie.

'*How* can you not have mentioned this?!'

'If you suddenly care so much about my family friends' gatherings, Emma, why don't you ask me about them next time.'

Really, the depth of some people's selfishness is astounding.

posted by EditingEmma 13.41

At the lunch table, I carried on waving my bone around and barking.

'So, Faith, what's he like?'

She rolled her eyes. 'Nice.'

'And?'

'Why don't you speak to him and find out yourself.'

'I'd love to.'

'If I give you his number, will you stop talking about this?'

'Er… yes.'

'Promise?'

'Yes.'

'Right. Here it is.'

She put it in my phone. We were silent for a moment.

'Can I really just… message him?'

She dropped her head onto the table. 'Ughhh. You promised.'

'*All right, all right.* Sorry.'

posted by EditingEmma 15.05

Decision Made

Steph always knows exactly what to do:

> Steph, can I really just message him out of the blue?
> 14.49
>
> Go forth. Be brave. Be bold. 14.50
>
> Also if he doesn't reply then you can always pretend it
> was a prank 14.50
>
> Ingenious!! 14.51

posted by EditingEmma 18.06

Sitting staring at my phone. I have a message all typed out:

Hi Alex. My name's Emma Nash in the year below, I'm

*friends with Faith. Anyway I hope you don't think this is
weird but she gave me your number and I just wanted to
say hi – really liked your performance as Hamlet. I cried.
You were great. x*

Too formal? I think so.

*Hi Alex. I'm Emma in the year below, I'm friends with
Faith. Anyway I hope you don't think this is weird but
she gave me your number and I just wanted to say
hi – really liked your performance as Hamlet. I cried.
You were great. x*

Maybe don't tell him that I cried. A bit fan-girlish. I should
probably lose the word 'weird' too. That will imply that I
am weird and seed it in his brain. I have no need to justify
myself. I'm messaging him because I *want* to message him,
and that's OK.

*Hi Alex. I'm Emma in the year below, I'm friends with Faith.
I hope you don't mind but she gave me your number and
I just wanted to say hi. How are you? x*

There. One confident, casual message born of nerves and
fretting. To send or not to send, that is the question…

posted by EditingEmma 18.35

'Steph, I SENT IT.'

'OHMYGOD. What?!'

'What do you mean WHAT?! You told me to!!!'

'Yeah, but I didn't think you'd *actually* do it.'

She's so supportive.

posted by EditingEmma 18.51

Oh God. Now the waiting. This is *awful*. I'm just staring at my phone, lying on the bed. It's sort of like tweeting a slightly risqué joke that you're not entirely sure you can pull off, and waiting to see if anyone validates it with a like. Except a thousand times more nerve-wracking. And you can't delete it. THERE IS NO GOING BACK.

Mum popped her head round the door. 'You're being awfully quiet... What are you doing?'

'Research.'

She snorted.

'I am, actually, Mother. Very important research.'

'Don't even *think* about using my debit card. I'll see it on my statement if you do,' she warned darkly, retreating from the room.

Yes, but three months later you wouldn't have a clue whether it was you or not, would you? That's why *normal* people have online banking.

posted by EditingEmma 19.22

He's Replied

He's replied. He'srepliedhe'srepliedhe'srepliedhe'sreplied.
Oh hi yeah I,'ve seen u around. I'm gd thanks, u? 19.19
SUCCESS! I mean, he abbreviated 'good' to 'gd' and 'you' to 'u' but no one's perfect.

posted by EditingEmma 21.27

I Am Completely Useless: A Realisation

Been messaging back and forth for a little while. Then Alex asked:

> So what kinda stuff do u like doing?!? 20.59

Hmmm. OK, so not pretending that I'm into water sports this time. Right, so, the truth, yes... The truth.

Oh my God. What AM I into?!?! I have ZERO special talents or skills. I can't even cook pasta.

I stomped downstairs to the living room.

'Mum, WHY didn't you make me keep going to football with Steph? Or guitar? Or swimming?!'

'Because you didn't want to.'

'Well, that's just not good enough, is it!! Where do you think Britney Spears would be now if her mum hadn't pushed her to keep singing at a young age?!'

'Probably a lot calmer, happier and more stable.'

'Who the hell cares about *that*?!'

'You were a very stubborn child. You used to stage naked protests.'

'I... what?!'

'You'd take off your clothes and say 'I can't go, I'm naked.' Then if I ever managed to get you there, fully clothed, you'd take them off again. Most of the classes asked me not to bring you back.'

> If I'm honest...watching TV. I'm really good at it, too. What about you? 21.10

I'm an unaccomplished, talentless drone, with a penchant for taking off my clothes in public. Take it or leave it.

Me toooo! And video games. 21.12

Hmm. That didn't go too badly.

I hope you don't think I'm lame but you have really pretty eyes :) 21.19

The memory of Leon telling me that I have pretty eyes and making me walk around with my eyes closed, because it wasn't fair on all the other eyes, drifts through my mind… Then he kissed each eyelid and slowly down my face, to my mouth…

Can't do any more of this today. Shoved my phone in my drawer. I'm going to go and have a good cry to some dramatic music. Maybe Kate Bush.

Thursday, 25 September

posted by EditingEmma 08.58

Faith's Family is NOT Religious (And They Still Maybe Mind Her Being Gay)
I was walking to Chapel with Faith, and she dropped a bombshell.

'Faith, do you think you'd still be afraid to tell your parents you were gay if they weren't Catholic?'

'My parents aren't Catholic.'

'What? What do you mean?'

'They're *not* Catholic.'

'What are they then??'

'Nothing, really. They go to church sometimes but I'm not sure if they actually believe.'

'Then why are you and your sister called Faith and Hope?!'

'They just liked the names.'

'Well this is a bit of a shock, Faith. First, you're friends with Alex Griffin, now you're not Catholic.'

'I can't believe you thought I was CATHOLIC... Oh my God.'

Silence.

'Is that why you asked my dad if he used to dream of being the Pope?!'

posted by EditingEmma 11.15

The Subtle, Coded Communication That is 'Eye Contact'
Alex Griffin is on the other side of the Sixth Form Centre, playing pool with his friends, and we KEEP making meaningful eye contact.

'Why don't you go over and say hi?' asked Gracie.

'I don't need to, Gracie, we're saying so much already.'

'Like what?' she asked, genuinely interested. She has so much to learn from me.

'OK, so, earlier, one of the girls he was playing leant across him and he looked at me as if to say, "Don't worry, she's just a friend."'

'Right.'

'And all the other looks have basically just meant… *I fancy you*. But deeper than that.'

Gracie looked over at Alex.

'Are you sure it doesn't just mean that you're looking at him, so he looks back at you?'

I sighed. 'Of course, not everyone can communicate in this way. You have to be a natural, like *moi*.'

posted by EditingEmma 18.15
Should I add Alex on Facebook? I mean, we're already speaking on WhatsApp, but Facebook friending is sort of taking things to the next level. It's basically the real world.

Making the move...

posted by EditingEmma 20.35

Hmm, my Friend Request has still not been accepted. So he's no Laurence Myer, then.

posted by EditingEmma 22.04

Friend Request accepted!!! He's online. Is he going to say hello...? If only there was some kind of messenger that notified you when people logged on and off. Is it worth a shot anyway?

Logging on.

Logging off.

Logging on...

Nothing. Hmm. I may have to rethink my strategy. This would be so much easier if we actually had the same circle of online friends. Then I could like loads of things, and it would come up in his most recent activity.

... Though we do have *one* mutual friend I can think of...

posted by EditingEmma 22.29

Faith:

I don't know what you're doing or why but STOP hounding me with notifications 22.17

FINE. Who else are we mutually friends with... ? Hmm. A few people from the year above... Eeny meeny... miny... moe. Sorry, Steven Lucy, prepare to be inundated with unwanted attention.

posted by EditingEmma 22.55

For the past five minutes I've been liking EVERYTHING on Steven Lucy's page. It is almost exclusively stuff about sea life (did you know scientists have discovered the first bio-fluorescent reptile?) but still I am met with SILENCE. Zero. Squat. I'm actually feeling quite rejected. Did our loaded glances across the Sixth Form Centre mean *nothing* to him?!

Evidence: It is much harder to catch people's attention online than in the real world, without being able to physically place yourself in their field of vision.

posted by EditingEmma 22.59

Steven: Hi ;)

NO STEVEN. YOU ARE THE BAIT, NOT THE FISH.

posted by EditingEmma 23.07

I'm actually feeling a little hurt. I added him, so I categorically CANNOT be the one to say hello. There is an etiquette in internet socialising and that would definitely be going against the rules. I am aware that relentlessly stalking our mutual friends in the hopes that he'll see my name come up and speak to me is more desperate than just saying hello in the first place, but no one *knows* about that. You can do whatever you want as long as people don't *know*.

Friday, 26 September

posted by EditingEmma 10.13

Possibly The Most Insulting Thing Anyone's Ever Said To Me
'If I were a Pokemon, what do you think I'd be?' chimed Steph.

'Umm… Flareon.'

She shone with pride.

'What about me?'

'Jigglypuff.'

'What, a pink, useless ball?!'

'Well…'

'I can't believe I gave you *Flareon* and you're giving me *Jigglypuff.*'

'All right, you'd be Ninetales.'

'No, no, it's too late now.'

I will never get over this.

posted by EditingEmma 11.02

Message from Alex asking me what I was up to. It felt a little anticlimactic after all last night's efforts. I suppose I *might* have been excited about it, if it wasn't written like 'wuu2?'

and if Leon hadn't walked past arm in arm with Apple at that exact moment.

posted by EditingEmma 11.14
Messaged Alex back and asked if he wanted to meet up this weekend. He said:

> OK. I could come to the park by my house. 10.59

Hmm. Not exactly brimming with enthusiasm, I'll admit… But then, neither am I. I'm getting the vibe that Alex is not going to meet the criteria I originally set out (*'an at least 50 per cent functional relationship'*). So really it just depends how desperate I am for some seedy physical contact in a park.

posted by EditingEmma 13.58
Quite desperate, apparently. I just replied and said yes. But I did think about it for at least eleven minutes.

posted by EditingEmma 15.50

Online Stalking When Someone's in the Room: Acceptable or Not?
So I'm in FT. Apple is also in the room…baking and giggling and chatting. I can see people nodding emphatically at whatever she's saying. I started stalking her on my phone and occasionally looking up to stare at the back of her head, but then I started to feel like Glenn Close, sitting turning a light switch on, and off, and on, and off…

Why does it feel OK to stalk someone on the internet when they're not in the room, but not OK if they are in the room? It's exactly the same action. Really, when you think about it, it changes nothing whether she's in the room or not.

Logically, I see no reason to not continue stalking.

posted by EditingEmma 00.51

Actual Stalking: Definitely Not Acceptable

I was just drifting off to sleep… When Mum came crashing through the door.

'Are you dressed?'

'What?'

'Are you decent?'

'Yes, I'm wearing a ball gown under here.'

'Oh, shut up.'

'Why??'

Then she threw a black wig at me. The one Steph bought when she was an emo.

'Put this on. We're going out.'

'Again… why??'

'We're on a mission.'

Half an hour later we were driving really slowly past Olly's house… Mum had sunglasses on, and it was pitch black. Sort of worrying, really.

'Mum. There's probably at least an 85 per cent chance of you crashing.'

'I won't.'

'Hmm, not reassured. This is *definitely* not how I want to be found dead and remembered. Stalking a stripper in the middle of the night, wearing a wig that makes me look like Alice Cooper.'

Fifteen minutes later we were still driving round.

'What exactly are we looking for, Mum?'

'I don't know… signs that he's lying.'

'About what?'

'Well, he might be married, I don't know, do I?'

Silence. We circled his road for the fourth time.

'Mum, this is ridiculous. All the lights are off and I left my night-vision goggles at spy school.'

'I'm looking for his car. I can't see it.'

'What kind of car is it?'

'Errr…it's red.'

'There are about five red cars.'

'No, I don't think any of them are his.'

'You can't even remember what car it is!!'

'They look different.'

'But they *could* be his?'

'I don't think so, no.'

Silence.

'I don't think he even lives here… The prick.'

I was just pointing out that she might be jumping to conclusions, when his front door opened and she sped off like a madwoman, skewing my wig.

'Why did you do that?? We didn't even see who it was!'

'What if it was him and he saw me? That would be awful!!!'

Evidence: Stalking in real life is more difficult, as well as more frowned upon than internet stalking.

Emma Nash @Em_Nasher
Tonight I learned that neither me, nor my mother, will ever have a career in espionage

Saturday, 27 September

posted by EditingEmma 09.37

When I got back last night I fell asleep attempting to masturbate over Alex. In my defence it was very late thanks to Mum's night-time escapades, but I have never *once* fallen asleep masturbating! Am I losing my sex drive?? Have I peaked already?! Will I never have the chance to share my urges with anyone other than me?

I suppose if I no longer have the urges, I'll no longer care. Like being dead.

posted by EditingEmma 09.55

I'm meeting Alex at half-one, but I've told Mum that I'm going shopping up town with Faith. I just can't be bothered with the hassle of telling her since she got all weird about Paolo. When I came down she said,

'Why are you up so early?'

I said, 'A bird flew into my window.'

posted by EditingEmma 11.34

Messaged Faith.

If my mum calls later, I'm at yours but on the toilet. And I
didn't end up buying anything xx 11.29
No. I told you not to use me as an excuse. X 11.31
She can be such a downer sometimes.

posted by EditingEmma 13.31
Messaged Steph:
Heading for the park now 13.18
Circling around the park a few times so that I'm not so
on time 13.27
Hahah! Hope he's not a Paolo. Sx 13.28

posted by EditingEmma 13.37

**The Paranoia of Meeting People You've Not Really Met
Before**
There have been a couple of boys pass by who I thought might
be Alex in the distance, but they both carried on walking.

Oh God. Maybe it was him and he did recognise me, but
decided to walk away anyway?

Maybe he's forgotten?

Maybe I got the wrong day?

Maybe this was all an elaborate joke?

Maybe I should calm down as he's only seven minutes
late. I'm turning into my Mum.

posted by EditingEmma 13.46
Is he there yet? 13.40
Not yet. 13.43

Wait. Oh my God. I think this might be it. 13.44

A car is pulling up. 13.44

?!?! 13.45

And a middle-aged woman is getting out. Clearly not for me. 13.45

Though, she does seem to be heading towards me... 13.46

posted by EditingEmma 14.29

I'm Never EVER Meeting Anyone Again EVER

Scrap that, I'm never leaving the house again, ever. Aghh- hhh!!! After the car pulled up... No. I can't even write it. The wound is still too raw.

posted by EditingEmma 15.05

What Happened

If I just write it down, maybe it will help. Maybe it won't seem so bad.

The car pulled up and the woman got out. Then... a small boy got out of the car from the other side. He trailed along behind her and they both started heading for me.

I kept thinking... they MUST have the wrong person.

But then they KEPT coming towards me.

Even when the woman stopped abruptly in front of me, I still couldn't quite believe that they were coming to meet me. I thought maybe they were going to ask me for directions.

She was very groomed and wearing a cream suit, and she put her hand on one hip.

'Aren't you a bit old, my love?' She frowned.

It was only then that the reality hit.

Oh no, I thought. No no no no no no no. Please no.

I looked at the small boy, cowering just behind her.

'Alex?' I whimpered.

He didn't say anything. He was just frozen in horror.

'Uh, this is Charlie. Alex's brother,' the woman said.

Writing it down didn't help.

posted by EditingEmma 15.22

Speaking About It Didn't Help, Either

Phoned Steph.

'Steph.'

'Emma.'

'Steph. I belong in the seventies.'

'What?'

'I should be locked behind bars.'

'What are you talking about?'

'Alex. He was… not Alex.'

'I still don't understand.'

I took a deep breath.

'I've been talking to his YOUNGER BROTHER. He was THIRTEEN.'

I hung up on her because she couldn't stop laughing. I half felt like joining in but the overwhelming feeling of wanting to sink into the ground took over. Five minutes later, she phoned back.

'I'm sorry, I'm sorry, I'll stop now. What *happened*?!'

'He turned up with his *mum*.'

More laughter. I hung up again.

Then my mum called.

'Where are you?' she said through gritted teeth.

My heart plummeted.

'On the train.'

'From where?'

'Shopping with Faith. I already told you.'

'Oh, *really*. Because I happen to know Faith's at home, doing her homework.'

Oh God. Think. Must turn it around. Play hurt and hard done by.

'Were you SPYING on me? First Olly and now ME? I can't believe you!!! I can't believe you wouldn't trust me!!'

'Yeah, well, evidently with good reason. I bumped into Faith's mum and dad on the high street, and they had no knowledge whatsoever of a shopping trip.'

Oh God. There really is no getting out of this one.

'I don't believe this… Faith must have a DOPPELGÄNGER.'

It might have worked on *The Vampire Diaries*.

posted by EditingEmma 15.33

Faith phoned.

'Oh my God, Emma!! DON'T GO TO MEET ALEX!!! Stop!! Turn around! Go home!'

'Faith. You're a bit late.'

'Oh no.'

'Oh yes.'

'Oh NO.'

'Oh yes.'

'I'm SO sorry!!! I just heard my parents talking about how Jane was taking Charlie on his first date to the park today and how cute it was... and my heart stopped. Emma, I swear to God, that *was* his number, honestly. He must have given his old phone to his little brother. I'm sooooo so sorry!!!'

'It's all right, Faith. These things happen.'

'Do they?'

'For a moment can you just... pretend they do?'

'Oh sure, sure. Yes. These things happen all the time.'

posted by EditingEmma 15.47

Lingering on the path to our house, which at the moment looks about as much fun as the Bates Motel.

posted by EditingEmma 16.08

How To End Up Grounded

When I went to put the key in the lock the door opened by itself... and Mum was standing behind it, looking very grave.

'Explain,' she barked.

'I went to meet a friend.'

'What *friend*?'

'His name's Alex.'

'How come I've never heard of this *Alex*?'

'I don't need to tell you everything, Mum. We're not Rory and Lorelai.'

'When it involves you going God knows where to meet God knows who, you *do* need to tell me.'

'Not God knows where to meet God knows who... To the park. To meet Alex.'

'The park?!' she exclaimed. 'The PARK?! Were there even people around, you stupid, stupid girl?!'

'YES, Mum. About fifty parents pushing their children on swings.'

(How apt.)

'And how do you know this *Alex*? Hmm?'

'He's friends with Faith.'

'Mmm. Just like that Paolo boy was friends with Jess? I'm not an idiot, Emma. You didn't go out all summer and now you're meeting boys left, right and centre.'

'I went out a *bit*...'

'I mean, what are you playing at? WHY are you meeting random strangers off the internet?'

'I'm not meeting *random strangers*.'

'Oh really?' She held up her phone. There was a picture of me trying to fit an entire burger in my mouth, and underneath it said '*Emma Nash. 18 Years Old. Spirit Pokemon: Jigglypuff.*'

'Oh my God. Mum... what *is* that?!'

'You tell me.'

'I have *no idea*.'

'No more lies, Emma, OK?'

'I swear. I'm not lying. I've never seen that before in my life... I don't know...'

Then I stopped.

Steph.

'Go upstairs. I've heard enough.'

'No really, listen...'

'Just go upstairs.'

'Mum, WHY would I use that picture? Why would I refer to myself as a JIGGLYPUFF?!'

'I have no idea what that even means.'

'Why do you ask me to *explain*, then not listen to me?!'

'I decided I don't want to hear it.'

'Ugh, even if I *was* doing it, which I'm *not*, YOU do it all the time!!!'

'I am an ADULT. Those websites are NOT for people your age. That's why there's a little click box that says 'I am 18 years and over.' Or did you just miss that?'

'All right, fine, so in one and a bit years it would be OK, would it? What's the difference, really?'

'One and a bit years is the difference.'

'All right, fine, well when you tell people that you're thirty-nine I'm going to point out the five and a bit years difference there.'

'GO UPSTAIRS NOW.'

And now I'm in my room, which is minus one laptop.

'Mum, where's my laptop?!' I call out.

Mum storms in. 'Aha, if you think I'm letting you anywhere *near* that computer you've got another thing coming.'

I can just go on my phone. Ha.

An Hour Later

I can't say the exact time, because Mum has taken my phone. And I don't own a watch, because who owns a watch? I am writing from a scruffy old notebook, stuffed at the back of my wardrobe. My hands are all covered in dust.

So, she barged back in and snatched my phone right out of my hands. 'I'll be taking this too.'

'How dare you!! Give that back!'

Desperation. Fear.

'I'm only using it to talk to Steph, honest. I... I... It doesn't even have the internet!'

'Do you think I was born yesterday?' she snorted and stalked off.

'No. I think you were born forty-four and a bit years ago!!' I called after her.

My cheap shot fired into the cold, technology-barren wasteland.

Then once again I heard footsteps thundering along the hallway. She stood in the doorway rubbing her temples. She was shaking.

'Do you even know how dangerous what you've been doing is, Emma? Going to meet complete strangers, and I'd have no idea where you were. You're a young, vulnerable girl, you're a target. People put up different pictures, people lie about their age. Not just like I do, I mean really lie. You could have been going to meet someone really dangerous today, Emma.'

I wanted to laugh out loud at the irony.

'Mum...'

But again, she left before I could get another word in. Does she not realise I was born in the twenty-first century? That I've seen Catfish? That I've grown up on internet safety workshops? That in Year 7 we did a somewhat disturbing play where Crazy Holly pretended to be a predator lurking on the other end of a computer?! I know, OF COURSE, that what she's saying would be true, if she was right. (Though somehow her warnings can't carry any weight accompanied by the image of Baby Charlie wielding a knife at me.) But I'm not an idiot, I was being *totally safe*. Agh, why didn't I just tell her about the stupid 'date' before I left?!

I'm going to KILL Steph when I see her.

God, my hand hurts... I think the last time I opened this book I must have been about ten or eleven. I'm just looking at all my old drawings of different outfits and little bits of material stuck in like a scrapbook. There's a bit of my old duvet I tried to make into a mermaid tail, and I thought Mum wouldn't notice. (She did notice.) It's sort of giving me the urge to cry, though I'm not sure why.

I Will Never Be Able to Masturbate Again

I can't because every time I try I see Baby Charlie. Stopitstopitstopit. I've tried doing it with Mr Allen but every time he morphs back into Charlie. What kind of cruel world is this where a) I have no one to have sex with except in my own mind, and b) even in my own mind I cannot choose who I want.

Gave up. My mind is too clouded. Sometimes I wish I

could just look at porn and get on with it, instead of having to use my 'imagination'. It's such an effort. But me and Steph watched porn once and very quickly turned it off again.

The Five Stages of Phoneless Grief

1 – Boredom
I have absolutely nothing to do except twiddle my thumbs and think about what a crappy day this is. Found an old to-do list that says 'Make Mum a hot cross loaf'. I don't remember this happening... Did I bake?! Who am I?!

Oh, no, it says 'Make Mum buy a hot cross loaf.' That makes much more sense. Identity crisis over.

Apple's GREAT at baking. Ugh. What a boring skill.

God, look at me... mocking Anna for taking an interest in something. There's absolutely nothing wrong with baking and I am just a bitter old lemon. At least she HAS a skill. Maybe I should be thinking less about masturbation and more about how I feel when someone asks me what I like doing and the only answer I can come up with is 'watching TV'. I could easily answer for Faith (art) or Steph (sports). I have nothing. Sitting here in this room, stripped down to just... me, that is really, painfully obvious.

2 – Isolation

I REALLY want to talk to someone, even if it's just to have Steph laugh at me again. I keep having the urge to reach out to someone with a message, or even just look at some pictures and comment on something. I think of everything going on without me. Everyone contacting each other and having fun whilst I am here, being left out. Totally invisible and forgotten. I start thinking about how lonely I feel, how deeply, deeply lonely, and I start crying uncontrollably. Because that's the truth, isn't it? I am alone. Everything is carrying on without me because no one really cares. Leon definitely doesn't. All this time I've been keeping us alive in my head, but that's not real. It's just an illusion created by the fact that I still, technically, know what he's doing. So do his other 567 Facebook friends.

3 – Frustration

I am sobbing so, so hard I can't breathe. I can't face being left alone, without any distractions. I can't face myself. It occurs to me how ludicrous it is that I'm feeling like this. But that just makes me feel even lower.

4 – Rage

And now I'm just angry. How dare Mum cut me off from everyone, from my life, what gives her the right to lock me up here whilst she can go around doing whatever she wants?! She's such a hypocrite.

Left the house. I'm sitting on a wall a few roads away, watching some kids kick a ball around. When she realises

I'm gone she'll be sick with worry and I won't have a phone that she can contact me on.

Ha-ha.

5 – Inevitable Descent into Madness

I keep walking across roads without even looking. I don't care if a car hits me or not. I feel blank. And also like that would really teach Mum if I got killed or seriously injured. I'm just wandering up and down the high street. Bored and a little bit cold because I left without a jacket.

I hear some guy say, 'Listen, mate, if I HAD a fridge...'

At least I've got a fridge.

What am I doing? I feel more alone than I've ever felt before in my life. I sit down by a wall and start sobbing again. People keep asking me if I'm OK and it just makes me cry more. A couple of people assume I am homeless and give me money. I hear one girl say, 'What if she's been mugged or something?'

I hear a car screeching to a halt and I know it's Mum before I even look up. She slams out of the car and drags me up off the floor by my arm (which really hurt).

'Go away!!' I yell. 'I don't know you!!'

'Get in the car, Emma,' she warns. I can see that she's been crying.

'You can't make me,' I say.

Am now in the car driving home.

Neither of us says anything.

Back in My Room

Now with the 'Emma lock' on the front door. Caged in like a prisoner. Slamming out of the house and walking around like Cathy on the moors distracted me for a brief period but the loneliness has taken over again. I'm also not sure the Cathy reference works because then Heathcliff would have to be my laptop. It's just not as romantic somehow.

Lying very still on my bed, trying to stay calm.

Doodling with some pens and paper in my room. Is this what I've been reduced to? I doodle a little Leon and Emma. In paper world we are together, and we have nothing to do in the vast expanse of white except kiss. And I'm wearing an amazing dress.

It really is an amazing dress.

I've sketched out the dress on another sheet of paper, in more detail. It's black with a couple of see-through stripes. I remember that I used to do this a lot, and I was quite good at it (well, as good as it's possible for ten-year-olds to be at anything). It feels a bit weird. It's been so long since I designed anything... I remember one time I made Mum this really gross, mint green skirt out of a pair of old kitchen curtains and made her wear it. And every time she took it off I cried, so she wore it to the cinema with Heather.

Thinking back, she probably took it off en route to the cinema.

Still sketching

How did I forget that I liked doing this so much? When

did I stop? Why haven't I even thought about this in years? What happened?

Possibly it was when I got a mobile phone.

I've made a couple of designs that I'm really happy with. Childishly, I really want to go and show them to Mum but I think she's probably still upset from earlier.

Going to Bed

For a moment I feel peaceful and safe in my room, like nothing matters because the outside world can't touch me and I am enough. Alone and secure in my own company. But just for a moment, and then my fingers burn to type.

Admiring my drawings before I go to sleep. This was definitely a more positive use for my time than crying on the street. I maybe feel a little bit, slightly, almost imperceptibly, better about myself.

On the downside, I'm still unable to masturbate successfully.

Sunday 28th September

Woke up from a dream where I was kissing Leon (obviously) but then he started getting smaller and smaller and disappearing in my arms, and then I looked down and there was a baby sitting on the floor. Then the social services lady from The Sims came to take the baby away, and then Steph appeared shaking her head and saying that she couldn't be my friend any more.

I feel so dirty.

Now I've got all my paper and pens spread out on the floor. I'm hoping to block out the fact that somewhere, out there in the world, is a small, scared thirteen-year-old I have technically been out with. I've been designing a shirt. Mum came in and looked over my shoulder.

'That's pretty,' she said.

Trying to Make Clothes

Mum suggested that we go to Cloth House so I can start actually making the stuff I've been sketching. It was actually really... nice. We avoided all other topics, and just talked about fabric. Now we're back with loads of lovely materials... She's got her old sewing machine down from the attic, and we've put it in the front room. I've ripped out pictures from magazines and stuck them on the wall around the window.

Failing to Make Clothes

I was feeling quite positive, looking at the space I've created. It's almost like having my own studio. Then I started attempting to make stuff and felt instantly grumpy again. I've messed up almost all of the fabric we bought earlier. Why didn't I make a first attempt using old sheets or something??! I even used to do that when I was a kid. I thought as you got older you were supposed to learn stuff, but it turns out I've actually LOST wisdom over the years. I forgot all about leaving a centimetre allowance for stitching and just started sewing bits together. They look AWFUL. I was just sitting staring at it in a ragged heap on the floor when Mum came in and said,

'I guess it's harder to make stuff than it is to imagine it.'

'That's helpful, thanks,' I said through gritted teeth.

'You probably should have made a toile.'

'A what?'

'First attempt.'

'You don't say.'

But I have nothing else to do so I may as well keep going.

My emotions are going round and round in circles. One minute I feel tragically invisible and angry at the world for going on without me. Then I feel angry at myself for being so pathetic, and realising that my only apparent source of self-esteem is from outside myself. From the amount of likes

I get. From Leon. Why doesn't it come from me? Then I stop thinking for a while, and carry on attempting to sew things (and failing), and then it starts all over again.

Hours Later
I have spent nearly five hours attempting to make clothes and all I've got to show for it is a single sleeve. Nonetheless, it is a good sleeve and I am immensely proud of it.

A Glimpse into the Dark Ages
Mum comes into my room holding a brick or something.

'Are you going to kill me with that?' I ask.

'Don't tempt me.'

'What is it?'

'This is for you to take to school.'

I look closer at the black object. 'Is that… Is that a phone?'

'No, it's a puppy.'

'No offence, Mum, but I don't want to carry around some dinosaur phone from the eighties or whenever you grew up.'

'I would have been so lucky to have a mobile phone when I was a teenager, Emma.'

I put the phone in my blazer pocket and it looks like a massive, square boob. I burst out laughing.

'Mum, I can't go into school with this…'

'You're taking it. But not until tomorrow morning,' she said, snatching it back.

This is absolutely ridiculous.

Going to Bed

With my sleeve. Now beside the plaster. I wonder what Leon has been doing this weekend? I have no idea. I can't check. And he does actually feel ever so slightly distanced from me. Like he's standing a millimetre further away than he was before. Maybe I should block his profiles when I'm allowed the internet back.

Then again there are lots of things people should do which they absolutely never will. Like hoovering under the bed.

Monday, 29 September

posted by EditingEmma 08.37

Registration

ON A COMPUTERRRR. In spite of my productive week-end, I'm so happy to see other human beings I could cry. I hugged Gracie really tight when I saw her and she looked very startled. I *almost* hugged Mr Morris and I even forgave Steph. When I came in she grovelled like a worm.

'Emma!! You're alive!!'

I sat down next to Gracie.

'What is that buzzing sound?'

'Emma, I'M SORRY.'

'Can you hear that, Gracie?'

Then Steph came and sat on my lap.

'I'M SORRY. IT WAS A JOKE. FORGIVE ME. EMMAEMMAEMMAEMMAEMMA.'

Then she *licked my forehead*.

'Ugh!!!' I pushed her off.

'Aha!' she said. 'You spoke!'

Then she threatened to follow me around licking me and my belongings all day, and resistance seemed futile.

In the middle of pulling my things out of my bag and dangling them in front of her tongue, Steph came across dinosaur phone.

'What is *that*?' she shrieked.

'Emma, give me the walkie-talkie,' said Mr Morris, taking it from me. 'This isn't allowed.'

'That's my phone.'

He raised one fluffy eyebrow at me.

'No, really,' I said.

posted by EditingEmma 11.12

Break

No one's said *anything* about the Alex–Charlie incident, which is highly unusual. Faith clearly instructed Steph and Gracie not to mention it.

I wonder how long that will last.

posted by EditingEmma 13.17

Five hours in total. Real Alex just came into the Sixth Form Centre and headed for the pool table. He looked over here and Gracie was practically wetting herself.

'So... what do you think *that* look said, Emma? I fancy you or... I heard she preys on thirteen-year-old boys?'

Can't say I blame her. Oh God. I can still see his brother's terrified little face peeking up at me from behind his mum.

Where can I hide?!

posted by EditingEmma 13.51

Hiding Like a Mole in the Ground
Found refuge in the 'Tech Lab' i.e. Laurence Myer's Lair. I've never been in here before. It's actually quite calming... Apart from Laurence Myer staring at me over the ridge of his computer.

At Home
I started making the dress I designed on Saturday. Still not finding this part as easy as the designing. I was wearing my second, slightly mangled attempt and feeling quite pleased that it at least sort of resembled what I drew, and Mum came in and laughed.

I thought I might start off a bit easier, and make a pattern from a pre-existing dress. Then I had a light-bulb moment. MY BLANKY DRESS. I can recreate it!!

I've laid out the dress on the floor, and have started to lovingly draw around it. I'm so excited!

Tuesday, 30 September

Damn You Steph

Steph was being very cagey, and then I spotted her phone under the desk, her screen full of boy pictures.

'Is that... Steph, did you not delete that yet?!'

'Er...'

'STEPH. Please delete it NOW. I mean it!!'

'OK, OK. I promise I will. I just wanted to have a *look*.'

'NO.'

'Come oon. Play with me!'

'I'm *really* not in the mood. Plus Mum would *kill* me.'

'She's already grounded you and taken away your phone. What can she do?'

'Home school me.'

Then Gracie looked over Steph's shoulder. 'Oh my God! I know that boy. He went to my brother's college. Oh that's so weird!'

And before long they were all crowded round Steph's phone, *giggling*.

'"I'll probably kiss you on the first date",' Faith read.

'Do I have a say in this? Because that sounds like sexual harassment.'

'Myles Henderson *loves food, drink and sleep*,' Gracie suggested.

'Yes, we have so much in common… I am also a human being.'

'What about him?' Faith pointed at a boy holding a puppy. Steph clicked on him and read,

'"*I am a keen racist*." Do you think he's trying to be funny?'

'Hmm, either way I'd rather go out with the dog,' replied Faith.

'What about him?' Steph's eyes widened at a good-looking boy, who also looked like he knew it.

'"Hilarious dude. Six-day per week gym routine. Give me a bench and I can press the world",' Faith read.

'Ooh!' exclaimed Steph.

'You're joking, right?'

'No. He's got a really nice body.'

'And about fifty pictures of his really nice body.'

'What's your point?'

'Oh look, "Luke" looks quite normal.'

'Yes, not to be confused with the last Luke who "love wild girl!!!!!!"'

'I suppose it's better than "Donz" who simply says "hi, women".'

'Enticing.'

'Oh my God. Emma, LOOK!'

'What?'

'It's Charles Manson boy! We saw him on Jess's Tinder, remember?'

'Ugh, he looks creepy!!' squealed Gracie.

'Oh, I know him!' said Crazy Holly, elbowing her way in. (Of course she does.)

'Are you OK, Emma?' asked Faith.

'I'm fine, sorry,' I mumbled.

But I'm not really fine. I want to be having fun like normal, and joke around about Charles Manson boy. But today, all I keep thinking about is Charles Manson boy in reality. He's probably just lonely, looking to find someone. And here we all are sitting mocking him. Like he's not a person... Like he's completely disposable. One glance and someone says 'no' and dismisses another human being with an entire life and mess of feelings in the tap of a finger. *No. No. No. No. No. No. No.* It isn't so much like dating as a game.

If this is what I've got to look forward to in adult life then count me out. Not that it matters, because I'm never going on another date anyway. Ever.

posted by EditingEmma 13.43

I'm in the Tech Lab again because I can't watch Leon and Apple any more. He was leaning all over her and they looked very... *together*. Mr Morris walked past and told them to stop 'canoodling', but they didn't. Does no one have any respect for teacher authority any more?? He gave her a Chewit and she ate it without a second thought. Like it was just *food* to her.

I said, 'I bet she doesn't store all the wrappers under her bed like I do.'

Faith said, 'That's probably in her favour, Emma.'

I sat there in disbelief that I could be feeling this deeply, and no one else knows. No one else can *feel* what I am feeling. Why isn't there some tangible sense for other people's internal life? Why can't we smell when someone is feeling very sad, or happy? Everything would be much easier. Maybe then they would know how truly awful they are making me feel and go and do their 'canoodling' somewhere private.

'Emma, you have to stop staring at them.' Steph's voice penetrated my somber shroud. 'You are the least subtle person.'

So maybe people notice a bit.

posted by EditingEmma 13.57

Steph came bounding into the computer room.

'Emma!! Emma!!' she called.

'You're not allowed to talk in here,' someone muttered.

'Oh, *sorry*,' she stage-whispered, putting her finger over her lips.

She clambered over to me, waving her phone around.

'I'm not interested,' I whispered.

'Look!'

She shoved her phone in my face. There was a picture of 'Greg Seymour'.

'Is that… ?'

'Yes!'

Oh my God… Greg.

'I was on your Facebook changing your age to make the, er, joke profile.' She looked sheepish. 'And he added you. Forgot to tell you, soz.'

I paused for a moment. 'Why would he do that? I yelled in his face and puked on his coat.'

'I know, I was confused as well. But I thought...'

'What? You thought *what*?'

'Might as well say hi?'

'STEPH!!!!' I hissed.

'Anyway, he just said hi back, KBYE,' she said, retreating from the room. 'You really should change your password now and again!' she called over her shoulder.

'My' Conversation with Greg

Emma: Hey :)

Greg: Well you're keen ;) only two weeks later!

Emma: Haha. Well, same to you...

Greg: Ooo yeah awkward, was kind of avoiding you but, since you couldn't keep away... :/

Then we *exchanged numbers*.

I swear to God, if I had more friends I'd consider getting Steph arrested for fraud.

posted by EditingEmma 21.00

I'M BACK

Moaned so much about dinosaur phone that Mum gave me back my regular phone. But she called my network and froze my data. I was pretty impressed. Obviously I can still connect through Wi-Fi, but she was halfway there.

posted by EditingEmma 21.29

For some reason, I'm still thinking about Greg. Here's my internal debate:

Reasons Not to Talk to Greg
1. I've gone past caring about dates.
2. I was a bit put off by how drunk and full on he was at first.
3. I'm technically still grounded.

Reasons to Talk to Greg
1) Though I do feel lethargic about dating, I'm nonetheless still very horny.
2) Although he was full on, he was quite sweet, and it's not like I can talk about being drunk, is it? Why was I so harsh? Hadn't I resolved to give some different people a chance? Isn't that what this whole blog is about?
3) Really, if Mum wants me not to lie about my whereabouts, she shouldn't ground me and then I wouldn't need to.

Hmm. I'll sleep on it.

Wednesday, 1 October

posted by EditingEmma 10.19

In English. We're still talking about the 'dangers of knowledge' in *Frankenstein*. How much more can we possibly analyse this?

'But is it science *itself* that is the danger, or what it becomes through abuse by society?'

I've already written an entire essay on this. Why do we only read one book a term? Are they *trying* to bore us? It's almost like she's *forcing* me to blog instead...

My Actual Conversation with Greg

Earlier on I got a message from an unknown number. My heart started pounding and I didn't open the message for a good thirty seconds, just to savour the excitement... which is when I realised I must have shockingly little excitement in my life. Anyway, it was Greg.

So, did you have fun at Andy's party? x 09.42

Did he *see* me at the party? Best to just gloss over that.

Yeah, did you? 09.45

Well, I can't remember anything past 11... So that means I probably did 09.45

Uh huh 09.47

Teacher has seen me on my phone so gotta go 09.47

See you 09.47

Oh OK, see you xx 09.48

Of course, I was in Maths so could've got up and done karaoke if I felt like it. But basically, what he's saying is he doesn't remember kissing me, or more likely he doesn't *want* to remember. So I thought it best to just end our conversation there. I'm never going to find the answer to the world's dating problems, no one wants to date me in the first place. Except a thirteen-year-old who brings his mum along for moral support.

posted by EditingEmma 23.38

I was just drifting off when my phone buzzed. Recording it here before I fall asleep again. Too tired to analyse it.

Hi, it's Greg. I think I might have offended you earlier…
I was really drunk, and I don't remember a lot, but I do remember one thing… Night night x 23.27

And then:

Do you want to go for a coffee tomorrow after school? x 23.29

OK sure. Where shall I meet you? 23.32

I'll come to pick you up after school? See you 4.00? x 23.33

OK, see you then. Night. X 23.34

Thursday, 2 October

posted by EditingEmma 07.34

Woke up and remembered that I basically sleepwalked myself into a date today. Huh.

posted by EditingEmma 11.16

Confusing Feelings For Older Men

Mr Allen was talking about his time in a Buddhist retreat in India really passionately. Now there is a man who feels things deeply. I considered my feelings for him a little while. He half makes me want to take my top off and lie out before him on the desk, and he half terrifies me and makes me want to wrap myself in bundles of cotton wool. He also sort of makes me want to sit on his knee and receive lots of praise for my homework, but let's not explore that too much.

posted by EditingEmma 13.15

I paid lots of attention in French today. If I'm going to be a big star in the world of design and fly over to Paris Fashion Week, I'm going to need to know French. I haven't thought about my 'coffee date' much. Probably because it definitely can't go any worse than the last one. Although, that's what I thought about meeting Alex, and that really *was* worse than the date with Paolo.

But at least I have seen and spoken with Greg, and ascertained that he is not a child in disguise.

posted by EditingEmma 16.02

The bell went two minutes ago and Mr Crispin is still talking. What's wrong with him!!! Does he think he's teaching a class of people who don't have lives?? Who are here voluntarily??! I've packed up all my things and am standing by the door with my hand hovering over the handle.

> Emma Nash @Em_Nasher
> Freedom!!! I can't believe I lost three minutes of valuable
> time talking about triangles

posted by EditingEmma 16.11

At the Gates

I sort of wish everyone was still around to see me getting into an older boy's car. What's the point of doing something cool if you don't have an audience? It would be like having a really, really funny thought and then not tweeting it.

posted by EditingEmma 19.58

Date Number 4

When Greg's car rolled up I was incredibly relieved that the gates were deserted. It's this sort of pea-green box-shaped thing that looks like it might collapse any second. There were bits of dirty smoke coming out of the back pipe.

He rolled down the window, (manually, of course)…

Finally, after about a year of rolling, his face appeared through the cloud of pollution.

'Are you going to get in?'

I don't know, am I? I thought. *Is this coffee worth risking my life?* I concluded no, but sheer awkwardness pushed me on. I tried not to imagine what Mum would say if she saw. I told her I was at home watching *Deal or No Deal*.

We drove along, very slowly. The engine was making questionable noises and I was beginning to long for Noel Edmonds' face. (You really have got to admire a man who can fake enthusiasm hundreds of times for people opening boxes at random, pretending like there are lots of different 'methods'.)

I realised that Greg and I hadn't spoken in twenty seconds, so I said this to him.

'Oh, I applied for that,' he said.

Of course he did.

Once we parked the 'car', we took a stroll along… my high street!! What an exciting destination. I probably could have walked there faster.

'Where do you want to go?' I asked.

'I thought we'd go to Costa?' he replied.

'Costa? I don't think there's a Costa on this road…'

'There is.'

'I've lived here all my life, and I've never seen it… '

Then Waitrose loomed in front of us and Greg started walking in. *Is he taking me shopping?* I wondered. *Am I going to hold the sack of potatoes whilst he scouts for a good bit of chicken breast?* Then I saw. There's a small Costa at the back of Waitrose. Greg looked very smug, like he'd won a game. Five minutes later, we were wedged in between an old couple 'taking time out from the frantic shop floor' and a middle-aged man explaining to his wife how cucumber had never 'agreed' with him. Whatever this was, it definitely wasn't winning.

Then came the strange part. Despite being in the middle of a supermarket, fearing running into my friends' parents or, worse, my mum, we actually started *getting along*. Maybe the surroundings were so bleak I forgot to be nervous.

'So wait, you broke your arm *three times* in six months?!'

'Yes. I swear!'

'I don't believe you.'

'It was my mum's fault.'

'What? She pushed you down the stairs?'

'She cut dairy out of our diet. She's a massive hypochondriac so she sometimes picks up the *Daily Mail* for affirmation. It said that there was "new evidence to suggest dairy gives you cancer".'

'The *Daily Mail* says everything gives you cancer.'

'Well *I* know that.'

'So how did your breaks happen?'

'Oh... you know...'

Trying to pick up a bag with my foot, and falling over.

Doing an overly complicated clappy-hands game with Steph, and falling over.

Rolling around on the floor pretending to be 'en-sausaged' and squishing my hand under my arse.

'… sports injuries, mostly.'

He nodded.

(I know, I know. I said I was going to be completely myself from now on, but there's definitely a fine, but very important line between being yourself and too much yourself.)

I can't remember the rest of our conversation in detail but I know that it barely stopped flowing, once we got started… Then suddenly I saw the time.

'CRAP. I have to go.'

Greg drove me home as fast as he could (which wasn't very fast). The whole time I was praying that Mum wasn't back and watching out the window for me. I made Greg park on the road next to us, which I told him was our road. I *was* going to explain, but then saying, 'Oh, could you just secretly drop me round the corner because I'm actually grounded and if my mum sees me out in a boy's car she might implode.' seemed like it might highlight our age difference.

'So, which one's your house?' he asked.

'Er… .that one.' I pointed to some random house.

'OK, well, bye, Emma.'

'Bye, Greg.'

Are we going to kiss?

'We should do this again.'

'Yes… definitely.'

How long are you supposed to wait for a kiss to happen, before leaving?

Then his head whacked me in the face. It was nice, I think. At least, I wasn't thinking about getting stabbed in the bum this time. Although my head is throbbing a little bit from where he crashed into me.

When I got out of the car, he didn't immediately drive off. It dawned on me that he was one of those people who waits to see that someone's gone inside, and my heart sank. I was going to have to walk up to the house I pointed at. The next five minutes went like this:

Maybe if I walk really, really slowly he'll get bored.

GO HOME, GREG.

Oh God. Walking up to the front door of no.17 Mornington Road.

I hope they don't have a dog.

Mock fumbling for keys.

Mock can't find them.

Oh, gonna have to pretend to ring the bell...

Then Greg rang me from the car, a puzzled expression on his face.

'Are you all right?'

'Yes... forgotten my keys but it's OK, my mum's just about to let me in. I think she's just getting out of the bath. You can go.'

'OK then. Bye, Emma.'

'Bye!'

I waved cheerily as he drove away, and waited until his car turned the corner before I bolted.

After all that, I might not have bothered. Mum still isn't back anyway.

posted by EditingEmma 21.38

When your mum is always out and you're at home watching *Gilmore Girls* and drinking your ninth cup of tea it's pretty sad.

Thoughts on *Gilmore Girls*

This show would be nothing without Kirk.

Why does everyone think Rory's so nice? She clearly isn't.

Why is Lorelai so mean about her parents? They're not even *that* bad.

Oh God. They're starting to annoy me as much as my own family members. Maybe I've watched it too many times?

Not possible.

posted by EditingEmma 22.20

Mum came in.

'Did you have a date? How was it?'

'Oh… only all right.'

'Do you think you'll see him again?'

'No. Why bother?'

'Not Olly?'

'No… not Olly.'

'Well, you look lovely.'

She smiled.

Friday 3rd October

posted by EditingEmma 08.40

Woke up this morning to a really intense message from Greg.

Miss you already when can I see you?xx 07.23

Woahhh. Way too much for this early in the morning. And this early in the relationship. If you could even call it that. I'm in registration now, avoiding replying.

'So my parents said I could have a party for my birthday,' Gracie announced.

'Didn't they say that about a month ago?' I asked.

'Yeah, but I had to check everyone could come before I invited people.'

'Isn't checking that people can come sort of the same as inviting them?'

'No. Because when some people couldn't come I moved the date. Three times.'

She never asked me whether I could come...

Who are these mysterious people that she will move party dates around for??

posted by EditingEmma 10.21

In Art
'Faith, did Gracie clear party dates with you?'
   'Yeah. Why?'
Mystery solved.

posted by EditingEmma 13.48

Lunchtime
Gracie continued to spread her joyous news.
   'Steph, I'm having a birthday party the weekend after next. It's an under-the-sea theme.'
   'I thought your birthday was ages ago?'
   'It was,' I said, 'but she had to wait until Faith could make it.'
   Gracie went all pink. 'And *other* people.'
   Then she got out her guest list. I looked at Steph. She looked at me.
   'This has twenty people on it,' I said.
   'Yes.' Gracie nodded.
   'Including Boring Susan,' I continued.
   'Yes? So?'
   'Nothing.'
   Pause.
   'Was Boring Susan one of the other people you checked could make it before me?'
   She rolled her eyes.
   'So where did Greg take you?'

'Costa.'

'There's no… Wait. Do you mean the Costa at the back of *Waitrose*?'

'He sent me a really full-on message this morning,' I said, changing the subject as Gracie smirked away.

'Let's see!!' cried Steph, looking at my phone. 'Wow, bit intense.'

'It is, isn't it?'

'Kind of sweet though. You should see him tonight.'

'Bit soon, isn't it?'

'I guess. What else are you doing?'

'Point taken.'

Tonight?x 13.32

Ooo miss spontaneous. I'll come get you at 7ish?xx 13.33

I don't think it was so much spontaneous as it was realising I had nothing to do on a Friday night except wait for Mum to get in from salsa.

posted by EditingEmma 15.08

The Enigma of Manic Messagers

Those weirdly impressive people who, somehow, never ever run out of things to say over their phone. Greg keeps messaging me things like… 'Lol wait until you get to apply for uni, it's so stresssfulllll' and 'ahhh kill me maths is so boring' and 'Lol my friend Jim is choking on a bit of apple.' Has he forgotten we're going to see each other later? Surely we're going to have nothing left to say? Why must we be in constant contact?

Why isn't he helping Jim, choking to death beside him, instead of messaging me about it?

posted by EditingEmma 15.43

'You should invite him to Gracie's party!!' exclaimed Steph.

Gracie looked up and said, 'Oh, no, don't. It would be awkward. I don't think my brother's really *friends* with him.'

I ignored Gracie and invited him. OK, so it's not *technically* my house to invite people to, but *technically* it's not really hers either. If she wants to get her parents, the legal homeowners, to ring me and tell me I can't bring him… well, then that would be a different story.

posted by EditingEmma 23.03

Back from Greg's house now, which was mostly spent making out on Greg's bed. I have three things which I want to discuss:

Love vs Being Horny

I'm still not 100 per cent sure how I feel about Greg, but I was getting ridiculously horny. More than when I was with Leon. Is that weird? Kissing Leon was kind of like kissing an angel. It felt like some other-worldly, sublime, sacred experience and it was all about how my heart and soul were feeling. My vagina didn't get much of a look in. But now it's *all* about the vagina. Can there be both?

Picturing One Person When You're Kissing Another
I realise I need to *stop* thinking about Leon when I'm kissing someone else. My brain's going, *STOP IT. STOP IT. STOP IT.* But sometimes he just creeps in. It's a very odd experience. If you get way too into it and then open your eyes, it's quite surprising.

Dating Older Boys
It's becoming clear to me that there are things they will never understand. My first clue was when we were watching *Adventure Time* and Greg started trying to get me to go upstairs.

'But… your mum's in.'

'So?'

And then we went. And his mother didn't burst out of the kitchen with a STOP sign or a fire extinguisher. Huh.

Later on I said, 'You should probably take me home now.'

'What?! It's only nine!'

'Yes, but my mum will be back soon.'

He was baffled.

'So?'

Then I was baffled.

He drove me home, and we sat outside (the wrong house) in the car. He seemed all 'hurt' by me going home, as if it was *my* choice. It was then that I concluded I'd rather make it look like my choice than him think I'm some little girl who has to do what her mum tells her all the time, so I sort of… went with it.

'Bye then,' he whimpered, looking all sad.

'Bye, see you Sunday,' I said and climbed out with purpose, as if I'd got really important things to be getting on with. I think it worked, because now he keeps messaging me like, 'I know you're really busy, but...' and all I'm doing is looking at the Style section on Zoella's blog, and pondering whether I should wear more hats.

Saturday, 4 October

posted by EditingEmma 16.07
Took another trip to Cloth House and bought a selection of different materials. I'm going to have A MILLION blanky dresses. I'm making a 'toile' this time because I'm fancy and experienced, now.

posted by EditingEmma 23.47

Coming Out Is Easier Said Than Done
We went round to Faith's house earlier. Every time you turn a corner something wedding-y leaps out at you. Hope was in the living room flicking through a bridal magazine.

'Emma!' she said, turning the page towards me. 'You're good with fashion. What's your opinion on veils?'

'Pretty, but given they were originally used to wrap women up like presents, questionable.'

'Uh-huh.'

Upstairs, I found Steph waggling her phone at Faith... her new victim.

'Don't you want to play with it even a little bit??' she nagged.

'Not especially. You've got it set to "woman looking for man" which makes it significantly less fun for me.'

'Well, we'd change that, duh.'

'Look, I don't want to think about it. I'm going to be alone for ever. Can we drop it now?'

'I heard Boring Susan got with a girl at Abby Matthews' party at the beginning of summer,' suggested Gracie.

'Boring Susan?!' exclaimed Faith. 'You're giving me BORING SUSAN?!'

'Well, I was just saying…'

'Just because two people are both gay, doesn't mean they automatically like each other. That would be like me trying to pawn you off with… Willie Thomas, just because he's a guy.'

Gracie's lip wobbled. We were all a little awkward for a moment… it's usually Faith who lightens the atmosphere, but she was still staring at Gracie incredulously.

'Is Boring Susan really the only other lesbian in our year?' Steph said, breaking the silence.

'She's not necessarily a lesbian. She just got with a girl,' I answered.

'Jess said she has a bunch of friends who are only just coming out as bi or gay now, and she's twenty, so I suppose there probably are other lesbians, they just don't know it yet.'

'They *know* it. They just haven't accepted it yet,' said Faith, bitterly. 'God, I can't wait for the day when being gay isn't something to "accept".'

We were silent again.

'But don't you think, you know, maybe trying to find

other people who *have* accepted it… might be a good idea?'
I said, gently.

'I can't just *date*, like you guys can.'

'Do you think your parents might see you?'

'Maybe. Or my sister. Or one of her friends.'

'Would they mind?'

'No. But them finding out is one step closer to my parents
finding out.'

'Don't you think you're being a bit extreme?'

'No.'

Then she, very sternly, showed us a sketch she'd been
doing of a fox in her garden. Conversation *closed*. It's so
frustrating!! She knows who she is but she feels she has to
hide it from her family. She wants a relationship but she's not
prepared to start looking for one. But she's right. I suppose
it's easy for me to look at her and say, yes, you should start
dating, you should come out to your parents, when really
I have no idea what it's like to be in her place. I guess it's
something that will only happen in her own time. But I just
want her to be happy. . . It's so, so unfair!!

Sunday, 5 October

posted by EditingEmma 21.53

I spent the afternoon at Greg's house and two very important things have come out of it:

1) I Am Someone's Girlfriend

We were standing in his kitchen making toast and his mum walked in. She sort of looks like the older, female version of him, so obviously gross images of me making out with her kept coming into my head and I had to dig my nails really hard into my hand to make them stop. She was just taking off her top (in my horrible head that taunts me so) when I heard Greg say, '. . . my girlfriend.'

My first thought was: Would he still want me to be his 'girlfriend' if I told him I accidentally imagined his mother without her top on?

Then later I kept noticing that whenever I went somewhere he'd sort of… follow me. I went into the kitchen again to get a Petits Filous and he got up too. As I was opening it, he crept up and hugged me from behind. Will I ever be able to eat a Petits Filous in peace again? It was really very difficult with his arms around me. Am I allowed to tell him to get off? 'Please leave me alone as you are hindering my yoghurt experience.' What are the boundaries here?

I'm still not quite sure how I feel about the whole thing. Leon always left me alone to enjoy my food but then, Leon did 'ghost' me. I've been round in circles, but my conclusion is that whilst it's a bit fast, it's probably a nice thing.

2) My Vagina Has Been Touched by a Third Party

His hands slid downwards, and I instinctively pulled them back up… But I'm not sure why… I *definitely* wanted to let him…

<u>Bedroom Thoughts</u>

Why did I stop him, when basically all I think about is my horniness?

Am I ready?

I think I might be ready.

Screw it. I'm way too horny. Decision made. I'm putting his hands back.

Hmm. Is this enjoyable?

Not enjoyable *as such*. I mean, it's OK.

Not nearly as good as when I do it myself, but OK.

Of course, the moment was slightly ruined when Mum rang in the middle reminding me that there was leftover pie in the fridge. No one wants to think about pie when a guy's hands are in their jeans. Well . . maybe some girls who really, really like pie.

Then he drove me home and kissed me goodnight. It was a little bit awkward. And now I feel kind of sordid, even though I don't think I have a reason to.

Or is this just the feeling of womanhood?

posted by EditingEmma 23.10

Proof the Movies Have Messed Us All Up
I always thought that the first time another person did that it would be more romantic. Although, now, thinking about it, I'm not sure why. Touching someone else's genitals is not a particularly romantic thing to do. I told Steph about it on the phone.

'I have been touched inappropriately by someone OTHER THAN MYSELF.'

'Oh my God. What was it like?'

'At times I didn't really feel much. He may as well have been rubbing my elbow. But it was pleasant enough…Sort of like going on Rumba Rapids at Thorpe Park, instead of Stealth.'

Monday 6th October

posted by EditingEmma 13.54

Do Boys Say Things Just to Get You to Do Stuff?
I was standing by the tuck shop with Gracie, and she said, 'Do you think that's why he called you his girlfriend? So he could get you to do stuff?'

'Well, *now* I do…'

And now it's all I can think about. So I thought I'd just get it out in the open:

Did you call me your girlfriend so that I'd do stuff with you? 13.43

No. What the hell, Emma? I'm really hurt that you asked that. I like you. We don't have to do stuff if you don't want. 13.44

You don't have to be my girlfriend if you don't want, either… x 13.44

I do want to be :) 13.50

I think? I don't know? I do, but I'd still rather be Leon's girlfriend given the choice. Does that count? It has to, otherwise I'll never be *anyone's* girlfriend.

:) I'll take you out somewhere on Friday? xx 18.51

That's nice.

Hopefully not to the Waitrose Costa again.

posted by EditingEmma 20.03

Are Face-to-Face Break-Ups Still a Necessity?
I've often wondered this. People keep relationships going on video chats, but is it OK to end one on them? Laurence Myer clearly thinks not.

> **Laurence:** So. Do we need to talk?
>
> **Emma:** Sure... About what?
>
> **Laurence:** Oh, well if you don't know then I guess it doesn't matter.

Silence.

> **Laurence:** So who's that guy you got into a car with?

Oh Jeez. I rang Steph.

'Steph, I think I need to break up with Laurence Myer.'

'But you're not going out with Laurence Myer.'

'Yes, but I think *he* thinks we're going out.'

'But if you break up with him then aren't you sort of going along with it?'

'I guess.'

'You can't do that. You have to let him down gently without actually conceding to a relationship status.'

'Right. How do I do that?'

'I have no idea.'

> **Laurence:** ?

'How about… Laurence, the boy in the car is my boyfriend. You are not.'

'Is that you trying to be gentle?'

'Hmm. How about… Though I enjoyed our *singular* date, and thank you heartily for the Minstrels, I didn't think we really connected. We're very… different.'

'Yes! That's better! Take out the "singular".'

'Right. I'm going in for the kill. Ripping off the Band-Aid.'

Emma: I enjoyed our date, and thank you heartily for the Minstrels, but I feel like we're very different.

Laurence: We both liked the film?

Emma: Oh, no, not that… Just, I felt like we didn't really connect?

I was sweating profusely by this point. That's when he said:

Laurence: Are you breaking up with me over the internet?

Evidence: Face-to-face break-ups are ALWAYS a necessity. Even if you have communicated with a person almost solely through the internet, it does not eliminate the need for them.

And even if you weren't properly going out with them in the first place.

I am not proud of this, but my need to avoid awkwardness took over:

Emma: Look, you want the truth… I just thought you weren't looking for a girlfriend, and now I'm seeing someone else

Laurence: Why did you think that?

Emma: Someone told me

Laurence: Who?

Emma: I'm afraid I can't reveal my sources

Laurence: They lied. It's not true

Emma: OK, well, I know that now, but I didn't...

Laurence: OK

Emma: Gotta go byeeeee

Despite this truly stressful interaction, I am feeling a bit relieved. At least I won't have to hide from him in the tuck shop any more or have dreams about drowning in pools of Minstrels.

Tuesday, 7 October

posted by EditingEmma 10.14

What Counts as a Break-Up?
This morning Gracie said to me, 'You've kind of had your
first break-up.'

'What about Leon?'

'Not sure a ghosting counts.'

'But... it's still a *breakup*.'

She bit her lip. 'OK, well, you've had your first break-up
that you initiated, then.'

posted by EditingEmma 10.38

In Maths
Crazy Holly is sitting at the front of the class on her mobile
phone. Just casually chatting away whilst Mr Crispin tries to
teach us about triangles... I mean, we all talk and message
each other, but actually speaking on your phone is kind of
taking it to a new level. He keeps glancing in her direction
and says 'hypotheses' instead of 'isosceles'. I put up my hand.

'Sir, what's a hypotheses triangle? You haven't mentioned that one before.'

Five minutes later, she is still on her phone. Mr Crispin is getting more and more agitated and making less and less sense. Is he going to say something? Surely, he must *have* to say something this time.

We have lift off!

Mr Crispin says politely, 'Can you stop talking, please?'

Holly looks up briefly, as if remembering where she is, and replies, 'Sorry, sir.'

. . . And then goes instantly back to talking on her phone.

Mr Crispin sits down, apparently defeated. We hear him say, quietly, from behind his book,

'You will be sorry.'

posted by EditingEmma 13.09

I Might Have to Have My Third Break-Up

Greg rang me at break and I made the mistake of telling him about the Laurence thing. I honestly didn't think it would bother him. Why would it? I thought he would find it funny but he got all weird and silent and I had to keep saying, 'Are you still there?' 'Are you still there?' And he'd say, 'Yes,' but then not say anything else. And what I really wanted to say was, 'OK, well if you're not going to talk can I go and talk to my friends?' but I sensed I should stay on the phone. Ten minutes later, he messaged me saying: 'Might not be able to do Friday any more.' No kiss.

Then he kept messaging me. I was so distracted in French

I didn't know whether Madame Fournier was talking about lungs or apples. He said, 'Think you should come over tonight and talk about this?' Talk about *what?* How I fake broke up with someone who I was fake going out with?

Then he said, 'I just don't get why you'd go along with it? You must have feelings for him.' Jeeez.

I did ask Mum if I could go over to Greg's tonight, and this is how it went:

Me: 'Can I go over to Greg's tonight? xx'

Mum: 'No.'

Me: 'But we have some issues to work through.'

Mum: 'I have pie for you to work through.'

Me: 'This is more important than pie!!'

Mum: 'If you have issues after going out for a week, end it now.'

So I called Greg: 'I'm really sorry, my mum says I can't come over tonight.'

'Oh. I see.'

'Sorry… I can still do Friday?'

'Don't bother,' he said, and hung up.

Aghh!

posted by EditingEmma 13.50

Yet More Strange Boy Behaviour

I was just innocently eating my post-lunch cookie when I turned round and Leon was standing right behind me. Watching me. I wish I could say I played it cool but he took me by surprise, and I got chocolate chip caught in my throat.

'Did you tell Laurence that I told you he didn't want a girlfriend?'

'No,' I said uncertainly, my face burning up.

'I know you, Emma.'

'OK...'

'I mean...' His cheeks flared a little, too. 'I mean I know when you're lying.'

'I'm not lying.'

He just looked at me ironically. I felt my bottled-up anger rising to the surface, but I wasn't going to give him the satisfaction of getting worked up this time. I said, in a calm and measured tone,

'How could you have done? We're not even speaking.'

'That's what I said.'

'Good. Then you've answered your own question.'

He looked at me for a second, and then... he leant down and took a bite of my cookie. He TOOK A BITE OF MY COOKIE. Then he turned and walked away.

How DARE he!! Who does he think he is?! I am still RAGING about this.

posted by EditingEmma 16.45

Analysing Strange Boy Behaviour

My rage has deflated. He bit my cookie... Surely that must mean something?!

'Steph, what do you think it means?' I asked her earlier.

'That he really likes cookies?'

I'm not sure this is an adequate conclusion.

posted by EditingEmma 19.33

I definitely did *not* save the rest of the cookie and put it in my bag because it has his saliva on it. That is definitely not something I would do.

Mum came in from work.

'Why are you staring at a half-eaten cookie?'

'I'm not staring at it. I'm just... staring near it.'

'You're not being funny, are you?' she asked.

'I like to think I'm quite funny... Maybe not like Tina Fey level...'

'I mean about your food.'

'What?'

'Are you eating properly?'

I paused, trying to work out what she meant. 'Are you asking me if I have an eating disorder?'

'Yes.'

'Mum, I think anorexia is a bit more serious than *leaving half a cookie*.'

'All right, no need to bite my head off, I was just concerned.'

I finally ate it. It tasted of Leon's sweet saliva and my own bitter self-hatred.

posted by EditingEmma 23.25

The Phenomenon of Having a Conversation With Yourself
My phone went off. Wonder who that could be.

Wish you could've come over tonight :(

Still no kiss. He acts like it's my fault. Arghhh. Then half an hour later he sent another one.

Wow. Am taking your not replying to mean you're really upset with me.

Actually, I got distracted by a half-eaten baked good.

I don't want to keep fighting like this any more.

Has he forgotten that I haven't replied to him? I think he's fighting with himself.

All right, let's go out on Friday. I'll cancel my plans, it's fine.

Whatever. Sure.

Evidence: If you don't reply for long enough, sometimes problems just resolve themselves.

Wednesday, 8 October

Emma Nash @Em_Nasher

Ms Parker put some paperclips on the table. 'Now girls, be sensible with these...' Ha.

Emma Nash @Em_Nasher

Steph has made me a lovely pair of paperclip glasses & paperclip hair extensions.

Emma Nash @Em_Nasher

I wonder what the paperclips were for, anyway?

posted by EditingEmma 11.18

Gracie Doubles My Problems

'Are you still on that app, Emma?' Gracie asked me, this morning.

'I was never on it.'

'OK, is your joke profile still on it?'

'Errr, I told Steph to delete it. Why?'

'Well, I don't know. You're in a relationship now.' She says the word 'relationship' like it has quotation marks around it.

'It's not like I used it.'

'OK.'

Then later I got a message from Greg saying, 'Well this is just taking the piss. Now Andy tells me you're on a DATING APP. Are we even together at all?' I showed Gracie my phone. She at least had the decency to look embarrassed.

'Why? Was it a secret?' she simpered.

posted by EditingEmma 19.00

Tried calling Greg but no answer. I have yet another *stye*. I think this one is Greg's fault. The rest of my evening was spent finishing off my new old dress, and it looks SO GOOD if I do say so myself. It's in a really nice, dark blue and green paisley.

Emma Nash @Em_Nasher

It's finally complete! My favourite dress, take 2. The heaving, screaming labour is over and I am now a proud mother

Steph Brent @Brentsy

@Em_Nasher Congrats. You're gross

Thursday 9th October

posted by EditingEmma 10.05

Just walked past Mr Morris in the hall. I smile and wave…
and he completely ignores me!! Just stares straight through
me like I am a ghost!! I know I was late again today, but
there's really no need to be so *rude*.

Maybe it's because I'm wearing sunglasses.

posted by EditingEmma 11.04

'Why are you wearing sunglasses?' asked Steph.

'It's back.'

'What is?'

'The stye.'

'Oh.'

Silence.

'I think it probably looks less stupid than the sunglasses.'

posted by EditingEmma 11.20

I can't believe this just happened. I can't believe it!! Leon
walked past and said hello to me. LEON SAID HELLO TO
ME. And he SMILED. I can't believe it. Maybe it's all going

to be all right?? Maybe we're going to make up?? I don't even care about us going out, I just want to be his friend again!!

I can't do anything properly I'm so excited. I put eyeliner on one eye and not the other. I took my sunglasses off and put them on some small boy's head.

posted by EditingEmma 13.08

The Art of Annoying Your Friends
'He said… "Hello, Emma."'
    'Reeallly? And what did you say?'
    'I said… "Hi."'
    'Did you??'
    'Yes.'
    Pause.
    'Just so you know, I am aware of your sarcasm, but I'm too happy to care.'

posted by EditingEmma 13.55
Greg phones.
    'Emma, look, I just called to say sorry about yesterday.'
    'Oh sure, whatever, it's fine!'
    'Oh… OK, well, I just wanted to say I'm sorry if I came across a bit—' he laughs '—insane. I just really like you and I was disappointed not to be able to see you before Friday. And then I got all paranoid about the ex, and the app. But if you say it was Steph then I believe you.'
    'It's no problem, Greg, really!'
    'OK… So will you delete it?'

'Of course!'

posted by EditingEmma 17.47

Deleting Your Dating App (Even If It Was a Prank): A New Key Relationship Step?

So we all know the main steps in a relationship. There's the first date, first kiss, first-time sex, moving in, maybe marriage, kids and then turning into old people who either vaguely tolerate each other or get divorced. Right. I think I've discovered a new step… deleting your dating app.

Greg offered to come by in his car and drop me home. He said that it was just because he 'wanted me to get home safe' but I walk home every other day and he's never cared before, so I assume he wanted to check I deleted my stupid fake profile. But that's fine, Leon said hello to me and everything is so gravy that I am swimming in gravy. Bathing in gravy. Drowning in gravy.

I got in his car and we chatted for a bit, but he was clearly on edge. So I got out Steph's phone and deleted it in front of him. It was weirdly ceremonial. Greg looked all solemn and I sort of felt like I was taking part in a holy ritual, and at any moment he might say, 'Bless you, my child, you are cleansed of your blasphemous online promiscuity and can once again be pure.'

I sort of wanted to laugh at the complete ludicrousness of the situation, but at least the bloody thing is DEFINITELY gone now. I suppose it's nice that he cares? It might even have been romantic, if Steph hadn't been looming over the car waiting to get her phone back.

posted by EditingEmma 18.50

I'm feeling really guilty, now, about a moment we had in the car.

'You're in a good mood,' Greg said.

'Er…'

'You make me happy too,' he said, then kissed me.

Oh God. Greg is really nice. How comes he can say things like 'you make me happy' and it kind of makes me feel good, but only really in the way that you feel good when someone in the girls' bathroom says 'I like your top,' and then Leon says 'hello' and I feel like I'm floating above the clouds? It's so unfair!!!

posted by EditingEmma 22.36

My Mother is Bonkers

If it wasn't confirmed before, it is now. I was just going to brush my teeth, when I stumble across something in a plastic bag in the hall.

'Why are you leaving things out in the dark?!' I yell out to Mum. 'You could have killed me!!!'

'If I was lucky,' she shouts back.

I turn on the light to inspect the mysterious object. I open the bag and see… a head. An actual HEAD. Not a human head, obviously, but the head of a stuffed camel.

Who am I living with?!?

I go into Mum's room and brandish the head.

'Mum, what the hell is this?!'

She looks sheepish and doesn't say anything.

'Why have you beheaded your stuffed camel?!'

Still no answer.

'Are you completely unbalanced? What is this?!'

'Don't go snooping in my private things!!' she barks.

'Don't leave your private things in the corridor!!'

'I had to leave it out to remind me.'

'Remind you what?'

She goes quiet again.

'Remind you *what*?!'

'To drop it off.'

Oh no. She can't be serious.

'Are you… Are you referencing *The Godfather*?'

'Olly is half Italian.'

'So this is what… revenge? A threat on his life?'

'Just a statement.'

'You know that they used a horse, right, not a camel?'

'Well, he didn't buy me a *horse*, he bought me a *camel*, so it will do.'

'You're not… You're not going to actually put it in his bed, are you?'

'Oh no. Just leave it on his doorstep.'

'Yes… that's much better.'

And now I'm in bed. Not sleeping. I feel too guilty about the camel. I can feel it sitting out there in the darkness, mourning its body… Oh God. What did she do with the body? I took a picture of the poor thing.

Emma Nash @Em_Nasher

Going to think twice next time before finishing off Mum's

fancy yoghurt, that's for sure

Steph Brent @Brentsy

@Em_Nasher OH MY GOD. Did your mum do that?!?!

Holly Barnet @HoHoHo

@Em_Nasher @Brentsy Cool

Friday, 10 October

posted by EditingEmma 08.01

Mum drove off with the decapitated camel head in the back of her car. There's a sentence I'll never say again.

I hope.

posted by EditingEmma 11.20

Am I a Doormat?

Earlier on, I saw Leon (and Apple) walking towards me and I smiled, but he just looked straight through me… I mean, what?! I thought we were speaking again?! I told Faith about it.

'Here's an idea, Emma, why don't *you* try speaking to *him*? Why is it always him who gets to make the rules?'

'I… What do you mean?'

'I mean always act normal with him. Speak to him when he's ignoring you. Or if he's been ignoring you, ignore him when he speaks again. Or at least comment on it. You can't just let him have his own way with you whenever he wants!! Don't be a doormat.'

I considered this for a moment. It does sound infinitely sensible.

'I don't think he treats me like a *doormat*...'

'He does.'

'No, he...'

'Yes—' she pointed to a little piece of mud on the floor '—that is you, there, getting stepped on.'

A few minutes later, Steph came over and sat down with us.

'Why are you staring intensely at the floor?'

'I am that piece of mud,' I replied.

'I see.'

'She's coming to terms with some realisations,' Faith said.

posted by EditingEmma 13.15

So am I still picking you up at 7?x 13.04

Why would our plans have changed since the last time we spoke, yesterday?

posted by EditingEmma 22.56

Welcome to Adulthood

I've just arrived back from a date where we went to an actual *restaurant*. Greg and I sat across from each other like actual *adults*, next to other actual *adults*. It was kind of nice I guess, but weird. Leon would never have taken me to a weird fancy restaurant. He would have got me a big tub of pic 'n' mix (and he knows all the ones I like, too) and we'd just sit in his room watching a terrible film with him shoving sweets down the back of my top. I kept thinking about this, all the way through my starter.

<u>Starter Thoughts</u>

SHUT UP. You're not on a date with Leon!! Do you know why? Because he doesn't like you!! Focus on the date you're actually on, with the person who does like you!!

Greg has a little piece of tomato on his nose and I can't stop staring at it.

What if he tries to kiss me? What will I do?

I mean, obviously, I'll duck.

After, we went back to Greg's house. Thankfully the little piece of tomato had mysteriously disappeared.

'So why didn't you text me back until this evening?' He lifted his eyebrows accusingly.

'Er…'

Then we just ended up kissing on his bed. It seems like kissing is the safest thing to do, because whenever we talk we seem to fight. And that's how I came to encounter a penis.

The Penis Encounter

We were just making out all normal and then… he started taking his trousers off. Here's how it went down in my head:

Am I supposed to counter-move? Because I'm on my period and my massive sanitary towel will be plainly visible.

OH MY GOD. I'VE STILL NOT SHAVED MY LEGS.

Steph was right. I want to be bold and feminist and bare my hairy legs to the world but now it's come down to it I'm gripped with terror.

Can I get them out? It felt so much easier in theory! Aghhhhh.

Well, now we're just making out with me fully clothed and him in his pants. It's a little bit awkward.

THE PANTS ARE OFF. THE PANTS ARE OFF. OH MY GOD. I HAVE SEEN A PENIS IN REAL LIFE AND IT IS TERRIFYING.

After ten seconds of looking at it, I know, deep down in my soul, that I will never, *ever*, get used to the sight of a human penis.

Should I touch it? Oh my God. I haven't even properly acquainted myself with it visually yet, let alone physically.

Moving nearer…

It slapped my hand. IT SLAPPED MY HAND. I've been rejected by the penis.

I'm not prepared for this.

I quickly withdrew.

'Greg, I just don't think I'm ready.'

'Oh my God. I'm so sorry. I just thought. Because you know. We'd already done stuff, so…'

'Er, yes, I can see why you'd think that. But… no.'

'Of course, I'm so sorry. I'll just, er, put these back on.'

Then he put his trousers back on in silence, and we didn't mention it again for the rest of the evening. I feel like I've been through an ordeal. And a little bit confused. It's not like I *definitely* didn't want to. I kind of did. At least, I've thought about it before and thought I did. But in the moment I felt all overwhelmed and weird.

Saturday, 11 October

posted by EditingEmma 13.46

The 'Am I Ready?' Question
Steph is round.

'That sounds horrendous,' she said.

'Thanks, I feel much better now.'

'So… you're not ready to do stuff with him?'

'Well, er… I'm ready for him to do stuff to *me*.'

Steph laughed.

'I always thought there was either an I'm ready or I'm not ready. How can I be half ready?!'

Steph thought for a moment, then said, 'Because you're a selfish lover?'

'Exactly. That's what it sounds like, isn't it? If a guy said that to me, I'd tell him to piss off.'

'Me too.'

'So am I allowed to say that? It's how I feel.'

'I don't know. I can tell you what Faith would say.'

'Go on.'

'She'd say, "Emma, that's OK, but until you feel ready to

reciprocate, maybe you shouldn't do anything at all, because you don't want to be a user".'

'Hmm.'

I've thought about this for a while and I've concluded that, whilst Steph-channelling-Faith made a good point, I think that Greg seems to want to touch me quite a lot. Therefore, denying him that would be denying us both.

Sunday, 12 October

posted by EditingEmma 15.00

SUCCESS

I've done it!!! I've finished the dress that I designed and it looks the same as it did in my head!! I feel so good about myself and I am *never* buying clothes again. (Only partially because Mum won't buy me lots of new clothes, but her purse strings seem very loose when it comes to buying me fabrics to make things with.) I posted a picture of it and I've never gotten so many likes. Even Mum came in as I was standing admiring it in the mirror and said,

'Oh wow! That looks lovely. I can't believe you made that.'

Still not sure how I feel about her praising me. It is alien and unnatural and I felt the urge to hug her, but also to counter it by saying something mean.

Anyway, I'm going to wear the dress to Gracie's party. Which is technically under-the-sea themed but I'm sure there must be some kind of black-with-see-through-stripes sea creature I can go as.

posted by EditingEmma 19.10
Found it!!! A banded sea krait. Perfect!!

posted by EditingEmma 19.58

I Will Never Be a Banded Sea Krait
Gracie called.

'So, I've changed the theme to *Great Gatsby*.'

'What, noooo! Why?!'

'Don't you think we're a bit old for under-the-sea? It is my seventeenth.'

'I think you shouldn't worry about how something looks, you should just do what you want…'

'Well, what I want to do is *Gatsby*.'

'But… but… I was coming as a banded sea krait.'

'A *what*?'

'Oh, never mind.'

I'll just put on a feather boa or something, then take it off after five minutes.

Monday, 13 October

posted by EditingEmma 08.55

Sitting on a Wall Near Chapel

Missed registration. Again. I came panting up to the Chapel, where Dr Penzik was standing 'monitoring' the students as they passed. He obnoxiously put an arm out in front of me as I tried to walk in.

'Emma, where's your blazer?'

'Oh, er…' I looked at my blazer-less arms. 'At home on the bannister?'

'You can't come in without your blazer.'

'Oh, great, thanks, Dr Penzik!' I said, and ran off to sit on the wall. I'd never have worn my blazer if I knew it was a get-out-of-Chapel-free card. On the way here I walked past Mr Morris.

'Oh, Mr Morris, I'm really sorry I was late today. I promise it won't happen again! This week, anyway.'

He stopped, furrowing his brow in confusion and anger. 'I'm not Mr Morris,' he said solemnly.

Has he lost his mind?

I can hear Chapel going on without me. It's so satisfying

not to have to mouth along to the hymns for once. Faith says that I'd find it less boring if I actually tried singing, and thinking about what the hymns mean, but I don't believe her.

posted by EditingEmma 10.15

In Art
Sitting next to Faith. We're supposed to be having 'quiet sketching' time.

    I saw a penis 10.13
    She raised her eyebrows.
    What was it like? 10.14
    A worm 10.15

posted by EditingEmma 11.17

The Catterfly: True or False?
I was discussing it with Faith and Steph, when Crazy Holly enlightened me.

    'What do you mean it slapped your hand?'
    'I don't know how else to say it.'
    'Why was it moving?'
    'I don't know!!'
    'Was it hard?'
    'Kind of.'
    'What do you mean kind of? Isn't it either hard or… not?'
    'No… I mean… That's what I thought too. But obviously not.'
    'Maybe Greg just has a weird penis.'

Then Holly came ambling over. 'Excuse me, ladies, I couldn't help but overhear your conversation. I think what you're talking about is a phenomenon I like to term *the catterfly.*'

We stared blankly.

'If a caterpillar is changing into a butterfly, what is it?'

'Er... a catterfly?'

'Exactly.'

More staring.

'So, the catterfly in question is neither a caterpillar nor a butterfly. It is in a *transitional stage.*'

'Holly, what are you talking about?'

'A semi-erection.'

I'm still absorbing this new information. That is, if it's true. Can I really trust what Crazy Holly says? She did go out with that guy who was in prison. But I'm not sure they ever actually met.

posted by EditingEmma 13.11

The Catterfly: True

Looked it up on the internet. Apparently it is a real thing!!! Why do they never teach you these things in sex ed? What did I even learn that was useful? All I know is how babies are made and I don't want a baby. Oh my God. Why did he only have a semi?! Do I not merit a full erection?

I was walking around with Faith.

'Faith, you're so lucky you'll never have to deal with this.'

'Why, because I'll never be with anyone ever?' she sighed.

'No, because when you DO start seeing someone, which you WILL, you'll already know what to do because you've got a vagina.'

posted by EditingEmma 13.45

A Revelation

'Did you notice anything weird about Mr Morris today?' I asked Steph.

'No,' she said absently, closely examining her chipped nail polish, 'why?'

'He seems to be having an identity crisis. He stopped in the middle of the corridor and said, "I am not Mr Morris."'

'That is weird.'

I looked out the window and saw him walking across the courtyard.

'Who knows what's going on inside that bearded head… What trauma he's dealing with…'

Steph looked up from her fingernails. 'That's not Mr Morris.'

'What?'

She started laughing really, really hard. 'That's not Mr Morris!!!'

'What are you talking about?!'

'That's Mr Grant! He teaches Physics!'

'No… What?! You're lying!'

She was laughing so hard she couldn't even answer. Ten minutes later, she was still laughing and had turned a deep shade of red.

'All this time… You saying Mr Morris was ignoring you…' She sputtered.

'I'm still not convinced.'

'I should have known when you asked whether I thought Elijah Wood would ever be able to move on from Harry Potter.'

posted by EditingEmma 23.00

Still stressing over my inability to engender a full erection. I suppose it was only the first time… Maybe I shouldn't be too hard on myself. (Haha, 'hard' on myself.) All good practice for if I ever go there with Leon. DON'T THINK ABOUT THAT. NO. Get out of my head, Leon. Get out get out get out get out get out. Maybe I should write lines or something?

You will never touch Leon's penis. You will never touch Leon's penis. You will never touch Leon's penis. You will never touch Leon's penis. You will never touch Leon's penis. You will never touch Leon's penis. You will never touch Leon's penis. You will never touch Leon's penis. You will never touch Leon's penis. You will never touch Leon's penis. You will never touch Leon's penis. You will never touch Leon's penis. You will never touch Leon's penis.

Tuesday, 14 October

posted by EditingEmma 11.15

I came in this morning and walked slowly past 'Mr Morris' at his desk. (Could it be Mr Grant? Who knows?)

'Good morning, Mr Morris...' I said sceptically.

Steph burst out laughing on the other side of the room.

Now I'm stalking the staff room to see proof that Mr Morris has a double... And there they are. The twins. Standing by the biscuit table with their barely discernible features.

Who knew?

posted by EditingEmma 13.50

I Am Not a Doormat

I was walking around the grounds with Faith, and two figures came into view ahead.

'Look... it's Leon!'

'How can you tell?'

'I've watched him from a distance enough. I can pick him out of crowds within *seconds*.'

Faith paused. 'What's it like living in a constant game of *Where's Leon?*'

'Tiring.'

'Do you ever think that if you put all that energy into something else you might… I don't know, learn a language? Read Balzac's *Human Comedy*?'

'What is that?'

'Never mind.'

He got closer, and closer…

'Now's your chance, Emma,' encouraged Faith.

'Do you think?!'

'DO IT.'

'Do what?!'

'Act how YOU want to act. Set the terms!! Lay down the rules!! How do YOU want to greet him?!'

'By licking his neck?'

By this point Leon was a few metres away (with Apple, who turned out to be the second tiny speck). And… instead of waiting for Leon to do something… I said, 'Hi.'

OK, so it came across a touch aggressive, perhaps more like 'HI'… but I did it! Apple looked over, a bit bemused. Leon looked like a rabbit caught in headlights. But I stared him down. And…he lifted a hand at me!! (In what is officially the most begrudging wave I have ever seen, but still!!)

TRIUMPH. I SHALL NOT BE IGNORED.

posted by EditingEmma 18.17

Greg turned up at school to give me a lift home, which was really sweet, but then he asked if we could go back to mine and I said no because my mum was in, and he looked a little bit hurt. I suggested we 'drive somewhere and chat' instead and I think he thought I meant something dirty, because he looked all pleased and went and parked up by the forest. Thankfully I am a teenager and am, therefore, always feeling just a *little* bit horny. Even when watching wholesome Christmas movies or eating soup at Granddad's house or buying laxatives for my mum in Boots.

<u>Forest Thoughts</u>

Oh God, what if someone sees us? Stop panicking! Relax… Relax…

This is not very arousing. I always thought I'd be one of those fun, carefree people who can do stuff in public places but it turns out I'm not.

Maybe if I focus on Greg…

What a nice nose he has.

Noses are not very arousing either

It was really quite a challenge, but by combining the powers of my long and enduring sexual angst, and mental images of Mr Allen, I managed to conjure a *very small* orgasm. It was nothing like when I'm alone and was really more of a twitch, but there it was. An orgasm, all the same.

When we drove back home I kept thinking about where Greg's hands had been and how now they were on his steering wheel. Is he going to wipe it? It seems unsanitary.

And that is the story of my third, fairly unfulfilling sexual experience. At least Greg didn't get his penis out this time, so I didn't have to awkwardly decline it.

posted by EditingEmma 19.12

Maybe We Should All Just Stick to Masturbation
Discussed it with Faith:

'Are you going to do it again?' she asked.

'Probably.'

'But why, may I ask? I mean, if it's only all right?'

I thought. Hmm, she had a point.

'I guess…I mean, I enjoy it more physically when I do it myself. But with him it still gets rid of the horniness more. Just because there's someone else there, I guess.'

She pondered for a moment. 'Could he just stand in the room, while you do it?'

'I like your thinking.'

posted by EditingEmma 20.44

I've made Gracie a very special jumper that says 'Word Wizard' on it for her birthday, to wear when we play *Articulate*. She'll be spectacularly embarrassed when I give it to her in front of people, but also she'll love it, so it's a win-win.

Wednesday, 15 October

posted by EditingEmma 13.41

The Awkwardness of Dirty Messaging

Got a message from Greg.

I can't stop thinking about getting you off x 09.29

Not sure how I feel about this. It was 9.30 in the morning, for one thing. And for another it just doesn't *sound* like him. He would NEVER say this to my face... usually he's all sweet and sickly.

Evidence: Technology lets people say what they are really thinking.

I have no idea what to reply, but I suppose I must. Hmm... 'Thanks'? Or should I be apologetic? Like, 'I hope you find a way to focus on your lessons?' Or more dirty, sort of like... 'Wait until you feel a *real* orgasm?' No. That is a) creepy and b) will expose the fact that mine was only about a 2.0 on the Richter scale.

Really, if anyone 'got me off' the other day it's Mr Allen. I almost want to slip him a thank you note.

Eventually went with:

Me neither xx 13.40

Generic, whitewashing lies are always the right answer.

posted by EditingEmma 17.19

Big News

I was standing waiting for Mum to pick me up at the gates, scanning for Leon in case he stayed late for some unknown reason, when Leon actually appeared in the distance.

I expected him to just walk past, but he kept heading for me... I could see Mum pulling up and waving frantically in the corner of my eye but I pretended not to notice.

'Are you going to this?' he asked, brandishing a little shiny card from his pocket. I leaned in... it was an invitation!! A bloody invitation to Gracie's party!! With 'Gracie's Sweet Seventeenth' written across the top in gold, shiny letters.

'What!!' I said, grabbing it. 'I never got one of those! Is this... Is this handmade?! I don't believe this. That takes the piss.'

'So you're not going?'

'Oh, no, I'm *going*.'

'OK, cool.'

. . . Really?

'I'll pee on the invitation and give it back to her, if you like.' He grinned.

And I wanted to reply, I really did, but the only thing that came to mind was '*You can pee on me*' and then I saw Mum getting out of the car.

'Oh, gotta go!' I said, and ran off to a very angry mother.

So I made you wait for me when you'd been kind enough to offer me a lift. LET IT GO.

Anyway, Leon spoke to me again!! I'm trying to stay grounded and keep Faith's words in my head, like a leaden weight, but it's like I'm filled up with helium. I keep floating off.

posted by EditingEmma 19.49

Actual Big News
Disregard my last post. Something far more newsworthy has happened. Faith called.

'Emma, I did it!!!'

'You did what?'

'IT.'

'You had *sex?!*'

'Pah! No, but I came one step closer. I came out to my parents!!'

'Oh my God!! Faith, that's huuuuge!!'

'I know. I know. I can't believe it.'

'What happened??'

'I guess… I guess it started because I was thinking about how harsh I was being about you and the way Leon treats you. I mean, I was feeling all judgemental and on my moral high horse and then I suddenly realised, I'm not exactly standing up for myself, either. And then I started getting so angry about how I'm pretty sure my parents *know*, but they don't *want* to know, as if there's something *wrong* with me, and how we all go along just saying nothing… And then, I thought, I'm probably just going to continue saying nothing and then I got even angrier, and then I *did* say something!! Out of nowhere! I said something!!'

'What did you say?? What did *they* say??'

'So, my aunt came over for dinner and I was being very silent and thinking about all the things I just said.'

'Yes, yes??'

'And we were talking about Hope's wedding, obviously, as I imagine we will be constantly for the rest of our lives.'

'Yes?! YES?!'

'And then, she asked me if I had a boyfriend yet. And then my mum laughed and said, "Oh, she's only sixteen, plenty of time." And then my aunt laughed and said that if I was still single when I went to uni people would start thinking I was a lesbian.'

'NO.'

'Yes. She said those words. They were real words that came out of her mouth.'

'And what did you say???'

'I said, "And if I was, what would be wrong with that?" and looked straight at her, and she was all stuttery and flappy and her bob was jiggling. And she didn't say anything. And then I just got up and left the table.'

'Oh my God.'

'I know.'

'OH MY GOD.'

'I know.'

posted by EditingEmma 23.01

Sometimes Mothers Are Actually OK
I was telling Mum about Faith, and we were discussing how ridiculous her aunt is on so many levels.

'Basically every time I'm reminded homophobia is still a thing, I just feel really naive and shocked,' I finished.

'Naive is right,' said Mum.

'And what's wrong with being single, anyway?' I exclaimed.

'I feel like you should ask yourself the same question.'

'What do you mean?'

'Why do you keep dating obsessively?'

Awkward question which exposes me as a hypocrite = I'm going to turn it around on her.

'What about you? Why are *you* always on dates?'

'Well, it would be nice to meet someone. So I keep trying. But I'm not going to force myself to be with someone for the sake of it.'

She's backed me into a corner = I'm now going to change the subject.

'Also, *if you're still single when you go to uni*? She sounds like an old woman from the forties giving warnings about biological clocks,' I go on.

'As women, Emma, we're constantly put in a race against time to "achieve" things we're not given a moment to consider we might not want.'

Later on, I tiptoed into her room.

'Mum?'

'Yes?'

'You know how earlier you said you felt like women were all put under pressure by society and whatnot, I assume you partly mean marriage and children, I mean… You did want me, didn't you?'

'Oh Emma. Of course I wanted you. I wasn't talking about you. I just meant that a lot of people consider marriage and children to be the only path in life, like you're inferior if you're a certain age and you don't have them.'

'OK.'

'I never cared about marriage, I just wanted to be in love and have a… mutually caring relationship. It hasn't happened for me, and I'd rather be on my own, with you, than in something I settled for, and in some people's eyes that makes me a failure.'

'You're no failure, Mum. And you're more than enough parent for *ten* children.'

Emma Nash @Em_Nasher
Briefly felt affectionate about my mother until she woke me
up snoring in the next room. Now contemplating putting a
pillow over her head

Thursday, 16 October

posted by EditingEmma 08.37

I was just walking into school with Gracie, talking about her inexplicable love of fishing (apparently it is very 'relaxing') when Leon came up to me.

Leon came up to me.

'I'll trade you a bit of cookie for a Chewit,' he said.

I nodded, trying to look as calm as possible. We made the transfer. It's like nothing ever changed between us and I want to sing and dance and run and play with rabbits in fields.

posted by EditingEmma 11.18

Coming Out Really IS Easier Said Than Done

Faith slumped down next to me at break.

'*Incroyable*!' she said. 'I don't think my coming out has been acknowledged.'

'What do you mean?'

'Well, after I called you, my mum came into my room to give me pudding and said that I should apologise to Aunt Carol for my "little outburst" and then nothing else was said. This morning, she was completely normal and going about making eggs.'

'Were you acting normal?'

'I was looking into her eyes questioningly, and she looked back… completely blank. Like a ghost. Nothing.'

'That is so strange!! Do you think she's in denial, or really didn't pick up on the undertones of what you were saying?'

'I don't know. I thought it was pretty obvious, but maybe not.'

Silence.

'Was your mum really up at seven this morning making you eggs?'

'Yes.'

'Does she do that every day?'

'Yes.'

'That's amazing.'

'Your mum accepts you for who you are. You win.'

'I'm sorry, Faith, I know it wasn't easy for you to say something.'

'Thanks, I'm sorry too. It just confirms everything I thought. It's impossible.'

'No!! It's not impossible!! Next time you just have to, er, leave them no room for doubt?'

'They don't want to hear it, Emma.'

This sucks so much I can't really put it into words.

posted by EditingEmma 13.15

In the loos. I was in the Sixth Form Centre getting my coat, about to go off with the others for lunch, and I noticed that Apple and her friends were staring at me and pointing.

'Did I do something?' I whispered to Gracie.

'Haven't you seen?' she whispered back.

'Seen what?'

'*Seriously?*'

'Seriously what?'

'Seriously all you do is stalk Leon and you miss *this*?'

'MISS WHAT?'

She showed me her phone.

Leon Naylor is single.

42 mins

And now this is what the inside of my brain looks like:

Leon Naylor is single.

Leon Naylor is single.

Leon Naylor is single.

Leon Naylor is single.

Leon Naylor is single.

Leon Naylor is single.

Leon Naylor is single.

Leon Naylor is single.

Leon Naylor is single.

Leon Naylor is single.

posted by EditingEmma 13.58

I was about to take a bite of this lovely, congealed rice pudding the school has served us, when Leon sat down next to me.

Leon sat down next to me.

'Is everything OK with… Anna?' I asked. (Had to concentrate so hard to use her real name.)

'We broke up,' he said, matter-of-factly.

'Oh,' I said, trying to sound sad when I actually felt like what I imagine someone who's just been injected with a jug-full of heroin feels like. 'What happened?'

'Oh. We're not actually very similar, you know?'

I do know. I do.

posted by EditingEmma 17.14

Even triple Biology could not dampen my mood. He said 'we're not similar'. That's probably because he can make at least five different facial expressions. Did he imply that me and him *are* similar?

Let's not get carried away.

Lalalalalalala.

posted by EditingEmma 22.05

My phone rang. I looked down and saw Greg's name and for a moment it felt like something from a past life. I'm not answering.

He's ringing again. I should probably answer.

'Hello, you,' he says cheerily.

'Hi!'

I sound strained.

'I just remembered, are we still going to that party on Saturday?'

Crap. No.

'What party?'

'I had "party with Emma" written in my phone calendar.'

'Is that because every day with me is a party?'

He laughs. 'It's better than a party.'

Nononono don't be nice to me. I am sludge. Horrible sludge!!

'So what are you doing Saturday?'

'Oh, er… just hanging out with my friends. I said I'd go round to Gracie's.'

Not a complete lie. I *will* be at Gracie's.

Oh God. I'm in bed but I already know that I won't be able to sleep. My stomach's churning from a mixture of elation and guilt.

Friday, 17 October

posted by EditingEmma 13.40

The Plan

I was walking along with Faith. I tried to ask how she was feeling, but as usual she completely shut me down.

'Is Greg coming tomorrow?' she asked.

I decided to play her at her own game.

'No. Did you know that hummingbirds can see UV light? So they can probably see a bunch of colours that we can't.'

'Why isn't he coming?'

'Oh, I don't know, he has cricket or something. Did you know that hummingbirds eat two or three times their own weight every day? That's like us eating a full fridge of food.'

'You're terrible at changing the subject.'

'Why are you so disinterested in hummingbirds?'

'Why isn't Greg coming?'

'. . . I may have uninvited him.'

'There we go.'

Then I laid out my flawless and clearly well-thought-out

plan (which I made up ten minutes ago) for Faith, which makes me TECHNICALLY <u>neither a liar nor a cheater.</u>

Tell Leon that me and Greg broke up.

Don't invite Greg to the party (to see how it goes with Leon).

If it looks like something *is* going to happen, then I can break up with Greg. And then I won't technically have lied to Leon, or cheated on Greg.

If it looks like it *isn't* going to happen, then I can tell Leon that me and Greg got back together, which means the first lie is voided and I obviously won't be a cheater.

'Just a couple of flaws in your flawless plan, Emma.'

'Please, do lay out your concerns and I will show you that they are wrong.'

'Well, aside from obvious moral deficiency.'

'That's a given.'

'How will you know something is going to happen before it happens?'

'Er… I'll get the vibes.'

'What if you get the vibes, and then break up with Greg and still nothing happens?'

'. . . I'll only do it if I'm getting very *strong* vibes.'

'But if you're getting *strong* vibes, then how will you stop the thing from happening before it's too late and you become a cheater?'

'I'll say I have to pee and then run out and phone Greg very quickly.'

'This is going to be a circus.'

posted by EditingEmma 16.35

I'd just come out of FT and was walking along with Gracie, when Leon sprang up beside me.

'What's in that?' he said, pointing at my FT tin.

'A jam roly-poly.'

'It's actually a burnt jam roly-poly,' Gracie interjected.

'Let's see it, then.'

He lifted up the lid and stared in. 'That can't be edible.'

'It's not,' said Gracie.

Leon picked up the roly-poly and started laughing.

'Can I?'

'Sure.'

Then he walked off into the distance, swinging my blackened cylindrical baked good in the air.

'Surely he can't be planning on eating that. Anna bakes such nice things,' said Gracie.

And I wished I had it back to use as a weapon.

posted by EditingEmma 20.34

Round at Steph's. I keep thinking about Leon walking around out there, holding my jam poly-poly. It seems significant somehow. Greg messaged:

> Wish I could've seen you tonight x 19.16
>
> Me too. Sorry, had to help Steph with this project though xx 19.41

A lie, but I put two kisses at the end which sort of makes up for it.

posted by EditingEmma 23.51

Even spooning Steph can't put me to sleep. In nine minutes
it will be the day of the party. A day that I potentially have
another sacred, incomparable kiss with Leon. Or potentially
mess it up with a really nice boy, for someone who, as Faith
put it, 'treats me like a piece of mud on the floor'.

Saturday, 18 October

posted by EditingEmma 11.01

THE DAY OF THE PARTY

I'm so anxious, I constantly feel like I might poo. Steph made me a bacon sandwich and my nerves are so strong that eating it was more disgusting than pleasurable, but I couldn't face myself if I said no to a bacon sandwich. What would that make me?

I've made Steph run through the plan with me so many times I think she's grown to hate me a little. Especially when I made her role-play as Greg.

posted by EditingEmma 18.16

At Gracie's

Her parents just left. As they went out they glanced at me all frightened, then looked at Gracie as if to say, *Please don't let her throw up on the spare room floor again*. Which is probably fair enough, really.

Anyway, Gracie is *particularly* stressy today, because she's all worried not enough people are coming.

I said, 'That's what happens when you only invite twenty people and five of them can't come.'

Then she shoved me. She *shoved* me!!! AND she invited Greg!!! She just walked into the room, announcing, 'By the way, I told my brother he could bring Greg tonight.'

'WHAT???'

We all stared at her.

'Look, my brother *asked*, I couldn't really say no, could I?'

'I thought you said Andy and Greg "weren't really friends".'

She didn't answer that, and replied, 'If you want me to, I can go and explain to Andy why he can't come?'

She knew she had me there and looked really smug. Aghh!! There's no way Andy *asked* if Greg could come! She's so only doing this to raise numbers for her stupid party!!

posted by EditingEmma 19.28

Eating dinner in silence, as a protest.

posted by EditingEmma 19.38

No one seemed to care about my silent protest, so I joined back in with the conversation. But I purposefully didn't enjoy it.

posted by EditingEmma 19.45

If you think about it, maybe it's actually *better* for my plan that both Greg and Leon are coming to the party. If I'm getting the vibes from Leon, then I can break up with Greg face to face instead of over the phone. As concluded in my previous post, no one wants to be dumped via any form of technology. What was I thinking?! This way will be much nicer.

Much nicer.

Yes. It will all be fine. Probably. I'm not a horrible person. I mean, I give to charity. Specifically, to the bees. Where would the bees be without my kind donations? (Kind donations that actually come from my mother because I don't make any money.)

AHHH who am I kidding!!! This isn't nicer in any way!! This is horrible!

posted by EditingEmma 20.27

Putting on Make-up in Gracie's Room
Me: 'How can I draw a moustache on her without her noticing?'

Steph: 'In her sleep?'

Me: 'It's not really bedtime.'

Steph: 'Crush some sleeping pills and put them in her vodka?'

Me: 'I said I want to draw on her, Steph, not kill her.'

Then Faith said, 'Guys, she's allowed to invite who she wants to her party. It's her house.'

I stared at her.

'Don't look at me like that, Emma. Why don't you just tell Leon the truth before he gets here?'

'I can't.'

'Fine, then break up with Greg before he gets here.'

'. . . I can't.'

'Well then, it's your mess. Don't blame Gracie.'

And she walked off to the bathroom... I gazed after her with an open mouth. Well, now that's two friends crossed off the list of people I will be speaking to tonight.

Steph said, 'Wow, I didn't know your mouth was that big. Can I try to throw things into it?'

I can't make it three people off the list, or I might have no one to talk to...

Emma Nash @Em_Nasher

.@Brentsy attempting to get Maltesers in my mouth. That's 17 to the floor, 0 into my mouth

posted by EditingEmma 20.59

Why Doing Stuff Just for You = A Confidence Boost
I put on my dress that I made and Faith said, 'That's nice. Where did you get it?'

And then I got to say, 'Oh, actually, I made it myself.'

BEST FEELING EVER.

I'm feeling really warm and happy... I know it sounds silly but this dress is something separate from any other aspect of my life, not for anyone else, just for me... Something *I've* achieved. I feel... proud of myself for something. Which never happens.

posted by EditingEmma 21.14

I'm even *enjoying* putting on make-up to go with it. I feel like I'm expressing myself, rather than just drudgingly trying to make myself look better. For a moment I actually felt sorry for the other half of the population that feel they can't do this, rather than the other way around.

Gracie saw it and got even more moody because I look nothing like a character out of *The Great Gatsby*. But even she said it was nice! And she *loved* her 'Word Wizard' jumper. She pretended like it was really lame in front of Andy and Babs (who, in his own words, is here early 'cause the party don't start 'til he walks in'), but there was true glee in her eyes.

posted by EditingEmma 21.35

Greg is here. Back to feeling awful about myself. Should I break up with him now?!

posted by EditingEmma 23.39

It's eleven-thirty and I'm already minesweeping in the kitchen like a lonely, minesweeping gremlin.

When Greg got here he bent down to kiss me.

'You look amazing,' he murmured, 'and your dress is really nice.'

I smiled weakly and pretended I was really interested in what Gracie was saying. Which wasn't convincing because she was just stressing about whether her flapper headdress 'looked authentic'. After a while, Greg said, 'Emma, can I talk to you?'

'Err… Sure. Go for it.'

He led me by the hand to Andy's room and shut the door. For a blissful moment I thought maybe he was going to break up with me and I wouldn't have to worry any more. But he didn't.

'Why did you lie to me about what you were doing tonight?'

'I didn't.'

'You said you were hanging out with your friends.'

'I *am* hanging out with my friends.'

'And about a hundred other people.'

'A hundred? You clearly haven't seen the guest list.'

He raised an eyebrow. 'Are you annoyed at me, Emma?'

'I don't know… er… why might I be annoyed at you?'

'Is it because I went to that party without you? It would have been hard to bring you, because it was at a club and you don't have ID.'

I paused. 'It… could be.'

'I just don't want our age difference to get in the way of something really good.'

Age difference!! Yes!! That's something I can use. He's just handing me break-up lines on a plate.

'I should go see if Gracie needs any help,' I said, and left the room. When I went downstairs she was actually struggling to put up a giant poster of a big pair of eyes, so I held one end. The room does actually look really nice. She's got stands with little mini-macaroons and vases with feathers in and a pink champagne fountain.

Then Leon arrived.

<u>Thoughts on Leon's Arrival</u>

I wonder when my Daisy will get here?

She's here. I mean, he's here. Leon is here. Leon is here. Leon is here.

Thank God I'm talking to Holly and not someone who cares whether I'm listening.

He's taken off his coat and now he's moving towards the drinks table.

He's picking up a pink champagne.

And sipping it.

He's been in the room for two minutes now.

And now three.

He's turning around and OH MY GOD he caught my eye.

Just for a second everything stopped and it was like everything between us was somehow said in that look. But I don't want to overanalyse it as, er, I have been known to misinterpret eye contact before.

Anyway, I carried on like a human-tracking device. I'm always aware of exactly where he is in the room. Even when he's behind me. And he kept looking over at me too. It was amazing, only constant surveillance was making my 'pretending not to have a boyfriend' act a little harder. I was standing very far away from Greg and every time he came near me I pretended that I was incredibly interested in something on the other side of the room. Then I'd walk away leaving him looking like a lost bunny… Oh God.

At this point I'm thinking, Why *did I think this plan would work??* They both kept looking at me all deceived and it was making me almost feel like I *might* have the beginnings of a conscience. Then Greg strode towards me in a purposeful and slightly aggressive manner. I pretended to be really interested in a painting of a fruit bowl and ran over to it, but he followed me.

'Emma, why are you ignoring me?'

'What? I'm not.'

'You are, though.'

'What do you think this painter was thinking about when he painted this?'

'Fruit.'

'Interesting… Interesting… I think he was thinking about his mother.'

'*Emma*,' he said, grabbing my arm.

I'm not exactly Tinkerbell so I went crashing sideways into the table. Which meant, of course, that everyone started staring at us. Including Leon.

'What's going on with you?' he pressed me.

I glanced sideways at Leon, who was frowning.

'Well, after that violent outburst, I don't think I want to talk to you.'

'It was an accident! I'm sorry.'

'Well… Sorry doesn't always cut the mustard, Greg.'

I walked off.

(Cut the mustard?)

And that's how I ended up downing other people's dirty leftover drinks in the gutter where I belong. I hope no one here has the flu. Or mouth herpes.

Gracie just came over to me and said, 'Greg went home. I hope you're happy.'

'I'm THRILLED,' I replied, trying to be sarcastic and casual, but definitely coming off like a raving madwoman by shouting and throwing my arms around.

I'm a horrible person. And a confused person. I do really like Greg. What am I doing?

posted by EditingEmma 00.29

And now it's half-twelve, and I'm crying alone in the garden. This party just gets better and better. Leon came over to me when I was in the kitchen. I pushed the weird potion I was making out of different people's drinks away.

'Emma, are you OK? What happened with you and that boy? Was that Greg?'

He looked genuinely concerned.

'Yes… He, er, he's having trouble accepting the break-up.'

He nodded.

'Well, I hope you're OK.'

'I think I am… thanks.'

I looked into his eyes for a second too long, and he stared back. Could this really be happening?? Then he looked away and stared down at the floor.

'You looked so funny when you went flying over that table… I mean, it kind of reminded me of that hippo that fell off that truck and died, the way you just lay there.'

'I didn't just *lie* there.'

'You did,' he said, laughing.

And for some reason, it wasn't funny. In that moment I couldn't laugh at myself. My heart snapped in two and I just stood there watching him laugh at me, getting further

and further away. I felt the reality of the situation. I was
'the friend' and I always would be. Someone he could liken
to a fallen, dead hippo without a second thought. My eyes
welled up with tears.

'Screw you, Leon,' I said, suddenly vaguely aware of my
words slurring, 'I wish the hippo was alive instead of you.'

And I ran off, trying not to run in a way that could be
compared to another kind of lumpish animal. And now here
I am. It seemed like a very good idea at the time. But it's very
cold and the house seems very far away. I'm sitting on the
swing, crying silently.

Probably not silently. I'm sniffling a lot. And wailing at
intervals.

posted by EditingEmma 03.36

I saw Leon step out onto the patio, looking for me. Someone
pointed down the end of the garden and he turned around,
searching the shadows. He came and sat on the swing next
to me. I want to write down everything that just happened
because I don't want to forget any of it. Even the bad parts:

I'm too drunk for my heart to start pounding, or to feel
nervous in any way. I just feel all sorts of things at once.
Like I want to hit him and scream at him and kiss him and
cradle him. But it's bigger than him… it's just like the world
is too huge and empty but also full of too many possibilities
and feelings and it's all opening up for me and it's *too much*
and I'm really really alive and present in this moment but
at the same time I've got no idea what I'm doing and I'm
just kicking around like a bug on its back that can't get up.

And for no apparent reason I just start swinging. Really, really hard, manic swinging. I'm vaguely aware of him beside me and at some point he starts swinging too. We're both just swinging… Swinging is a funny word. I'm not sure how long we swung for. But my brain fills with the words just keep *swinging* just keep *swinging* just keep *swinging* and it seems easier for a while, somehow, as if there's no room in it for my actual thoughts.

Then I have to stop because I'm out of breath. Leon stops too and says, 'Are you quite finished?'

'Yes,' I wheeze.

'You're really red,' he says. 'Like, really, really red. It's dark and I can still see your face shining into the night.'

'Well…' I take a long breath, 'I'm no hockey captain.'

'Shut up, Emma.'

'Don't tell me to shut up!'

And I start crying again. Then he gets up and stands by my swing and pushes the hair out of my face. And then he kneels in the grass and puts his arms around my waist, and rests his head on my stomach. And I breathe in his hair, which smells like bubbles and biscuits and soap all at the same time, which doesn't sound appealing but it's incredible. And it's so much better in real life than when I'm walking around and think I smell it. And I'm running my hands through his soft, long dark hair and it's not in my imagination, it's HAPPENING.

And then somehow he's kissing me. And it's not just kissing like the act of kissing, he's kissing *me* and I'm kissing *him*. It's frantic yet soft and beautiful. And I'm a bit snotty and gross but he doesn't seem to care, and he starts kissing the tears from my cheek and I could go on for ever. I'm not aware of anything else, I've got no idea how long we've been kissing for. Sometimes we stop. And then I realise we've started again.

Later on, who knows how much later, we're lying in the grass next to each other. I'm lying in the crook of his arm and looking up at the sky, which feels big in a good way, now. We're just talking about EVERYTHING. A vague outline of our conversation:

'I'm sorry about Biology...' he sighs, 'I just... I was embarrassed.'

'Embarrassed of what?'

'You know.'

'Of *what*?'

'Don't make me say it.'

'I'm serious, Leon. I have no idea what you mean.'

He pauses. 'When you came up behind me. I was... looking at your Twitter.'

I could laugh out loud at the irony.

'I didn't see. I swear.'

We're silent for a moment.

'When you tweeted about making dinner that time, I really wanted to come and save your fingers, by the way.'

The back of my throat prickles with tears.

'Can I ask one thing?' he says. 'Why did your mum behead a stuffed camel?'

I laugh, and tell him.

'OH MY GOD. I can't believe I missed that.'

'Me neither.' I take a breath, and ask what I've been wanting to ask for four months, 'Why did you?'

He looks uncomfortable. 'We weren't speaking.'

'Yes. I know. But... *why* weren't we speaking?'

'I'm sorry.'

'That's not a reason.'

'I don't know. I was upset.'

'*You* were upset? But you're the one who broke up with *me*.'

'I don't know, I just... felt really angry with you. For making me feel like that.'

'Like what?'

'Like... I don't know, Emma!'

'You do know.'

'Confused, unsure. Freaked out. Confused. I don't know.'

'I don't know how *I* can have confused *you*. I think it's pretty obvious that I like you. I even got a sympathy spot where you have that little mole on your cheek.'

He doesn't say anything.

'Do you like me, Leon?'

'I do like you. I like you a lot.'

'Do you like Apple?'

'Huh?'

'Appananna. Anna.'

He pauses. 'I like her in a different way.'

I feel my guts wrenching and rage or vomit or both bubbling away inside me. *Sound casual.*

'Different how?'

'It's easier with her.'

'Easier how?'

'Well, for one thing, she doesn't interrogate me.'

'I'm not *interrogating* you. I think I deserve some answers.'

Silence. He sighs.

'You're right. I should never have asked you to go out with me, Emma.'

I feel like someone just speared me through the stomach. I try to get up and he grabs my arm.

'No! Emma, sit down. I was worried about ruining our friendship but then it just sort of happened anyway. And when it happened I was still worrying.'

'So you thought the solution to saving a friendship would be to ignore me?'

'I thought that breaking up with you would really ruin it.'

'Leon, ignoring someone *is* breaking up with someone.'

'It isn't.'

'It is. It's just doing it in a cowardly way.'

'It isn't. It isn't really breaking up with someone.'

'OK, well, if ignoring me isn't breaking up with me, then going out with someone else *definitely* is.'

He pauses. 'I never really wanted to break up with you.'

'Well, what did you want?'

'I don't know.'

He stays silent.

'What do you want now?'

He looks at me, and kisses me.

Then I remember us not talking for a long time. We just lie on our backs looking at the stars. Eventually, Leon says, 'It's getting cold. We should go in.'

My chest tightens at the thought of him leaving. At the thought of this ending.

'I'm not cold,' I say, shivering.

'I've got to go home soon.'

'OK.'

And now he's gone home. When he left he kissed me goodbye just like we were really together.

Actually, most people have gone home. When did the party end?

posted by EditingEmma 04.08

We're all in Gracie's room. Steph is listening to me babble. Faith is asleep. Gracie is irritable because she found a Malteser in her bed and keeps shhing me.

He likes me. He kissed me and he likes me. I will not go to sleep. This happiness will not be wasted on sleep. Should I have told him about my sympathy spot? Probably not.

Who cares?

posted by EditingEmma 04.25

Three messages from Greg. I'll just pretend I don't see them. If I don't read them, they could theoretically say anything, and only by opening them will I make them bad. Like Schrödinger's messages.

posted by EditingEmma 05.37

Still Up and Smiling

On the way to the bathroom, I ran into Steph in the corridor.

'Emma… what are you doing?'

'Peeing,' I said dreamily.

'Great,' she said and walked past me.

I can *hear* myself being unbearable, if only I could *care*…

Then on the way back I ran into Gracie's brother, also on his way to the bathroom. He smiled awkwardly and went past me. Hmm, even from the depths of my dark and all-encompassing self involvement, I sense that wasn't a coincidence.

When she came back to bed, I asked, 'Steph… where were you?'

'When?'

'Just now.'

'I went to the kitchen for a drink.'

Damn, I wish I'd been paying enough attention to know whether she'd been in the room before or not. I sat up and pointed at Gracie, very attractively sleeping with her mouth open. Then I made a little penis gesture with my hand.

'Gracie has a penis…?'

'You know what I mean.'

Her eyes flashed. 'OK… fine. We can't talk about this here!!'

posted by EditingEmma 06.21

Ten minutes later, we were sitting under Gracie's kitchen table with a bucket of chocolate bites.

'What happened?!'

'So, he came up to me and he said he was really sorry that I had to find out about Jonno like that, but he thought I should know.'

'And??'

'And then he said he hoped I didn't hate him.'

'What did you say?'

'I said he was just the messenger and that he did me a favour. And then he said, I hope so, because you deserve to be treated much, much better than that. And then we stared at each other.'

'And you kissed??'

'No. Then Gracie came over and asked Andy to refill the champagne fountain. She gave me a warning look.'

'Stay away from my brother or DIE.'

'Yes. That kind of look. And then nothing happened until about an hour ago, when I went to the kitchen for some water, and his light was on. And he saw me go past and came out into the hallway, and we both knew what was going to happen.'

'And??'

'Then we kissed. But it was over really quickly. We heard a noise.'

'Gracie dislocating her jaw so she could devour you like a snake.'

'That might have been it.'

Back in bed now. I will never sleep again.

Sunday, 19 October

posted by EditingEmma 08.09

I did sleep. Very briefly. Until we were all woken up by *someone* in the room farting but no one will admit it was them. It definitely wasn't me. Or was it? Can people fart themselves awake?

I've only been awake two minutes and last night's magic has sort of faded. I have a headache (though not as bad as last time I was here), my mouth tastes like a small furry animal died in it, I feel vaguely socially embarrassed and ashamed though I'm not sure what for, and the intense, gnawing guilt about Greg is much, much harder to ignore.

Five messages from him. Oh God.

Emma Nash @Em_Nasher

Reviving hangover Coco Pops with @Brentsy and @GracieMorton1, @Faith18 has fallen asleep over the table

posted by EditingEmma 08.42

Andy came in, looking weary.

'Why are you up so early?' he croaked, rubbing his eyes.

I was about to say someone farted, but then I remembered Steph might potentially want to have sex with this person.

Her and Andy are trying to be subtle but it isn't working. He mawkishly offered her a Pop-Tart as if it was a bunch of flowers and she has suddenly become very austere. Whenever someone says something she considers it carefully and nods without really responding.

We that are true lovers run into strange capers...

posted by EditingEmma 09.00

Can't put it off any more. Going to have to read the messages.

> Am going home. Wasn't having much fun. You clearly don't want to see me so maybe we can talk tomorrow. Hope you have a fun evening. x 23.05
>
> Are you even going to reply? x 00.12
>
> I don't even know what I've done :S if we talk about it we can sort it out. x 01.45
>
> Please talk to me :(04.33
>
> I can't sleep. I really like you, Emma, but I'm angry and confused and you can't just ignore me. 04.48

Oh my God. I've done exactly what Leon did to me. How did that happen? And all I've been doing all term and all summer is rant on about finding someone who will treat me nicely and I actually found them... then treated them horribly.

posted by EditingEmma 09.27

Right. It's time to get it together and stop being such a repulsive person. Dialling Greg...

> And hanging up before it rings.
>
> Dialling Greg...
>
> And hanging up before it rings.

This is getting ridiculous. I can do this.

Greg is ringing. *Crap*. OK, breathe, breathe.

'Hello?'

'Emma, did you just try to call me?'

'Oh, no, sorry, accident.'

'OK.'

'But, I mean, er, I was going to call you. Are you otherwise engaged?'

'What?'

'I mean, er, are you free to talk?'

'I can talk.'

Silence.

'What's wrong, Emma? Why were you being so weird last night?'

'I… er, well…'

Moment of truth.

'I kind of felt like maybe you're not that into having a girlfriend right now.'

Agh. I'm a chicken. A snivelling, gutless, yellow-bellied chicken.

'Emma, don't do that. I know that's how you fobbed off that other guy you were dating. Don't do that to *me*.'

'OK, first things first, I was never "dating" Laurence Myer!!'

'Emma.'

'All right, I'm sorry. I guess I kind of… I kind of like someone else.'

Silence.

'I'm really sorry, Greg. I should have said something before.'

'I… How long have you liked him?'

Since before I wore a bra?

'Not very long.'

Silence.

'Is it Leon?'

'How did you…'

'The first time we met. You said I wasn't him.'

'Right, yeah.'

'I guess I should have known.'

Silence.

'I'm going back to bed. Bye, Emma.'

Well, that was extremely uncomfortable.

posted by EditingEmma 09.35

I feel horrible. But also like a huge weight has been lifted… Am I allowed to feel happy about the Leon thing now? Or would that still make me a bad person?

posted by EditingEmma 14.23

I can't help feeling happy. As I was leaving, I hugged Gracie's mum and apologised for the mess I made last time I was round. She didn't really say anything, only looked very startled. When I got back home I hugged Mum, too, and she eyed me with suspicion.

'Have you taken something?' she said.

Once I had thoroughly convinced her I wasn't high on

Ecstasy, she wandered off. Later on, she walked into the kitchen and I was buttering a plate instead of the toast.

'What's wrong with you?' she snapped. 'Has your brain fallen out?'

I think it might have.

posted by EditingEmma 22.31

In bed. Greg hasn't been in contact... I guess he's too angry. I probably wouldn't be in contact with me either. I can't sleep, even though I only slept for two hours last night. I get to see Leon tomorrow. I hope there will be more kissing.

Monday, 20 October

posted by EditingEmma 08.59

I floated into school on a cloud this morning. Walked past Mr Morris and said, 'Good morning Mr Morris! I'm very sorry I was late this morning and I'm sure I'm in big trouble, but I have to say, you really are an excellent teacher and role model in my life – for that I thank you.'

He looked stunned and said nothing. I'm 90 per cent sure it was him and not his twin. Oh well. I am continuing to spread the joy... lalala. I even smiled at a horrible little child who was throwing Skittles at passers-by. Lalala...

posted by EditingEmma 11.09

The sparkling rainbow following me around has faded a little. I suddenly feel really nervous going up to Leon...I don't know why. Saturday night feels like a *lifetime* ago. I'm sure I'm just being stupid. It will be fine. It has to be fine. I bought my Chewits security blanket and I'm going to walk past him holding them, very casually...

posted by EditingEmma 11.19

I did it. I walked past him. Nothing. *Nada*. Not so much as a glance. My tummy is all wobbly.

'What does this mean?' I asked Steph.

'Maybe he's gone off Chewits?' she replied.

Then Apple went over to him and he got a cookie out of his coat pocket and gave it to her. HE GOT A COOKIE OUT OF HIS COAT POCKET AND GAVE IT TO HER.

He couldn't be doing the same thing to me... *again*... could he? *Could he?*

I feel like people keep glancing over at me, and looking a bit... apprehensive? Even Abby Matthews gave me a grim smile, and we never speak. Does everyone know? I'm sitting with Faith with my head in my hands as she analyses the situation.

'It's like a really weird food game... Laurence running after you with Minstrels and you running after Leon with Chewits and him running after Apple with cookies...'

'Yes, it's a delicious feast of broken hearts.'

She pats me and says, 'You're feeling melodramatic today.'

Faith can be so cold.

posted by EditingEmma 11.45

In Maths

'I can't believe he's done this!! AGAIN!!' raged Steph, scaring Mr Crispin as he walked past.

'Me neither,' I said, staring into space.

'Do you think they're back together?? Agh, that's so...

shit, Emma. I can't believe he would do this and then get back together with her.'

'I…' My voice sounded blank. 'I really thought this time was different. I don't understand.'

'*I* understand.' Steph waved her fist around. 'I understand now how murders happen.'

I took the pen out of her hands before she accidentally stabbed Boring Susan in the back of the head.

posted by EditingEmma 12.45

Editing Emma Goes Public

I was just sitting in French, trying not to cry, when I got a message from Steph.

Check your notifications, NOW 12.26

Madame Fournier is really strict about phones, unlike Mr Crispin, so I had to wait until she turned around to the board before I could reply.

Later. With Madame F 12.34

Seriously Emma. Do it NOW 12.34

I excused myself to go to the loo. Madame Fournier rolled her eyes and made some comment about not being able to hold my bladder for forty minutes and that by the time I was her age I'd be peeing myself. But I got away. I was sceptical about what could be so bloody important. I thought, this had better not be something to do with *Game of Thrones*.

And now I'm in the toilets. Looking at what Steph meant. And I'm wishing it was something to do with *Game of Thrones*. It's my blog.

My blog.

On public.

My PRIVATE blog.

On PUBLIC.

Not all of it, just one of the worst possible posts that could ever have been uploaded… *Reasons Why Leon Naylor is Not Worth Any Girl's Time or Virginity.* There it is. Just sitting there on my screen. And everyone else's screens. For everyone to see. Oh my God… that's why Leon's not speaking to me. T*hat's* why people were staring at me at break-time.

I read back through my own words, slagging him off. Slagging off is an understatement. I call him stupid. I mock him for trying. I say his parents love his brother more, an insecurity he shared with me in confidence, that he's never told *anyone else*. I'm mortified by what I've written. Mortified that other people have seen this. That *Leon* has seen this.

I've set it back to private, obviously, but the damage is done. Steph commented on it about a million times saying 'EMMA. EMMA. DELETE. DELETE.'

What have I done? How did this happen?

posted by EditingEmma 13.30

Hiding in the toilets. I don't want to go out there. I can only imagine what people are saying about me. I bet everyone thinks I'm a massive bitch. Oh God. I'm so *humiliated*. Now I know what it feels like to be a celebrity and have all your private business aired in a magazine. I feel like someone's taken my deepest, weirdest daydream and played it out on a TV for everyone to watch.

I've turned off my phone so no one and nothing can reach me. I will stay in this cubicle making little loo roll dolls. Little loo roll dolls who would never judge me because they do not have thoughts. I will stay in here *for ever* with my harmless paper friends.

Or at least until English.

posted by EditingEmma 14.10

English

People abruptly stopped talking when I came in, but I heard the word 'disgusting'. Has *everyone* seen it?! I know it was bad but I'm not sure I'd call it *disgusting*.

I sat down next to Steph, hiding behind my hair. She was doodling on her folder and clearly trying to keep calm for me. Even Ms Parker had concern in her eyes when she handed me back my essay. She must have heard what people were saying.

I burrowed further into my seat. I could just *feel* everyone staring at me. Oh God, I was going to have to move schools. Except we all know that never works because *everything* ends up on the internet so whenever anyone does something really embarrassing it just *follows* them. FOR EVER. Could I make a clean break at uni?! What if I end up accidentally going to uni with Abby Matthews and she tells everyone there?! Should I apply to universities in Europe? Oh God, WHY DIDN'T I PAY MORE ATTENTION IN FRENCH.

'Steph, I can't take it!!'

'What?'

'Everyone *talking* about me!!'

She paused for a second, frowning. 'No they're not.'

'It's OK, Steph, you don't have to shield my feelings.'

'No, really. They're talking about this girl in Year 9 who did a poo on the bathroom floor.'

'I… What?!'

'She left it too late and just missed the toilet. Apparently it was just sitting there in the girls' loos all morning.'

We both sat there, imagining it.

'So no one's said anything?'

'Umm. I did hear Boring Susan say it was a bit weird, but then the poo thing happened and you kind of got over-shadowed.'

Overshadowed by a poo. Right. Well… that's a relief.

posted by EditingEmma 15.30

'….Were they *really* not talking about me?'

'Really, really not.'

'I just can't believe someone's poor bowel control is more interesting than my life.'

'Emma, is this really what you're focusing on right now? *Leon* cares. Leon. You know, the person you actually care about? Rather than fifty other people in our year you never speak to?'

She's right. Suddenly I feel like I've been punched in the stomach.

'He looked pretty upset, Emmy. He looked kind of, well, miserable.'

I'd take a hundred mean comments from Abby Matthews if it meant me and Leon were OK. We *have* to be OK.

posted by EditingEmma 16.34

As soon as the bell went, I ran to the gates to wait for Leon.
He was clearly trying to avoid me, because when I got there
he was practically running out of his class.

'Leon. LEON!' I called.

When he saw me, he moved even faster.

'Please talk to me.'

'I don't really want to, Emma.'

Then he walked away. And I just stood there watching
him go. Again.

posted by EditingEmma 22.25

How My Blog Could Possibly Have Gone Public

I've been racking my brains over this, and talked through it
with Steph, and we came down to three options.

I Did It By Mistake

Highly unlikely, but possible. It would be a bit of a coincidence given I wrote that post so long ago, and given its
content. There are a million posts on my blog about random
other crap and none of those went public. It feels planned.

Anna

I wouldn't normally be this paranoid, but I feel pretty sure
someone did this. I guess, she might have been upset about
Leon and realised that maybe I had something to do with it.
But it doesn't really seem like her. She's actually really nice.

And how on Earth would she have even known I was writing a blog, let alone have had access to it? Which led us to…

Greg
He's definitely upset with me. He definitely knows about my secret blog, and he was always asking to see it. Could I have left my log in details on his computer? Suffice to say, I've changed my password.

We concluded that it *must* have been Greg, it seems like the only feasible option. But I still can't believe he would do that… He's not *nasty*. I really need to phone him tomorrow, to talk.

Tuesday, 21 October

posted by EditingEmma 11.35

Sitting in the loos staring into space. I'm not even crying; I don't think I have any tears left. I should be in a lesson right now but I categorically don't care. Somehow yesterday I really thought, deep down, that we'd work it out. I was upset but I wasn't *worried*. I thought he was mad, and needed a bit of time… But it's over. It's actually over this time.

I finally got him to at least talk to me. All his friends were staring at us and he *hates* people making a scene. Which I was.

'Come on,' I said pleadingly. 'Please come with me?'

He took a deep breath.

'Fine.'

We went and sat on the wall, by Chapel. He was keeping his eyes fixed on his shoes.

'I'm sorry, Leon. I have no idea how that post went public.'

'It doesn't matter.'

'Well, it clearly *does* matter.'

He said nothing.

'It wasn't meant for anyone to see,' I said desperately. 'I was just… venting. Everybody vents.'

He was silent for a while. 'I'm stupid?'

'I didn't mean it.'

'*My parents love my brother more than me*?'

'Leon, I was upset. I was so, *so* upset. I had to find a way to deal with it somehow. I only said those things because... Because you'd gone away and I didn't know why. And because I like you so much.' My voice wobbled. *Don't cry, don't cry, don't cry.*

He sighed.

'Come on. This can't be unfixable. This is so, so stupid.'

He put his head in his hands. 'This is why I think... maybe I had it right over the summer. I don't know.'

Owch.

'What do you mean?'

'This is just too much, Emma.'

'Look, I'm sorry. I was *mad* at you. I mean, I shouldn't have said it, but don't you think I had a right to be mad at you?'

'Stop turning this around.'

'I... I'm *not* turning it around. I'm just explaining myself. It's not like I just wrote those things without a reason.'

'I can't do this,' was all he replied, still looking at the floor.

I sat for a moment. Was this really all I was going to get?

'I can't believe you're not taking *any* responsibility for this. Fine, punish me for what I wrote, but how can you not understand why I wrote it?'

Then he shrugged. He *shrugged* at me.

'I was *angry*,' I carried on, 'Which, by the way, I had every right to be!'

I was yelling by this point. He jumped down from the wall.

'Don't just walk away! Hey!' I grabbed him. 'You can't just do this! Just blame everything on me and then disappear again? This is NOT all my fault.'

He looked at me then. He looked from my left eye to my right, as if searching in me for something. I wanted so badly to give him whatever it was. He looked so profoundly sorrowful, and full of so many emotions that even then I thought that maybe I'd got through. That maybe we were going to be OK.

But then he looked away again, and walked off.

'Oh, right, yeah. Do what you do best. Communicate via telepathic waves. I'm still waiting for the ones you sent over summer to arrive, by the way,' I called after him.

And, once more, I had ended up literally chasing him around school.

posted by EditingEmma 13.55

Mystery Solved

I thought today couldn't get any worse, but oh, look at that. It did.

After lunch we all came back to the Sixth Form Centre.

I phoned Greg, and he mostly kept saying. 'What?? What??' and then finally, 'No, Emma, I did not put up your *diary* for everyone to read. If you don't mind, I have class.'

(Owch.)

When I hung up the phone Faith and Steph were staring expectantly. Gracie was looking down at her shoes, all pink.

She caught my eye briefly, and that's when I knew. It was her. I remembered logging on to her computer, in her room, but it didn't even occur to me that one of my friends would do this. Steph and Faith were looking between us, confused and wide-eyed, and I got up and left.

This is so, so much more hurtful than if it had been Greg. I feel like I've been punched in the stomach. *Why?* I know we fight a lot, but I thought when it came down to it we had each other's back. Why would she do this?! I don't even want to know. Nothing she says can ever take this back.

posted by EditingEmma 19.03
The rest of the day passed in a blur. Steph has rung about a million times, but I've turned off my phone and put myself to bed. Don't want to think about this horrible day. I don't want to think about anything any more.

Wednesday, 22 October

posted by EditingEmma 12.06

I told Mum I was sick this morning, and needed to stay home. Thankfully she's easy and believed me. She nodded fervently, feeling my forehead and declaring that 'her glands were up too'. I swear for a moment she almost considered staying home herself. I'm on the sofa watching *Working Girl*. Because 80s hair always puts me in a slightly better mood.

Couldn't eat anything this morning. I feel numb. I'm feeling so bad about so many things I hardly know what to think about.

posted by EditingEmma 19.20

Finally turned on my phone. For no other reason than because I thought Steph might be worried. As soon as it came on it started ringing.

'Emma, where have you been?!' she yelled.

'Zimbabwe. At home, obviously,' I said.

'DON'T do this again, Emma. Don't you DARE hide away again, and shut the world out. Shut *me* out.'

'I...'

'No. I don't want to hear it. Because you're better than this. You were doing *so well*. You seemed… happy for a while. And it wasn't to do with Leon. It was to do with *you*. So, this has happened and it's rubbish, but don't let it drag you down again. Don't let this ruin everything. Now what kind of mini-bites do you want?'

'Chocolate cornflake.'

'Great. I'm coming over.'

When Steph arrived we avoided the subject for a while, until she couldn't hold back any longer.

'Emma, about Gracie…'

'Ugh. Really? Are we really going to talk about this?'

'I think we have to.'

I stayed silent.

'Look, she did a bad thing and I'm not going to defend her. That's up to her. But you two will work it out, and… and… and maybe this hasn't gone so terribly.'

'You're going to have to explain that one to me.'

'Look. The things you said were bad, but they weren't… *that* bad. I mean, considering. Leon had *hurt* you. You shouldn't have to feel guilty about this, Emma.'

'Shouldn't I?'

'No. He's been such a prick, Emma. I'm sorry. I've refrained from saying it all this time. I know how much you like him. But he's a giant, prick-headed prick. Essentially, he treated you like mud, as Faith put it, and now he's treating you like mud again because you were angry about being treated that way in the first place. It's doubly prickish. And well… now at least you *know* it.'

And I know that she's right. We watched TV and ate heaps of chocolate and it felt, just for a while, like maybe the world didn't have to end after all.

Thursday, 23 October

posted by EditingEmma 13.22

Mum clocked that I wasn't sick when she caught me hot-flannelling my head and made me come in. Spent the day so far successfully avoiding Gracie. On my way to French, I passed Leon in the corridor. He looked down, and it was so infuriating that I stood in front of him so he couldn't get past me.

I said, 'We're done, Leon. As friends and as whatever we were. I don't need people like you in my life. Don't bother talking to me ever again.'

He kept his eyes on the floor the whole time and walked on.

Steph said, 'So you told someone who's not talking to you, to not bother talking to you?'

'Don't ruin my moment.'

posted by EditingEmma 16.13

Walking home alone. I waited at the gates for Steph and Faith, but Faith said we should wait for Gracie so I left.

'You can't avoid her for ever, Emma!!' she called after me.

'I can!' I shouted back.

'You have FT with her ALL AFTERNOON tomorrow!!'
Drat. She's right.

posted by EditingEmma 17.03

I notice that Gracie hasn't posted anything since we stopped speaking. Should I unfollow her on Twitter?

posted by EditingEmma 17.07

No. There are some things in life you can never get over and I think that may just be one of them.

posted by EditingEmma 17.35

Fighting with a compulsion to post a clip from *Bad Blood*. The urge is almost primal. But I feel like that would be returning to my less mature, summer self. Oh God. Looking back at some of my tweets about Leon from June:

> Emma Nash @Em_Nasher
> You're my first and last and I'm NOTHING to you

(Why Barry White?! Why?! I blame my mother for constantly playing Mellow Magic.) And then in my even more pathetic, sad moments:

> Emma Nash @Em_Nasher
> You should always give someone the chance to explain if
> they did something wrong, before you walk away
> Emma Nash @Em_Nasher
> What did I do wrong?

Who am I? I might as well be posting My Chemical Romance song lyrics.

In fact, that would have been less embarrassing.

Anyway, I have deleted all those cringe-worthy tweets. I will never again be attention-seeking on the internet, hoping that he will see and be persuaded to change his mind, and I will not sink to the level of having an internet-go at Gracie through Taylor Swift lyrics.

I fleetingly wonder what she's thinking, if she's upset or guilty, or satisfied? Then I go back to pretending she doesn't exist.

posted by EditingEmma 18.08
Heather is round for dinner, which is always a welcome distraction from misery. She left her glasses on the train, and her phone on the bus.

'It was only when I was looking out the window I realised my vision was a little blurry!' she chirruped, laughing away.

How?

Anyway, I see that she is now the proud new owner of the dinosaur phone.

posted by EditingEmma 18.53

THE CHEWITS ARE GONE
'Oh, by the way, Emma, you really need to clean your room more,' Mum said.

'What? Why? It's fine.'

'I had to throw away this gross bundle of rubbish from under your bed.'

'Ew, what rubbish?! I don't have *rubbish*.'

Then it hit me.

'Mum, WHY were you under my bed?!'

'I thought you might have some spare glasses to help Heather.'

'Well don't!! Don't go in my room and stay away from my things!! Agh, I can't believe you threw them away!!'

'Threw *what* away?!'

Now I'm in my room staring at the blank space under my bed where the Chewit wrapper collection used to be. I think this time last week I might have been more upset, but now it feels weirdly prophetic. I started crying loudly and gutturally. Mum came in.

'What on Earth is that noise? You're disturbing Heather.'

Then she saw me crying on the floor.

'Do you want to talk about it?' she asked.

I couldn't breathe properly or form words so I shook my head in response. Mum retreated slowly from the room.

posted by EditingEmma 19.44

The crying has stopped. I definitely feel a lot better this time around, Leon-wise. Comparatively, anyway. I still feel totally rejected and abandoned, but like my core being is still intact. Like he hasn't managed to get at some part of me, that he did before. He's treated me like I'm worthless but I don't feel worthless, if you see what I mean.

But Gracie… I keep going over it in my head. Gracie reading through my blog. Gracie clicking 'publish'. Gracie watching me cry at school and not saying anything. I just don't understand.

At least before, when it was just about Leon and Greg,

it was just... boys. Somehow this makes all that seem a bit... stupid. Now that the problem is my *friends* I feel worse than ever before. Like my foundations have been shaken and I'm not sure how I'll ever stand up again, let alone carry on.

posted by EditingEmma 20.15

Making another dress on the sewing machine. Still feeling numb but quite creative. Heather came in and peered at the designs and said it looked 'wonderful'. Earlier on I heard Heather describe a fridge magnet as 'wonderful' but I'm going to take the compliment anyway.

posted by EditingEmma 22.50

Faith called.

'Emma, I think you should talk to Gracie.'

I snorted.

'Look, I know you're upset, but so is she.'

'Oh, *boo-hoo*.'

'I know she did a bad thing. But... you aren't without fault here.'

'*Excuse* me?'

'You can be quite mean to her.'

'She's mean to me!!!'

'I know, but... look, just talk to her, all right?'

'No.'

'Emma, come on.'

'*No.*'

Friday, 24 October

posted by EditingEmma 14.35

In FT
Pretending Gracie doesn't exist is so much harder when she's sitting next to me. Why did I choose a recipe that only takes me fifteen minutes, AGAIN? Stupid syllabub. Now I'm just sitting here twiddling my thumbs, which is making my blatant ignoring even more obvious. I only picked it because I wanted to hear it over and over in conversation with Ms McElroy. But she said,

'So, Emma, how do you feel the syllabub emerged today? Tell me about the syllabub's journey.'

And I felt nothing. It's a sad day when the word 'syllabub' doesn't even elicit a smile.

posted by EditingEmma 15.07
My syllabub isn't very mousse-like. It's runny and yellow and looks like washing up liquid. Tastes like it too. Gracie would normally make fun of it, but she's concentrating really hard on her muffins rising in the oven. She looks like she's about to cry.

Oh God, I think *I* might cry.

posted by EditingEmma 16.50

Back Home
Gracie opened her mouth a few times, but then stopped herself. I could see her in the corner of my eye.

Eventually, I said, 'Sorry, did you want to look at my phone? There's probably loads on it you can humiliate me with. The passcode is 1989.'

I regretted it as soon as it came out of my mouth, because then Gracie really did cry, and so did I. Everyone was staring at us (including Apple, who looked deeply uncomfortable). Ms McElroy said we needed to go and 'express our emotions' and excused us from class. I'm pretty sure she thought we were actually crying over the failed syllabub.

I went into a cubicle and really let rip, in that sort of loud, snotty way that can also sound a bit like guffawing. I could hear Gracie sniffling outside. Then she came and squished in next to me, locking the door.

'Emma, I'm really sorry,' she choked.

'Why did you do it?' I asked, mascara running down my face.

'I just… ugh, it seems so silly now. I came upstairs and I was having a really crap evening. I felt really insecure because I thought no one was coming. And then when people did come I wasn't even having a good time. I don't know, I felt really lonely and just a bit socially out of it, you know? Like I'd been looking forward to this for so long. And… I don't know. I know it's silly, but I guess I'd been hoping that maybe *I'd* get with someone. And you were just running around between Greg and Leon and I just...You're really lucky.'

'*Lucky?*' I scoffed. I'd *never* thought about it like that before. 'Gracie, the only boy I've ever really liked pretends I don't even exist.'

'But Greg doesn't. Greg really likes you and you were treating him like he didn't even matter.'

I felt a stab of guilt.

'So what? This is punishment for my bad behaviour?'

'No! Maybe... I don't know. I just came upstairs, feeling sorry for myself and a bit annoyed at you, I guess. And then I saw that you'd left your blog open. I know I shouldn't have, but I started reading it, and, you know...'

I blinked. 'What?'

'"An Ode To Steph"? "Reasons That Faith Is One of The Best Humans I Know"?'

And suddenly it dawned on me.

'I mean... what about me, Emma? I'm your friend too. And then I shouldn't have, but I searched my name, and all that was coming up was just horrible, mean stuff. And the worst part is I knew it would be. I did it on purpose. I don't know why I even looked, when I knew it would make me upset.'

I knew the feeling.

'Is that all I am to you?' she went on. 'A joke?'

'No, of course not,' I said, feeling genuinely ashamed. 'It's just venting. Like the post about Leon. True friends are always horrible to each other. You know... like on *Girls*.'

'Am I your friend?' she asked.

'Am I yours?'

We sat in silence for a moment.

'I guess we've both been pretty crap,' I said.

'I'm sorry,' she said, and she looked so sad and small.

'I'm really sorry, too, Gracie.'

We were silent for a moment, and then we hugged. I could feel her wet cheeks soaking into my shirt.

'I'm sorry I ruined things for you and Leon,' she said into my shoulder.

'You didn't ruin it,' I said, 'he ruined it.'

When we got back into the classroom she patted me gingerly on the arm and said, 'I'll pour your syllabub down the drain for you if you like.'

And I knew we were going to be OK.

posted by EditingEmma 21.01

Inspecting my eyes for signs of another lurking stye. Thankfully there isn't one... yet, but it's only a matter of time. I probably deserve it for being so horrible to Greg.

Greg. I wonder what Greg's doing? Does he still like me? Or does he hate me?

Saturday, 25 October

posted by EditingEmma 12.06

Saw a picture of Greg, playing football with his friends. Posted twenty minutes ago. He *looks* okay. If only there was a way to know from it how he was *actually* feeling... I wonder if he's talking to other girls already? AGH, I need to stop thinking about this.

posted by EditingEmma 14.17

Fighting the compulsion to read Greg's comment conversations and try to detect potential flirtations. I called Faith.

'Do you think Greg is talking to other girls?'

'I think if he were, that would be his prerogative.'

'You're always right.'

'I know. *Don't* try and find out.'

'I won't...'

'Are you and Gracie all right now?'

'We've got a long way to go, but we will be.'

'Good. That's good. I have to go. Hope wants to look at me in various ugly bridesmaid dresses. Oh, by the way... GUESS WHAT.'

'What?'

'Guess.'

'You had sex?!'

'NO. Why do you always think that?'

'Sorry. It's my vagina talking.'

'Well, I signed up for this new sketch class on Saturdays, and there's this girl…'

'OH MY GOD.'

'What? You don't even know what I'm going to say yet.'

'Sorry, go on.'

'Well now it's going to be really anticlimactic. I followed her and we've been liking each other's tweets and I think she's really cool. But it could just be a friend thing for her. I don't know. That's it. That's my news.'

'OH MY GOD!!'

'Shut up.'

'No really, that's really great!!'

'It feels like she might like me. But I don't know…'

'She likes you.'

'She might not.'

'She likes you. I hope you have more luck with her than I did with Paolo. Or Alex.'

'Me too, no offence. Bye bye now. AND DON'T STALK GREG.'

'I won't!!!'

posted by EditingEmma 15.04

Opened the laptop.

posted by EditingEmma 15.06

Closed the laptop.

posted by EditingEmma 20.43

Went downstairs. Mum was sitting on the sofa crying into a bag of crisps watching *American Gigolo*. I sat on the sofa with her. It's not really a sad film but somehow her crying has made me cry, and I'm just so angry at the gross injustice Richard Gere is facing. Why is he being set up? He doesn't deserve this.

'Mum, why are you crying?'

'I don't know. Why are you?'

'You started it.'

I put my hand on her arm, which had my phone in it. She looked down.

'Who's that?' she asked.

It was a picture of Greg.

'Er, no one.'

'I thought you and Leon were back together.'

'What? Have you been spying on me again?'

'No. But you got in the bath with your socks on and I sensed he was back in your life.'

'Oh, well. We're not.'

'Are you with this Greg?'

'No. I'm not. I'm not with anyone.'

'Good,' she said.

'*Good?*' I snarled. 'Why is that *good?*'

'You shouldn't go out with someone you think is a consolation prize. It's not very respectful to them, or yourself.'

And this time I didn't feel like I could turn it around, or change the subject. I felt gripped with a sudden, paralysing fear.

'But what if everyone, for the rest of my life, is a consolation prize?'

She laughed. 'They won't be.'

'How do you *know*?'

'Because I know. Anyway, what's so bad about being single? Do you think my life is bad?'

'No,' I said, genuinely.

'Well then.'

I thought for a moment.

'Trust me. Trying to get over Leon by filling the gap with someone else is not going to work. And you don't *need* anyone else.'

I looked at her and realised she was speaking from experience. And that I should actually, for once, maybe, and I'm stressing the word *maybe*, listen to her.

'Are you OK, Mum?'

'Me? Yes, I'm OK, Emma. Are you OK?'

'I think so.'

Then she hugged me. And I let her. For a full two seconds.

posted by EditingEmma 22.31

In my room, thinking about what Mum said. Agh, I can't believe this has all gone so wrong!! In trying to change things all I seem to have done is make them worse! It was all a mistake from the start. This whole mission was flawed. Trying to distract myself through meeting other people didn't do

ANYTHING. All I did was go on some truly awful dates, or drag other people down with me.

Summary of Evidence

1) Maybe the people we don't speak to in real life, we don't speak to for a reason i.e. Laurence Myer.

2) If we alter our personalities online, it doesn't translate to the real world.

3) Keep in mind the other person may well be altering their ENTIRE IDENTITY.

4) Even if you DO meet someone you normally wouldn't have gone out with and end up liking them, the person you liked first is probably still the one you really want.

= FAIL.

posted by EditingEmma 23.05

AND, not only have I hurt lots of other people, but I STILL don't even like myself. Whoever I've been over the last few months I've barely liked more than the person I was over summer! I don't know who I was *then*, I don't know who I am *now*. God, what if this is just...me? I hope my mum was wrong in what she said about my dad, and that people really *can* change.

Emma Nash @Em_Nasher

Does anyone ever know who they are? Thirty-six-year-olds probably do. Probably

Sunday, 26 October

posted by EditingEmma 13.50

I was just sewing together a new top when I realised, the not liking myself thing isn't *entirely* true. I like myself is when I'm making clothes (and, er, not thinking or speaking). I like myself when I'm hanging out with my friends, and chatting about random, stupid stuff instead of complaining about Leon...

Maybe it's not so terrible after all. (I mean, still quite terrible, but not *so* terrible.) So yes, meeting someone else was a fail, but as Mum said: I DON'T NEED ANYONE ELSE. *Why* haven't I been focusing on all these other great things I have going on?!?!

After pondering for a while, and taking a lot of deep breaths, I've decided that she's right. I've been dating for all the wrong reasons and I don't think I should do any more of it for a while. I'm ending the mission and I'm not going to bother Greg again, either. What would be the point? Just because I can't have Leon, it doesn't mean I really want Greg.

I've drafted a sort of goodbye message to him. It says, 'I'm really sorry. Hope you're OK. x' Should I send it? It could be quite patronising. Or embarrassing, if he's completely forgotten about it by now.

posted by EditingEmma 14.18

Sent it anyway. I needed to say it. I feel a bit better about Greg, and a bit better about Leon, and a bit better about Gracie... Aghhhh. I really wanted a fresh start at the beginning of term, but I'm going to have to have *another* one after half-term!! Maybe that's just life... Fresh start after fresh start. Do things ever just get good and stay good?

posted by EditingEmma 21.03

New Day, New Blog

Well, it's not really a new day, technically it's nine o'clock at night. But any time is fine for an emotional 'new day,' I think. I have, once again, decided to take some action in my life. My reasons are four-fold:

1) The conclusion that trying to get over one person by going out with another doesn't work.
2) Having accidentally hurt not only Greg, but also myself and my friends, and not wanting to do that again.
3) Once again, finding that I don't like myself very much. And realising that in order to change this I should probably have a think about who *I* am, before I start trying to factor in somebody else.
4) Learning that general stalking is not necessarily a better use for the internet than stalking one person. BUT, in

doing so, accidentally rediscovering my love of fashion and designing.

For these reasons I have been once again redesigning my blog, because I am 'Editing Emma' in the present tense and therefore can never have too many drafts. Redesign is nearly complete, and I've made some new, better resolutions to go with my new, better blog.

Editing Emma

(The Secret Blog of a VERY Nearly Proper Person)

posted by Editing Emma 23.44

Today is the day. Today is the day that I, Emma Nash – in light of the above realisations – set upon a mission. I continue to be Editing Emma, only changing direction a little with my 'edits'… Because I do still want to make changes in my life, only clearly I was going about it the wrong way.

I've made a discovery, that I, in fact, smug as I was, have continued to use the internet incorrectly.

Here's why:

It is true that my Leon-stalking needed to stop. But replacing Leon by stalking other people doesn't count. You can't use other people to make changes in your life…Those changes have to come from you.

I scoffed at Steph and my Mum's terrible dating patterns whilst making my own terrible dating pattern: using boys to try and make me happy, and forgetting all the other things that make me happy.

For these reasons, I believe for a long time I have missed

out on what the internet has to offer. Over 50 per cent of people in THE WORLD have a presence on a social network, and this does mean we have access to get to know all kinds of people we would never have. It also means we can share our thoughts, ideas and interests with these different people we never would have met! I am determined to prove to myself in the quest to be an at least 50 per cent functional human being that, with the internet's help, it can and will be done. (I think. Maybe. Let's give it a try.)

NEW RESOLUTIONS
Don't worry so much about meeting someone else I like. Be a version of MYSELF that I like.

I will do this by:

A) Keeping on making clothes.

B) Focusing on my friendships.

C) Stopping stalking Leon AND boys in general (perhaps, with the exception of Mr Allen) and really, really trying to not use the internet as a place to mope, moan or unhealthily obsess.

Let this translate to an internet space that is just about me, without e-tweaking myself.

I will do this by:

A) Writing more private posts which AREN'T about Leon.

B) Making a Pinterest board for inspiration.

C) Making a brand new public blog, purely dedicated to my fashion pursuits.

Behold... my new blog(s).

Acknowledgments

First and foremost thank you to my Mum, best friend and first reader – if we were the last two people on Earth we'd probably be just fine. Or kill each other.

I couldn't have written this book without the countless laughs (and occasional arguments) shared with Nell, Rachel, Catie and Sarah, my best friends from school (or my 'muses.') We managed to put up with each other through the awkward and sometimes awful teenage years, as I imagine we will do for the rest of our lives.

Thank you also to my incredibly supportive boyfriend Patrick. I know I must have bored you to death asking you about the placement of EVERY SINGLE WORD but you never once showed it.

One person I will never be able to thank enough is Lauren Gardner at Bell Lomax Moreton, for believing in Emma from the beginning. Your input has been invaluable and your moral support kept me going through the whole excruciatingly

wracking process. (You even managed to make submis-
n fun?!)

A massive thank you to Anna Baggaley, (I still feel so amazed/
privileged that you wanted to add Emma to your very special
list!), the fab Lucy Richardson and the whole team at HQ
for being generally awesome and brilliant at what they do.

And to anyone else who's given me advice/guidance/let me
pick their brains along the way. Emma and I are eternally
grateful for your infinite wisdom .

HQ
One Place. Many Stories

The home of bold, innovative
and empowering publishing.

Follow us online

 @HQStories

 @HQStories

 HQStories

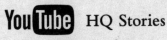 HQ Stories

 HQMusic